Death by the Devil's Hand

Michael L. Patton

Cover photo courtesy of Sicnag via Creative Commons.org.
Limited rights may apply. The image was significantly modified for
use on the cover.

DEDICATION

This book is dedicated to my uncle, Richard E. Droddy, who we lost in October of 2018. He was a man who loved his family, and his example helped to guide many of us who had the privilege of knowing him.

Michael L. Patton

Contents

Chapter One - Wednesday, June 8th...1

Chapter Two - Thursday, June 9th...13

Chapter Three - Monday, June 13th...21

Chapter Four - Tuesday, June 14th (Early AM).........................27

    Tuesday, June 14th (Morning)...31

    Tuesday, June 14th (Evening) 36

Chapter Five - Wednesday, June 15th 41

(Morning) 41

    Wednesday, June 15th (Late Afternoon) 52

Chapter Six - Thursday, June 16th...60

    Thursday, June 16th (Evening)...64

Chapter Seven - Friday, June 17th...68

    Friday, June 17th (Afternoon)...88

    Friday, June 17th (Evening) 98

Chapter Eight - Saturday, June 18th (Morning).....................109

    Saturday, June 18th (Afternoon) 143

    Saturday, June 18th (Evening) 148

Chapter Nine - Sunday, June 19th...152

Chapter Ten - Monday, June 20th 179

Chapter Eleven - Tuesday, June 21st...190

Chapter Twelve - Wednesday, June 22nd 196

Chapter Thirteen - Thursday, June 23rd...206

Chapter Fourteen - Friday, June 24th...212

Chapter Fifteen - Saturday, June 25th...222

Chapter Sixteen - Sunday, June 26th.......................................228

Chapter Seventeen - Monday, June 27th 238

ABOUT THE AUTHOR...242

ACKNOWLEDGMENTS

I have had help from a number of people in completing this novel. I would like to acknowledge the East Bay Writer's Group, which has helped and educated me tremendously. I greatly appreciate the patience and talents of my editor, Gene Roberts, who made the editing process so much easier than I thought possible. Thanks to my draft readers for their reviews of the early, painful versions. Thanks to my wacky friends for their antics that serve as the inspiration for many of the ideas in the books. Special thanks to my friend Greg Johnson for his tireless efforts on the design of the cover.

Chapter One - Wednesday, June 8th

Blackie adopted his nickname the day he ran away from home, but he wouldn't begin using it until later that night. It was given to him by his mother. She screamed it at him as he ran out the back door after catching him going through her purse stealing the money she'd saved for next month's rent. As the door slammed behind him for the last time, he could still hear her shouts.

"You blackhearted son of a bitch, get back here with my money!"

Frankie Ramirez was only sixteen but laughed as he thought to himself, you ought to know, Mama. You ought to know if I'm a son of a bitch. He stuffed the bills into his jean jacket pocket and cockily strutted to the highway. Once there, he stuck out his thumb to head west. The money wasn't much, a mere three hundred dollars, but it would get him out of Texas. His luck held as an old pickup stopped to give him a ride. He ran to the truck noticing rain was sweeping across the plains toward El Paso; the wind chased tumbleweeds in front of the storm. Frankie pictured himself as a tumbleweed always being pushed by violent winds. No more, he thought. I will be the wind in other people's lives.

The driver leaned across the seat and rolled down the window. "Where ya headed?"

"West," was all the boy answered. With that, the driver opened the door, and the hitchhiker climbed into the old Ford pickup.

"What do they call you?" The driver asked, trying to initiate conversation. He hoped the hitchhiker would help him stay awake on the seven hundred miles drive to Henderson, Nevada.

His passenger chuckled to himself, thinking of his mother's last words. Blackhearted son of a bitch! "Most call me Frankie," he said out of habit, not looking over at the driver.

"Well Frankie, I'm Bob. We got us a long stretch of Route 10 ahead of us to Phoenix. What kind of music do you like?" The driver wasn't sure if the kid was shy or what, but it was going to be a long drive with no conversation to break it up.

"It don't matter. I like all kinds of m-m-music." Still no eye contact. The kid didn't look nervous. He was slouched in the seat with his eyes on the road ahead.

"Okay. I listen to country mostly but feel free to find something else if you get tired of it. I'll let you know if I don't like it. We should be good as long as you don't put on some rap shit." The kid sat there with his left hand in his lap, the right hand fingers tapping on the armrest.

Frankie was lost in thought, thinking about how he got to this point in his life where he would jump in a stranger's truck and just go. It wasn't much of a life so far, he concluded. It mostly consisted of being dragged around by his mother from place to place in West Texas as a kid. He didn't remember his father, and most of the men who paraded through his life were mean and drunk, or God forbid, on drugs. They all used his mother and abused him to the point that now at sixteen he wanted to be out on his own rather than waiting to see what the next loser would bring. Frankie decided to never look back. He would reinvent himself and leave this sad, ugly world behind.

"Moving to a new job?" The driver asked, hoping to get the boy to engage in conversation. He could only guess the kid was in his late teens or early twenties. He was stocky but short, maybe five feet, six inches. Dark hair cut short on the sides and left longer at the top like the kids wore now. Probably got some Mexican blood, the driver decided.

"Nah, just visiting r-r-relatives in California. My uncle has an old truck he's gonna l-l-let me have." Frankie was surprised at how naturally and quickly the lies came off his tongue. He could be anyone he wanted now.

"Really? What kind of truck?" Finally, a spark of interest. He tried to keep the boy talking to help keep himself awake.

The idea came to him in a flash, "L-l-l-like this one." He could say anything now. Then he thought better of showing his hand. "It m-m-might be a year or two older."

"You can't beat these old Fords." The driver slapped the dash of his truck. "I bought this baby new. She's treated me really well. Driven this one all over most of the western states chasin' work. No sir, can't beat these old Fords. My Uncle Rick gave me my first one when I was about your age. It was an old '54 with a straight six, and I drove it everywhere. You a pretty good mechanic, kid?"

"I know a little," Frankie lied. "Helped my f-f-friend soup up his Camaro."

"Well, you learn all you can. If you take care of a truck, it'll treat you right," Bob responded as he wiped his large hand over his face, trying to brush away the fatigue. "Just like a woman, but you gotta treat 'em right." He looked over and saw his passenger's face showed a slight blush. "You gotta couple cute little senoritas back in El Paso you're chasing, Son?" The blush increased. Hmmm, the kid must be younger than he looks.

"A f-f-few," he tried to bluff, but his stutter gave him away. Frankie only stuttered when he was embarrassed, but it always significantly limited his success with girls. His confidence would dissolve in a trembling pool of stumbling consonants. He turned his face to the side window, humiliated.

Damn. Getting this boy to talk was like milking a mule. "You got a steady girlfriend, then?" he tried again.

"N-n-n-no." Now that it was out, the speech impediment took control.

Bob's frustration and fatigue got the best of him. "Hell, I ain't never met a stuttering Mexican before. Speak some Spanish for me so I can hear what it sounds like." Seething, Frankie flashed him a dark look and turned back to the window. There was no getting him to talk now. That was for sure. They drove in silence for a while.

"Aw, C'mon, kid. You gotta be able to take a little ribbin' once in a while. Otherwise, people will run roughshod over you." No response.

Bob continued to drive, shaking his head to clear the cobwebs now and then. It was close to two in the morning when they came to a truck stop near Eloy, Arizona, where Bob exited the highway. They pulled up near the main building that housed a restaurant and rest rooms. The kid watched as Bob weaved his way toward the entrance and disappeared into the building.

Minutes later, Bob walked out the entrance and became involved in an animated discussion with an old man.

Bob and the older man walked to the pickup and circled it slowly as they talked. Frankie laid his head back and pretended to be asleep. He held his right arm across his face as if shielding the light. Minutes passed. He lowered his arm slightly to peer and saw the men were back at the building

He watched Bob gesture several times at the truck, laugh and shake the older man's hand as they were joined by a younger man.

~~ Dan Williams and his Uncle Wally drove all day. They were delivering a set of telescope mounts to an astrophysicist at the Whipple Observatory on Mount Hopkins, south of Tucson, Arizona. Dan ran a custom machine shop which he recently relocated to Patterson, California. What started as a small machine shop on his maternal uncle's ranch, now occupied a 3200 square foot shop and made it closer for his customers in the Valley instead of having to drive an hour on winding mountain roads.

Dan was at the wheel of the heavy-duty flatbed truck he rented to haul the mounts and drove steadily for the last eight hours. It was well past midnight, and he was ready for a rest break. Dan's uncle was suddenly quiet. Usually, Wally would be talking about the trip, or the project, or telling stories from his endless cache of tales. However, when the pressure on his bladder built up enough, he would grow quiet. Dan saw a sign up ahead indicating a truck stop in five miles near Eloy.

"I think I'll push on into Tucson. It's only another hour. I think I can make it," Dan said not looking over. There was no response, but out of the corner of his eye, he noticed Wally's left leg start to bounce a little as his stress level went up.

After about two minutes another sign for the truck stop came into view. Wally finally said, "Well, I could use a restroom."

"Seriously?" Dan acted exasperated. "This trip's gonna take twice as long if we have to stop at every restroom and gas station on the way!" Syd, Dan's dog, lay on the back seat of the crew cab style truck. She raised her head when she heard the tone in his voice, but quickly figured out they were joking. Unconcerned, she lay her head back down, her eyes looking from one to the other as the exchange continued.

"Yeah, well I'm getting paid by the hour, so pull the hell over or suffer the consequences, Pal."

Dan passed the first exit that advertised a big truck stop and Wally became agitated.

"I thought you said you were stoppin'?" Wally insisted.

Dan sighed heavily and turned onto the next exit ramp. "I like this one better." Wally looked up to see a familiar sign with a Blue "T" and a red "A" leaning against each other.

"Huh, I hope you're not a big enough dumbass to think that because the signs have a T and an A on them, this is some kind of a stripper joint." Wally looked at his nephew derisively.

"Well, if it's not then it's false advertising." Dan laughed as he elbowed Wally. Wally looked at him unsure if he was kidding at first. Then Dan added, "I have their app on my phone and their diesel fuel prices were better than the others in the area."

They climbed out of the truck and walked into the men's room. Syd followed then sat outside the door waiting for them to exit.

"Man, not a minute too soon!" Dan said, still standing at the urinal while Wally washed his hands. A wet paper towel bounced off the side of his head and landed on his shoulder. When he emerged from the restroom, he saw Wally talking to someone standing near an older pickup.

"Yep, it's a '68," the stranger said as he and Wally circled the truck looking it over. "First year you could get the 390 engine. I've rebuilt it a couple times, and it still runs like a top." He was medium height with an average build but looked like he'd worked hard all his life. He squatted petting Syd who enjoyed the attention now that she knew he was a friend. "I got out of the Army late in 1968 and used my severance and savings to buy it as Ford was rolling out the '69's. They didn't change much, and I got a better deal."

"Oh, hey. This is Bob," Wally said to Dan. "He's driving this '68 F100 here. This is my nephew, Dan. He wasn't even born in '68." They all laughed and looked at the truck as a head popped up in the back window of the cab. "Hope yours is brighter than this one," he said nodding toward the old Ford while thumbing toward Dan.

"Just a hitchhiker I picked up near El Paso." He shook his head. "Mexican kid who don't talk much. Stutters. I hoped he'd help me stay awake. Needed someone to talk to, but he got his feelings hurt when I teased him and clammed up on me. I got so sleepy I needed to stop for a nap."

"You're not looking to sell that truck, are you? I've been looking for a new project. It would be in good hands," Wally assured him.

"No. I think I'll keep her." He rubbed his chin looking down. "I have a neighbor who has a similar one. I could check to see if he'd be interested in selling," Bob added.

"Is it nice as yours?"

"It was in pretty good shape when I last saw it. Been on the road for the last six months."

Bob shook his head likely thinking of all the time away from home.

Wally took out a pen and piece of paper and wrote his name and number. He handed it to Bob who stuffed in his jacket pocket. "Sure, let me know if he's interested, or if you change your mind."

"Will do."

"Well, pleased to meet you, Bob," Wally stuck out his hand. "You heading home to Nevada?"

"Yep, I been chasing work all over the southwest for the last two years. Finally found something in Vegas. I live in Henderson," Bob said as he stared intently at the ground in front of him. "Nice to meet you too."

As they walked away, Dan asked, "How'd you know he was from Nevada?"

"Plates on his truck."

Dan looked over at the pickup as he waited for Syd to complete her business in the area designated for pets. It had Nevada specialty plates which said '1968' with the word 'Veteran' underneath the numbers. He watched as Bob walked over to his truck, climbed in, and drove to a dimly lit corner of the lot. After pulling to the pumps and refueling Dan and Wally were back on the interstate heading south.

~~ Bob climbed into the driver's seat and pulled to the back of the lot away from most of the trucks, near where a Pizza Hut sat at an angle to the truck stop. Only two cars were in their lot. Bob shut off the engine and said almost in a whisper, "I gotta get some sleep, kid," as he opened his door and reached behind the seat.

"W-w-want me to drive for a while?" Frankie asked as he watched the flatbed truck exit the parking lot.

"Sorry, Pedro. Nobody drives ole Sweetpea here but yours truly. I gotta sleeping bag for me to stretch out in the bed. You can have the cab since you got them short Mexican legs. It'll be warmer for you in here too." Bob hoped the damned kid appreciated the fact that he offered it.

But Frankie was speechless at the number of insults he was forced to endure in such a short time. Frankie felt the truck lurch as Bob climbed into the back of the pickup and bedded down for the last time in his life.

Thinking back to the interaction between Bob and the two strangers, Frankie wondered what the two men said to Bob. How was it possible to interact with complete strangers so easily? Frankie was always mistrustful of people, but these men chatted easily, laughed, and went on their way. Having been raised to be seen and not heard, Frankie didn't understand how one day you were supposed to be able to communicate with ease. Every time he even tried to make his views known at home, his mother's latest would call him Dummy and tell him to shut up. How could he not stutter when he knew what would happen every time he tried to speak?

Frankie lay down across the truck's seat. The frigid night air invaded the cab immediately. He tried not to think about the temperature and managed to fall asleep briefly. When he awoke, his arm was draped over the edge of the seat, and his hand was touching something hard and cold. He looked underneath the seat and barely made out a tire iron in the dim light from the distant parking lot lights at the edge of the truck stop lot. It was so cold he retracted his hand immediately and tucked it under his other armpit attempting to warm his fingers.

The boy lay there shivering. The only warmth he felt was from the anger building inside him thinking about the insults and humiliation he suffered in such a short time from this stranger. Having been born in Texas, he wanted to go to the back of the truck, wake him, and tell him he was just as American as the old man's lily-white ass. Frankie thought back to all the times he was teased in school at the hands of some of his cruel classmates for stuttering. He was even unable to talk to a pretty girl at church. How would he ever make it on his own now? He was branded the minute he opened his mouth. Frankie felt so alone, angry, and vulnerable to assholes like Bob. He would change and take control. Now on his own, Frankie would become a different person, strong and confident. No one would laugh at his speech again! He would never show weakness.

Frankie reached under the seat and felt the cold, hard steel of the tire iron. He grasped it, testing its weight. Time to be as cold and hard as this metal, striking out at anyone who crossed him. He found himself moving out of the truck before he even realized what he was doing. No longer did he feel the cold night air or the hard asphalt beneath his feet. The weight of every slight and embarrassment was off his shoulders. He felt a lightness and a heat of being transformed. He glanced all around. No one was visible or watching. The tailgate was down, and he grabbed the bottom edge of the sleeping bag and dragged the heavy load onto the parking lot.

~~ Bob had no idea what was going on. Suddenly, it felt as if the truck was moving. He opened his eyes as his head slid off the edge of the tailgate and hit the asphalt hard dazing him. Before he could recover and try to open the sleeping bag, something hard struck his upper right arm shattering the humerus bone. The next two blows destroyed his left clavicle immobilizing the arm. He was defenseless and attempted to roll to escape the attack. Several kicks to the kidneys raised the level of pain to where he was sure he would pass out. He realized the assault happened so quickly he hadn't made a sound and the only thing he heard was the squeaking of his attacker's sneakers against the pavement.

"No!" he yelled. "Please, no!" He was face down now on the pavement, at the mercy of his attacker. The only response he heard was a dry laugh void of any mirth. "Who are you?" Bob pleaded. "Why?"

~~ "I'm ... the last person ... you're ever ... going to ... make fun of ...." Each pause was punctuated by another blow with the weapon. The first snapping his ankle, then crushing a knee, hip, ribs, and neck. Bob was rolled over, barely conscious now and saw a distorted face he barely recognized leaning into view.

"You can call me Blackie!"

A white-hot pain exploded in Bob's head, then darkness descended.

Blackie zipped the sleeping bag closed and wrapped the end over Bob's head. Most of the blood was contained within the confines of the bedroll. The area of the lot where Bob parked was mostly dark with no other vehicles. Traffic in the early morning hours consisted of large trucks, mostly parked on the other side of the truck stop. He dragged the sleeping bag to some dumpsters in the adjacent Pizza Hut parking lot. The backs of the two lots almost touched, and the dumpsters were only about twenty yards away. A wooden fence enclosed the dumpsters to hide them. Unable to lift Bob's body completely off the ground, he dragged the body between the two dumpsters and threw flattened cardboard boxes over it. A set of headlights swept across him from behind, and panic rose in his throat until he reminded himself he was not timid Frankie Ramirez anymore. Now he was Blackie. He was afraid of nothing and turned and strode confidently back to the truck. His truck. As he neared it, the realization hit him that he was in such a hurry he did not go through Bob's pockets to get the keys.

"Damn it! Stupid!" he cursed himself under his breath. He continued toward the truck, so he didn't look like a carnival duck at a shooting range, changing directions, and drawing attention. Waiting until the car sped down the entrance to the highway, he went back to retrieve the keyring. He felt sick at the idea of what he'd done and having to touch the dead body again.

"Stop it!" he blurted aloud at himself. Fear was a weakness coming from Frankie and his past. "I am Blackie now. I fear nothing. I will do whatever I need to do. The man mocked me and disrespected me. Bob deserved what he got, and I, Blackie will never show weakness again. Blackie does not stutter and takes what he wants."

Walking back to the dumpster area, Blackie slipped behind the gate without opening it completely again. He quickly went through Bob's pockets, grabbing his keys and wallet. The only other content was a small slip of paper with a name and phone number he stuffed back in Bob's jeans. He hurriedly spent time rearranging trash to better cover the body. The wallet contained more than a couple hundred dollars; it would help fund his adventure.

Leaving the wood pen, he heard, "Hey, get the hell out of there. You'll get sick stealing food from the garbage. Go on, git."

Blackie glared at the fast-food employee, threw him the finger, then lolled leisurely back to the truck and got in. The boy was beginning to like being Blackie.

Smiling as he drove west on I-10, Blackie repeated the name in his head. His confidence grew with each minute and each mile he put behind him. Near Phoenix, the sun was rising above the horizon behind him when he needed a restroom break and breakfast near Phoenix.

"Nice truck," said the gas station attendant when Blackie stopped to refill. "What is it? A '67?"

Looking down, the custom license plate gave him the answer. "Uh, no. '68." It occurred to him he should know more about the truck if it was now his. Blackie tried to open the glove box to look for the registration, but it was locked. He found the proper key on the ring and opened it. Inside, he discovered a small canvas bank bag and a .38 caliber revolver. Bob was old-school. The bag was also locked, but Blackie found the key on the keyring and opened it. He let out a celebratory whistle and started counting it.

Realizing where he was, he put it back to be checked later in private. Blackie quickly paid for the gas, then pulled off to an area with more privacy... He grabbed the bank bag and his heart raced as he counted nearly thirty thousand dollars in twenties, fifties and hundred-dollar bills. Blackie was a rich S.O.B.! He sauntered to the attached restaurant and ordered a huge meal.

Back on the highway, he contemplated his next move as he reached the western edge of Phoenix. Blackie saw a sign for Route 60 that said Las Vegas was 285 miles ahead. He smacked the steering wheel with the palm of his hand and shouted, "Vegas, Baby!

Chapter Two - Thursday, June 9th

.

Dan offered to mount the telescopes, but the scientist didn't want him or anyone else near their precious equipment. He and Wally made the mounts to detailed specifications and tested them against a dummy telescope they mocked up, but Dan wanted to work with the real thing. He had even installed a gantry crane that used a steel beam suspended the width of his shop to be able to move larger items around. His perfectionism made it difficult for him to let go, but Dan was outranked and given direct orders, so he backed off and sat watching. Walking up to the cab of the truck, he wore a look of frustration.

"Who peed in your cornflakes there, Big Fella?" His uncle didn't miss a chance to goad him.

"Well, they won't let us help mount the telescopes," Dan explained. "And I know these big-brained idiots will screw it up since they don't have the common sense of a signpost. They probably saw who was with me and figured they were better off with their blind monkeys." The telescopes had to be mounted on the stands that Dan had made, then lifted as a unit into the top of several smaller buildings with clamshell roofs that opened up for the observation of the night sky.

"Won't hurt my feelings to sit on the sidelines and laugh at them trying figure out which end of a screwdriver to use. I get paid the same either way," his uncle replied, failing to take the bait.

"Well, can you back the truck up to where they can unload it with the crane? I need the center of the bed even with the center of the boom. I'll direct you," Dan said pointing to the spot where he wanted the truck. He jumped off the running board and Wally slid over to the driver's seat. Syd jumped between the front seats onto the passenger seat to look out the window. Dan walked past the crane and turned, ready to direct Wally.

"Watch this Syd," Wally said causing her to glance back at him. "Where'd ja say you need her?" using his fake grandpa voice he screeched out the window. Syd cocked her head at the unusual sound coming from Wally.

"Right over here, Gramps," Dan played along. He could see out the corner of his eye that a few of the lab guys glanced over their shoulder. Wally made a big show of revving the diesel engine and grinding the gears. He popped the clutch, and the truck jumped backward going well beyond the center point of the crane. Syd spread her feet to keep from losing her balance and falling off the seat.

"How's zat?" he shouted.

"Not bad, Old Timer. Just a little past it. So I need you to move forward a bit." More revving and suddenly the truck was past where it started.

"Am I close?"

"Little too forward now. I need you to back up again," Dan said as if talking to a child. All the scientists stared at the spectacle before them. Wally shot further back this time. He locked the brakes, making the tires squeal.

"Good?" He couldn't make eye contact with Dan, or he would have started laughing.

"You're doing good, you're doing better. I believe you're sneaking up on it, Big Guy. Just a little more forward," Dan responded, biting his lip. By now, Syd moved over close to Wally and put her paw on his right arm, concerned something was wrong. In the rearview mirror, Wally saw that Joe, the project manager, walking toward Dan. He deftly let the clutch out and moved the truck smoothly to the exact spot Dan designated. He watched the guy frown looking from the rig to Dan, then shake his head, and walk back to where he started. Wally sat in the cab until he could get control of himself, and he watched Dan practically run into the building and make a right into the restroom inside the door.

After working with the crane operator to unload the truck, Wally and Dan were not even allowed to help install the mounts before the telescopes were installed.

Twenty minutes later, they stood watching. "Based on the drawings, you're putting that in backward," Wally said pointing to the middle mount the local team was bolting to steel base beams. Dan stood in front of him with the drawing open, and his finger touched the middle placement, a second behind Wally's realization. Joe glanced at them but continued on.

"He's right. That one is backward," Dan added. He spent hours getting the measurements perfect, and the pre-drilled holes were precise to the specifications. The locals continued to ignore them.

"I marked the front so we wouldn't mix them up because it's hard to see it," Wally tried again, to no avail. After a few seconds, he stepped closer. "Hey, dumbass!" Dan put his hand on his uncle's shoulder and gently pulled him back. Syd, who was relaxing on the flatbed truck stood to keep a better eye on things.

"Joe, are we working from the same drawings?" Dan showed him the orientation on the sketch. "We stamped in a small F on the front of the center pillar to help with the install. If you don't switch them, you will have to drill out the holes once the telescope is sitting on it. The engineer won't like it,"

Joe took out his tape measure and checked the mount. "Looks like you're right." Dan looked at his uncle, trying to signal him to hold his tongue. Too late...

"I'm glad I'm not the only dumbass in the room. It took me three times before I started stamping those suckers," Wally said smiling.

Joe laughed. "I guess it didn't free up enough time for you to practice your driving skills, though." He winked at Wally. Syd realizing the tension was broken, moved up closer to the cab where there was shade and laid down again.

"Aw, hell. I was driving a truck when you were still drooling on a sippy cup," Wally quipped. "Let me give you a hand spinning that thing around." Wally moved forward, and he and Dan helped install the rest of the mounts, with his uncle keeping them laughing telling stories about the dumb things he had done. They still didn't get to help with the delicate telescopes, but when they made suggestions the group listened, and by the end of the day they were all working as a team.

Dan, Syd, and Wally climbed into the truck a little before sunset to start the trip home. By ten that night they were nearing Phoenix.

"Let's hit that same truck stop and map out where we are going to find a motel for the night. I'm getting tired," Dan said as he moved to the exit ramp. As he pulled into a parking space, the truck faced the interstate. They saw police activity in the back of the parking lot near the Pizza Hut.

"You heard anything on the radio about what's going on over there?" Wally asked a semi-truck driver standing outside the restroom watching the activity.

"Supposed to have found a dead body over there by the trash bins. Sometime yesterday from the sound of it," the trucker responded, lifting his ball cap and scratching the top of his head. "I stopped in here last night on my way to El Paso."

"Yeah, we did too," Dan responded. "Scary. Thanks." He walked over to take Syd to the pet area.

"No problem," the trucker answered. "Y'all be safe now."

"Yes, sir. You too," Wally said with a nod.

~~ Blackie grew more excited as he drove into the Las Vegas city limits. With money in his pocket and a vehicle to drive, he felt his confidence growing. He could own this town. It took him a little while to find the strip. When he located it, Blackie drove up and down Las Vegas Boulevard to check it out. Frankie would have been gawking like a tourist, but Blackie simply cruised as his eyes caught it all with a stoic mask behind dark sunglasses. After the second tour of the area, he decided to buy lunch. He wanted something local, instead of one of the plastic tourist traps bursting out from the casinos competing for attention. He found a little joint on the older part of the strip. It sported a faded sign saying, 'Burt's Diner.' Inside, he sat at the counter, surprised to see slot machines at every other seat.

"What a crazy town," he mumbled to himself.

"Mornin', Darlin'," a redheaded waitress spoke as she approached and handed him a menu. "What can I get ya to drink?" She looked to be in her mid-to-late twenties, her tight uniform showing enough cleavage to distract the boy and garner more tips.

"Orange juice, please," Blackie answered and immediately chided himself for sounding as if he were asking

"You want any coffee, Darlin'?" She waggled the pot she carried in her left hand over his empty cup and looked at him through sexy but dismissive green eyes.

"Hell yeah," he answered perhaps a bit too enthusiastically. Tammy's eyes registered a flash of surprise followed by derision. She poured his coffee with a practiced flair.

"There ya go, Sweetheart," she purred and saw his face flush with embarrassment. She spun on her heels and took her time walking away while watching in the mirror behind the counter to make sure he was staring.

Blackie watched as the smooth turquoise fabric slid and stretched when she moved accentuating the roundness of her firm bottom. His eyes slid down her legs and were transfixed by a small red rose tattoo on her ankle. Realizing how long he was staring, he quickly looked up and saw her face in the mirror. Their eyes met for the briefest of seconds before he looked away. She held hers there just long enough to notice the redness deepen on his face. She could see the menu shake when he held it in front of him. She smiled, hoping to herself that the kid had enough money for a tip or her flirt would be wasted.

In reality, Tammy Dotson was thirty-three and was recently single. Again. The only thing she walked away with from a four-year relationship with Freddie was her breast implants. She convinced him she would be able to get into casino work and pay him back quickly. But her lack of talent killed her dreams of being a showgirl. Well, at least she walked away with something this time. She sashayed back to the kid at the counter. "What'll it be, Sweetie?"

Confidence! He tried to psyche himself into his new personality. "I'll take the Number Three breakfast," he said trying to use strong words instead of asking 'can I have.' However, his voice cracked, remembering too late to speak in a lower timbre.

"Sure, Sweetie. How would you like your eggs?"

"Over hard," he responded, remembering to sound in command.

"I took you for a man who likes 'em soft and jiggly," she leaned forward giving him a good look at her cleavage and noticed the red color expanding up his neck. "Toast, or biscuits, baby?"

"Huh?" he was so flustered he didn't hear the question

"Would you like toast or biscuits with your HARD eggs," she glanced down toward his lap, then back to his face.

"Biscuits," he finally got out. He felt the stirring in his crotch when the waitress looked down.

"Comin' right up, Handsome," she took the menu from his hand brushing his fingers slightly and placed it back in the chromed holder in front of him. She turned slowly and walked away. She figured if the kid had any money, she'd get a tip alright.

"Tammy, why are you teasing that boy?" It was Alice, the old battle-ax, queen bee of the waitresses. "You got him so flustered, he can't see straight."

"Oh, it won't hurt him. He was trying to act all grown up and tough, so I thought I'd have some fun," Tammy replied, acting as if it were trivial.

"Well, keep it under control." Alice gave Tammy a sideways glare as she grabbed the coffee pot. "I don't want this place to get a reputation." Her disapproving look continued until she turned toward the customers, then the fake smile she wore for customers re-emerged.

"Okay," came the reply with an innocent look. Tammy tended to her other patrons and got tied up with a regular who insisted on showing her the latest pictures of his grandson. She noticed as soon as the boy's order came up, Alice grabbed it and delivered it to him. "What a bitch!" she mumbled. Tammy did check on him a few times, to see how his meal came out, throwing in a few darlins and sweeties. When she caught him looking in the mirror, she winked at him, making him look away. She walked up to him with his bill, asking, "You see anything else you want, Sweetie?"

"No, thank you," he answered looking down instead of at her. Blackie reached into his pocket and pulled out a wad of bills. He did it intentionally to impress the waitress that he was a high roller. Her hand went up toward her mouth in a reaction of surprise, and her eyes widened even though she was half turned away from him. She spun back around and moved closer.

"Honey, you must be new in this part of town," she said in a hushed voice. "Don't ever flash that kind of cash if you don't want to get robbed." Her eyes darted to the right and left to see who was looking

Blackie pulled off a twenty and shoved the rest of the cash back into his pocket, looking in the mirror for any reaction nearby. Seeing none, he focused on her. "I can take care of myself." Their eyes met briefly, then he looked to his right as someone took a seat two stools away.

"I'm sure you can, baby," she cooed back. Tammy noticed his hand was shaking as he laid the money on the counter. She put her hand on his before he could pull it away. "Why don't you buy me dinner tomorrow night, I get off at four?" She let her touch linger a moment longer.

"What about tonight?" he asked feeling a surge of confidence.

"Well, okay, Baby." Her smile dripped with promise. "I like your enthusiasm." She gave his hand a slight squeeze and lightly raked her nails on his skin as she pulled away.

The warmth of her skin electrified him, and the hairs raised on the back of his neck. "Keep the change, Baby," he said. The check was only twelve dollars. He was trying to show confidence but almost stuttered on the word baby. He glanced up at her eyes, and they were locked onto his. Must keep my cool. After what seemed like an eternity, he said, "See you at four." He turned and walked away, trying not to trip on his way out the door. Once in his truck, he let out a whoop.

"What the hell was that?" It was Alice again who sidled up to Tammy, and they both watched him walk out.

"I'm not sure, yet," came the answer.

Chapter Three - Monday, June 13th

Dan and Wally were only home for a couple of days when the call came. Wally's cell phone rang as they were making a list of materials needed for a new project. "Hang on. It's that crazy old married woman I'm living with," Wally said holding up a finger. Into the phone, he said, "What's happening?" A pause, then, "Who? What do they want with me?" A puzzled look came over his face.

"What's going on?" Dan asked impatiently. Syd, sleeping on her bed in the corner of the shop, opened her eyes.

Wally raised his hand while listening. "Okay, well, text me the number." He rolled his eyes at Dan. "I will. I will. Okay, bye." Wally stared at the phone he held away from his head.

"What?" Dan insisted. A few seconds later Wally's phone made a dog barking sound indicating a text from his wife, Bobbie. Syd groaned and laid her head back down, closing her eyes.

"I got a call from a detective in Phoenix about a murder investigation," Wally said staring at the screen with a number showing. "Said I'm a person of interest in a murder." He stared at Dan confused. "S'posed to call him back. Bobbie just texted me the number. What do you reckon I oughtta do?"

"Call him," Dan said as if it were simple. "Find out what he wants."

"Remember what happened to you last time?" Wally said obviously shaken. "What if they think I did something?" He referenced Dan being a suspect in a local murder a few months back.

"Did you?"

"Hell no," Wally shot back. "You were with me the whole trip!"

"When did this thing supposedly happen?"

"How the hell should I know?" He began pacing, almost in a panic. Syd got up, walked to him and nuzzled his hand.

Dan put his hand on Wally's shoulder. "You want me to call for you? To find out what's going on?"

"You think that's okay?" Wally sat, suddenly exhausted and overwhelmed.

"Here. Give me the number," Dan said as he took Wally's phone. He dialed on his cell, and asked, "What's the detective's name?" His uncle simply stared at him. Frustrated, Dan scrolled through Aunt Bobby's message until he saw the name, Detective Bartlett.

"Phoenix PD," a woman's businesslike voice answered.

"Detective Bartlett, please."

"May I ask what this is regarding?" the professional manner continued.

"I'm not sure," Dan answered. "I received a call about a murder investigation."

"Your name?"

"Dan Williams."

"Thank you, Mr. Williams. I'll try to connect you." Dan was put on hold and heard occasional beeps indicating the call was being recorded. Finally, another female voice came on the phone.

"Mr. Williams, what can I do for you?"

Dan was thrown by the voice bordering on sultry. "Uh, I'm waiting to speak to Detective Bartlett," he finally managed to say.

"Speaking. Oh, just a minute. Did you say, Dan or Wally?" she asked. Dan heard papers shuffling and figured she was looking through her notes.

"Dan," he said when it sounded like she was back on the line. "Wally is my uncle, and I was calling to find out what this is about. I…"

"I can't discuss that Mr. Williams," she cut him off. "Please have your uncle call me if you would."

"Wait, he's here with me." Dan thought she might be hanging up. "Can I put him on speaker?"

"It's fine by me," she sounded impatient.

Dan pressed the speakerphone button and nodded to his uncle to talk.

"This is Wally Williams," he said tentatively.

The detective cut right to the chase. "Mr. Williams, can you tell me why we found your name and number on the body of an unidentified man who was recently murdered at a truck stop on I-10?"

Wally was utterly lost for a response. "Uh, uh. No, ma'am," he finally managed to blurt out.

"Do you know anyone in the Phoenix area?" she shot back.

"I, uh, have some relatives down that way."

"When was the last time you were in the Phoenix area, Mr. Williams?" She was riddling him with questions so quickly Wally was having trouble keeping up.

"Um…my nephew and I drove through there a couple of days ago," he responded, raising his eyebrows at Dan signaling him about saying too much.

"What day was the guy found?" Dan interrupted.

"I'm not at liberty to provide those details," Bartlett responded.

"And you said it was at a truck stop?" Dan was searching his memory.

"Yes."

"Near Eloy?"

"Yes, it was." The detective stopped abruptly making Dan wonder if she gave away more than she intended.

"Remember, we stopped in there, and you talked to a guy about a truck," he prodded his uncle's memory.

"Oh, yeah," Wally suddenly recalled. He spoke into the phone. "I talked to a guy about his pickup. It was just like one I used to have. A '68 F100. I asked him if he wanted to sell it. Is that the guy?"

"We don't know who the person is," she answered. "There was no ID on the body. Do you know his name?"

"I think it was Bob or Bill. Something short like that. Pretty sure it started with a B." Wally tried to think back.

"The truck had vanity plates on it!" Dan burst out. "They just said, 1968. And some kind of veteran indication too. Remember, Uncle?"

"That's right. And the plates were Nevada tags. He said he lived in Henderson, I think. I gave him my number because he said his neighbor owns a similar truck he might be selling."

"I'll need a statement from both of you. You may be the last people to see this man alive." The detective sounded encouraged about the lead on the victim's ID. "The body was found by two dumpsters." She held back the sleeping bag information.

"He said there was a Mexican kid with him," Wally added.

"Did you meet him, can you describe the younger man?"

"No. We only saw the back of his head through the rear truck window, Looked like he was asleep." Dan answered. "He said he picked the kid up around El Paso, Texas, and mentioned about the kid being shy."

"No. Bob said the kid stuttered and didn't talk much," Wally corrected. "Pretty sure it was Bob."

"Anyway, you should find the kid, and talk to him," Dan insisted.

"Why did you give him your home number and not your cell, Mr.Williams?

"Do you give your cell number out to strangers, Detective? Your personal one?" Wally shot back.

"Good point. Thank you for the information, gentlemen. If we need anything else can I use this number?" She responded. "I'll have these typed up and faxed to you for signature if that's okay?"

"Will email work? It's easier than a fax for me." Dan suggested since he didn't have a fax machine.

"That's fine," she responded. Dan gave her his email address. "And thank you for your time. I'll be in touch."

Wally sat, and Syd immediately put her head on his lap, trying to calm him. He stroked her ears absentmindedly and asked, "You really think it was that guy Bob?"

"I don't know, but it sure sounds like it could be," Dan answered.

~~ It was Alice who saw the boy swing into the parking lot at twenty minutes before four o'clock. "Tammy, your boy is back. You got a babysitting job tonight?"

"Screw you, you old cow," Tammy whispered to herself as she smiled at Alice from across the room. Twenty-five minutes later she hustled down the steps of the diner and almost bumped into Blackie as he headed for the door to enter.

"Hey…uh, hi. We still on for dinner?" Blackie asked nervously.

"Sure, Sweetie. But let's get out of here first. I would never eat in a joint like this." She took his right hand and spun him around. Tammy threaded her arm through his and moved in close like they were dating for years, whisking him back in the direction he'd come. "This your truck, Darlin'? It's kinda old for a young buck like you, ain't it?"

"Yeah, it's mine. It's a classic." He opened the driver's door and stood back waiting for her to slide in.

"Oh, I see you're not broke in yet. This ain't how you treat a lady," she glared at him disapprovingly above her sunglasses. Tammy walked around and stood by the passenger door until Blackie caught on, followed and opened it for her. She hopped up into the truck and lit a cigarette.

"Sorry," she heard him say as the door shut, then he walked back around the truck. She could see his lips moving as he mumbled something to himself.

As he climbed into the truck, she asked, "What's your name? I need to tell my roommate," she snapped his photo with her cellphone. She sent a text with the picture to someone.

"People call me Blackie,"

"Just Blackie. You mean like Madonna? What are you, a rapper?" she teased.

He laughed. "Yeah, something like that." He narrowed his eyes, trying to look mean and added, "I'm the badass those rappers wish they were."

She laughed and saw his face soften to a smile as he watched her. Tammy pulled a band out of her hair and let it fall to her shoulders, and then she scooted closer to him on the bench seat, grabbed his rearview mirror and primped as he drove.

She took him to a small Mediterranean restaurant on the outskirts of town. It was dark, romantic, and she knew the waiter who served them. Tammy ordered a bottle of wine, but he insisted on having a beer. When the waiter started to card him, she gave him a look that made him back off.

Between three beers, and her hand on his thigh, the boy already looked buzzed. Two more beers at her place, and he was down for the count.

Chapter Four - Tuesday, June 14ᵗʰ (Early AM)

Blackie woke up naked in bed. Someone was kicking the bottom of his foot, hard. Completely disoriented, not to mention hung over, he was sure he was back home and about to receive another beating from Julio, his mom's current boyfriend.

"Get up, Faggot!" a voice commanded him.

It was the wrong voice, not Julio. Perhaps his Mom brought home another loser last night. He sat on the edge of the bed trying to focus on his surroundings. This wasn't his room. A skinny, white guy with a pistol stood at the foot of the bed! Blackie turned around and looked at the bed searching for his clothes. A naked woman was backed up against the headboard, with her knees pulled up and her arms wrapped around them.

Suddenly, she was screamed at the white guy, "Freddie, don't kill him! Just take the money and go!"

Blackie was moving before he even thought about what to do. He stood and faced the man with the gun. There was no fear, only anger that someone would threaten him. As he moved toward the man, he spoke in a voice he barely recognized.

"You wanna kill me? Huh?"

The man was stunned by the transition. Blackie's eyes were wild with what looked like rage. Freddie took a step back and glanced down at Blackie's naked body. It was then the boy realized he had a semi-erection, probably caused by needing to pee. He continued walking until the gun was pressed against his chest, his eyes locked on the intruder's.

"Get back," Freddie said as he half-heartedly pressed forward with the gun.

"You ever kill a man?" Blackie asked. He saw uncertainty in the man's eyes. When the gunman glanced over at the woman on the

27

bed, Blackie grabbed the gun and wrenched it toward the floor. It went off. The bullet struck Freddie in the right knee, causing him to release his grip. Blackie used the pistol to club the intruder across the face. The combination of the blow and the bullet in his knee made him slump to the floor. The stranger's head bent at an angle when it hit against the baseboard. Without hesitation, Blackie kicked him under the chin with the heel of his foot. He heard the bones in the neck grate as it twisted. The body went limp, the head at a peculiar angle, eyes still wide with fear, then shock as he suffocated.

Blackie turned to face the bed. He saw surprise and fear on the woman's face before she gained control of herself and tried to smile. As he calmed down, memories of the previous night and dinner with Tammy flooded back. Blackie couldn't remember even coming to her apartment.

"Is he…." Tammy couldn't bring herself to say it. There was no response for a full minute.

Finally, Blackie nodded and looked at the gun in his hand. His knees became weak as he realized what happened, and he sat in a chair. Tammy slid to the near side of the bed.

"You okay, Darlin'?" she paused, and he saw her look at his crotch. "You look okay." She paused, "You get off on danger, don't you, Baby?" her voice was almost a whisper.

Blackie realized he now had a full erection. He stared down confused until it hit him. If she only knew. He realized he got off on killing. A satisfied smile on his face was her only answer.

"Oh, no. I've seen that look on you before." She nodded at his crotch. "You put that big thing away. You almost killed me with it last night." Then she looked at the body, fear and indecision covering her face. "We need to get rid of him. We're lucky my housemate is gone."

They wrapped the body in a sheet and carried it out to Freddie's car and tossed him in the trunk. Blackie followed her in his truck. After burying Freddie in the desert, they drove his car and left it in a remote casino parking lot careful to look for an area with no surveillance cameras, then he dropped Tammy off at work.

Blackie drove around the strip for hours, thinking and watching the tourists. So much happened in the past few days. He really liked Tammy. She had more class than anyone he'd known before, but he wondered what she was doing with him. He caught himself and knew she was attracted to the strong, determined Blackie. He marveled at how he walked right up to the intruder and snatched the gun away. He acted like a man, and now he must think like a man. Stop thinking like a scared little boy. That's what women liked.

Blackie thought back to his Mom's choices. She was always weak and ended up with men who beat and used her. He paid the price for it. At first, these men seemed strong and in charge, but as he got older he saw how weak they were and began to challenge them. In the beginning, it was in small ways. He took money from their pockets or wallet if they left it where he could get it. Soon, he ignored their commands directed at him and walked away as if they weren't even there. He had taken beatings for years but soon realized when he cried the men became more aggressive. When he stood up to them, most found a way to back down. Only one responded with violence, almost breaking Blackie's jaw in the process. After that, he always made sure there was a weapon within reach when he challenged the cowards.

Blackie pitied his mom, but soon his disrespect spilled over to include her. He despised what he considered weakness. Especially women who threw themselves at men to get what they wanted. Tammy's insistence on him opening her car door, showed class, and strength. He liked that.

Thinking back to what happened late last night, he wondered if he should leave town. "It was self-defense," he said aloud, trying to reassure himself. How did the guy get the drop on him in the first place? Blackie was a light sleeper after all the years of living with violent drunkards his mother brought home. Did the guy have a key?

What was it Tammy said to him? He pulled into a parking lot and sat watching the crowds walking the strip.

Finally, it came to him. Tammy said, "Just take the money and go."   The money. He turned the phrase over in his head. That meant the guy knew there was money. Was he set up?

Tuesday, June 14th (Morning)

Detective Angie Bartlett finally had a lead. Admittedly not much of one, but it was a place to start. Bob or Bill was not very specific, but the description of the truck and the plate at least got her started. She contacted the Nevada DMV and quickly got lucky, finding a 1968 Ford F-100 registered to an owner in Henderson. Finally, she had a name and address. The owner was Robert Foster, and his age and description matched the body they found at the dumpsters. When they emailed a copy of the picture from his license, she was able to positively identify Foster as the victim.

Bartlett sat at her desk and reviewed her notes. She put out an APB on the Ford in Arizona and asked her Nevada contacts to do the same. It shouldn't be too hard to find the truck with vanity plates. She wished there was a better description of the Mexican kid. Since Foster was in his sixties, 'kid' could be anyone from their teens to their thirties. It wasn't much to go on. The witness said Foster claimed the kid stuttered. That should narrow it down a bit.

Angie Bartlett was a tall, athletic brunette who bristled at being called 'pretty.' Her looks always kept her from being one of the guys, but she never focused on them or the limitations they created for her. Sometimes, she used them to break down barriers, so she considered it a wash. With a law degree and graduating in the top five at the academy, she was able to cut through most of the bullshit with her intellect. She also had studied several martial arts including Aikido and Judo since the age of eleven, and she carried herself with physical confidence. Word of her skills spread quickly throughout the academy when she broke the hand of their close quarters combat instructor.

Angie was riding on an elevator with two other cadets in front of her and the instructor behind her. Suddenly, she had the instructor's hand bent at the wrist, arm straight, with him bent over at the waist.

"Does this belong to you?" she asked him. "I found it on my ass." When he tried to get away, she applied more pressure to the wrist.

"Bitch!" By now the other two cadets were watching.

"Wrong answer," she responded as she increased the pressure on his wrist forcing him to his knees. She released him, and the other cadets stepped beside her.

"I wasn't going to hurt her," the instructor hissed at them.

"It wasn't her we were worried about," one of them replied. She couldn't help but smile. The instructor's employment ended the following day.

She sat at her desk, slamming down her third Diet Pepsi of the morning. Coffee was too bitter on her stomach. She pulled pictures on the internet of old Ford pickups. Her father was always a Chevy man, and since she was born in the early eighties, the truck was before her time. She was not much of a truck fan but loved the old muscle cars from the same era.

~~ Tammy panicked. Her hands shook so much all day at work that she kept dropping things. When a group of policemen came in the diner's door, Tammy almost cried. They sat at a booth, and even though she would typically serve that table, she asked someone else to take them. Her nerves were barely settling down a bit when she turned around to see one of them standing close, looking at her expectantly. He was a regular, named Pete.

"Tammy, can I talk to you?" he asked. She almost bolted for the door.

"About what?" she blurted. Her right hand flew up nervously and seemed to get tangled in her hair. She brought it back down to her waist and grabbed her right wrist with her left hand to try to control the errant appendage.

"What's going on? Are you alright?" A look of concern crossed his face.

To Tammy, it was a look of suspicion. "Uh, I'm fine." She briefly made eye contact trying to assess whether he believed her.

"You look as nervous as a cream puff at a weight loss meeting." He gave her a brief smile. "The guys are worried about you."

"I'm fine, really. I broke up with my boyfriend a couple weeks ago." She managed a weak smile. "Guess I'm still getting over it," she lied.

"Well, you let us know if we can do anything. The guy is not hassling you, is he?" Pete put his hand on her upper arm and gave a slight squeeze. "We'll take care of him if he does."

She stiffened. "No. No. I haven't seen Freddie since we broke up. There's no problem, there." She needed an alibi. "Haven't heard a peep in weeks. He's probably shacked up with some twenty-year-old with big boobs."

"You cheer up, now. We all come in here to see that smile of yours." He winked at her. "You sure didn't think it was the food, did ya?"

"Thanks, Darlin'." She gave him a hug.

"There ya go. You keep your chin up." Pete lifted her chin with his forefinger and smiled. He turned and walked back to the table where the others sat.

Tammy managed to get through her shift and left via the diner's back door. She had no idea where to go. Afraid to go back to her place, she caught a cab downtown to a lawyer's office she'd used to get a restraining order a few years ago. Tammy sat in the waiting room, biting her fingernails, trying to figure out how much to tell.

"Ms. Auer will see you now," the receptionist said, interrupting Tammy's thoughts. Once inside the private office, Tammy broke down. Tears ran down her face as she told the young lawyer everything. While mostly listening, the lawyer followed up with a few questions, and after a deep sigh began her advice.

"First you need to write me a check for a minimal amount to retain me and invoke attorney-client privilege. Let's say one hundred dollars." Tammy nodded. "Then find another place to stay for a while. It sounds like this guy is dangerous, or crazy, or both." She wrote a list of actions for Tammy to take.

"Did he force himself on you?" the lawyer asked.

"No. No, Blackie was so drunk after four or five beers that he passed out at my place." She nervously played with her hair. "I undressed him and put him to bed. But the next morning I did lead him to believe we had sex." She paused, and added, "To soothe his male ego."

"I've been there too." The lawyer smiled.

"How do I get rid of him? He knows where I work."

"Technically, you didn't have any part in the murder. And you can always claim you were under duress when you helped after the fact." She waited for an acknowledgment from Tammy. "So you could call the police if he shows up. Or we could go to them and report it, which is what I strongly recommend."

"I'll have to think about it." Tammy was terrible about making decisions under pressure, so she stalled for time.

"Don't wait too long. This guy sounds impulsive." As they walked to the door, the attorney hugged her, and held her by her upper arms, facing her. "You were one of my first clients. We're almost the same age, and in a way, you feel like a sister to me." She made sure Tammy was looking at her. "I want you to take care of yourself and call the cops if this guy gives you any trouble." Tammy nodded and stumbled out the office door with her head spinning.

She had no idea where to go or what to do next. She needed time to think. It was all coming at her too quickly. Grabbing a cab, she told the driver to drop her a few blocks from her apartment. She needed to get her car so she could stay mobile. Taking alleys and trying to keep out of sight, she cursed the turquoise uniform that screamed 'WAITRESS.' Carefully approaching the parking lot, she remained hidden behind a bush for a long time looking for any sign of the blue pickup, or the kid. She finally worked up the nerve to casually approach her gold colored Corolla and slip inside. She grabbed an old ball cap of Freddie's from the back seat to wear. Her large sunglasses were on the dash, and she added those too. Driving cautiously and trying not to draw attention to herself, it felt like she'd driven blocks before she was able to breathe.

Tammy wondered if she could trust the cop, Pete. On a whim, she decided to head to the police station. She parked the Toyota across the street at a muffler shop where she could watch the patrol cars going in and out. She'd seen the number of his unit on the front edge of the fender enough times to recognize him pulling into the lot. She would tell him Blackie killed Freddie and threatened her. Tammy sat for thirty minutes wondering when the shift change would start. Watching all the activity around the station made her nervous. She thought about calling the lawyer to ask if this was a good idea. As she picked up her phone to dial, Pete, pulled into the lot.

No! I should have my lawyer here. That's what she'd say. This was stupid. Tammy waited until he was in the building before leaving the lot.

Tuesday, June 14th (Evening)

When he went back to Tammy's work to pick her up, Blackie couldn't locate her. He was told she left, and Alice had no idea where she went. When he pressed, the manager was called and became suspicious. Blackie let it drop. She was not at her apartment when he went by there. He wondered if the police found the body already and arrested her. He needed to ask her about what she said to Freddie. Panic gnawed at him as he sat in the truck trying to decide what to do next. To make matters worse, a police car circled the block and seemed to be checking out the pickup more than usual. He needed a plan and a place to hide.

The first thing Blackie did was find a poorer neighborhood likely to contain some older cars. He cruised through a shopping center parking lot until he located an early model Ford pickup. It was green and not the same year as his, but close. Using the tools he found behind the seat, he removed the plates from the green pickup and put them on his truck. He also took the plates from a different car and put them on the other truck to keep the owner from noticing them being stolen.

The next stop was at a Walmart where he purchased six cans of white spray paint. He pulled behind the store and used them to change the looks of his truck. The factory color was light blue on the entire body. Blackie used the spray paint on the roof, and the side of the pickup below the chrome strip down the length of it below the door handles. It wasn't the best paint job, but it made the truck look entirely different.

He stepped back, admiring his work. "Not bad." It felt good to do something active to help move forward. No more waiting for Tammy or anyone. He would take charge and do what he wanted. He drove his newly disguised truck back to the strip. Cruising around he decided to take a chance on one of the more prominent casinos. With so many people there, he could blend in with the crowd.

Blackie parked between two box trucks near the loading dock. The truck was completely hidden from the street. He grabbed the small gym bag from behind the seat and headed for the entrance of the casino. He wished he could remember the night before with Tammy. She said they had some pretty intense sex. That would be nice to remember. He would need to back off on the beers from now on. He wandered through the smoke-filled casino for twenty minutes before he found the registration desk.

At the counter, he was determined to look like he knew what he was doing. Confidence! He pulled out Bob's wallet, which he was now using. Something wasn't right. Things had been moved around in the credit card slots. Blackie threw down Bob's credit card.

"I'd like a room."

"Sure, thing," the eager young clerk responded. "I'll just need some ID."

Blackie froze, then recovering, shook his head. "Damn. I think I left it in my other jacket in the car." He snatched the credit card back, spun and left the building. Shit!

Blackie drove around until he saw a business copy store. When he was in junior high, he and a friend used them to make fake ID's to try to get some beer. It would have worked if his friend hadn't giggled and made the store clerk suspicious. He had a passport photo taken and grabbed a brochure on the way out listing all the company's locations in Vegas. With his new picture and Bob's license, he drove to the next nearest store and reduced the photo to match the size he needed. Using the lamination machine, he pasted his picture over the existing one. It wasn't perfect if scrutinized, but it would do. The kid behind the counter was about his age and didn't bat an eye as he paid and left.

"Thanks, Dude," the kid said. "Hope it works for you."

Blackie nodded and left the store. Moving on to a different casino, he checked in, went up to his tenth-floor suite, laid across the bed, and was asleep in seconds. His last conscious thoughts were wondering if Tammy went through his wallet. Who else could have put the credit card in the wrong slot?

~~ Detective Bartlett was sitting at her desk when she got a call from Robert Foster's credit card company saying his card was just used in Las Vegas.

"Hey Verderosa, do you want to take a trip to Vegas?" Angie yelled over the partition.

"I'd love to, but tomorrow is my wedding anniversary," came the response. "I'd be a dead man if I ran off to Vegas now... especially if I went with you. Maybe Grant will go with you." Grant was their captain.

"I'd rather take my grandmother. Guess I'll have to suffer through Vegas all by myself." She made arrangements to fly out that night. "Hey, call and let this hotel know I'm coming, will you? I want to get up there before he bolts." He nodded and she handed him a yellow sticky note as she headed out.

She stopped at home for a small overnight bag, then drove to the airport. Bartlett was extremely practical when it came to her clothes, wearing mostly blue or gray sports coats and pants. Everything was basic colors and interchangeable. What makeup she used, which wasn't much, was already in her purse. The overnight bag contained a small lockable pistol case. She filled out an orange 'weapon' card the TSA required and put it in the bag with the gun case. Bartlett alerted the ticket clerk and was escorted to the TSA screener who verified the gun was secure. Then it was checked into the system so she could pick it up in Vegas. She wasn't about to go naked during an investigation.

Her flight was delayed, and she didn't get in until after midnight. Upon landing, Bartlett drove to the casino where they received the credit card hit. She checked in but decided to wait until morning to check with security when senior management personnel was more likely to be there.

Michael L. Patton

Chapter Five - Wednesday, June 15ᵗʰ
(Morning)

Dan still helped on the Rockin A when his Uncle Ed needed a hand, but most of his time was now dedicated to the machine shop in Patterson. He and Wally built a small apartment over the shop where he stayed during the week, but Dan still went back to his Hawk's Nest house in the hills on weekends. He felt it helped him stay focused on the right things when he returned to the ranch. The land Dan bought to erect the new building in Patterson had enough acreage he considered adding a house, but he would sorely miss Hawk's Nest, at least for now. It also let him use the weekends to help Ed with any projects that always seemed to crop up on a spread as big as the Rockin' A.

Since it was Wednesday, Dan was in his apartment above the shop getting dressed when he heard the alarm system chirp, then go silent. It likely meant Uncle Wally was getting an early start that morning.

"I wonder what could get that old goat moving this early," Dan said to Syd as they descended the stairs from the apartment into the shop. Syd ran ahead and found Wally in the small office sitting at the computer.

"Hey! If Aunt Bobbie doesn't let you surf porn at home, you can't do it here either," Dan teased. "I don't want you infecting my computer with some virus."

"I got your virus, Buddy," Wally growled.

"Maybe you should take an online course on manners."

"Leave me alone. I'm doing research here." He turned and looked at Dan. "Where would I look for registration information in another state?"

Dan frowned at his uncle. "Registration information. What are you researching?"

Wally pushed away from the desk and spun to face him. "I'm trying to find out about Bob's '68 F-100. See if I can find his address." Syd, seeing an opportunity, dropped a tennis ball in his lap.

"What in the world for? That don't have nothing to do with you."

He looked at Dan indignantly and tossed the ball for Syd. "Well, me and the Otters are going to a car show in Vegas in a few weeks. I thought I might cruise by to see if Bob was ok, or if it really was him they found."

'The Otters' was a hot rod club. Actually, it was a group of retirees who rented a warehouse in town to use as a garage where they worked on their cars, and it served as a gearhead clubhouse. They all chipped in for the rent and shared tools, labor, lies, and jokes. Rather than restore old cars, this group tended to modify them and try to outdo each other when it came to speed and spending. The guy with the fastest car who spent the least amount of money was the winner. This forced them to do most of the modifications themselves, as opposed to buying parts from a catalog. They shared machining equipment, welders, and lifts that let them do most of what they needed in their own shop. This caused the leader of one of the restoration-minded clubs to label them as the Other-side of the Tracks Racing club. Rather than get offended, they adopted the name which evolved to OTR, then the Otters because it was easier to say. The average age of the Otters was about '68, and as the old saying goes, if you put two of them in a room, you would get at least three opinions on any topic.

"You need to stay out of it, Uncle," Dan insisted. "Remember what happened to me last time we got near a murder case. I don't have time to be running to Vegas to bail your wrinkled old butt out of trouble."

"Last time I checked, it was a free country. Ain't nobody asking you for bail." He jutted out his chin to emphasize his point and tossed Syd's ever-returning ball again. "If you don't know where I can find the registration information, just say so." With that, he turned back to the computer.

"So how does the Otter brain trust plan to catch a killer?" Dan asked.

"I didn't say we were trying to find that guy. I said I wanted to check on Bob."

"As long as that's all you're doing." Dan lightly kicked the back of the chair Wally was in. "Now get to work. I'm not paying you to stalk dead guys."

"Ha! The entertainment value alone of watching you screw things up around here qualifies me as overpaid." Wally rose from the desk, and they went to work. They decided to quit at three o'clock because Dan was taking a trailer load of gravel out to a friend's house in the town of Newman.

"You need any help with this?" Wally asked as they walked toward Dan's truck which already had the load attached. The trailer was made from an old pickup bed that was cut off, with a hitch welded to it.

"No, I've got this, Uncle. You could hurt yourself shoveling." Wally saw the twinkle in his eye before he even spoke. "You should go home and take your old man nap. You're on borrowed time as it is."

"I thought that thing dumped," Wally said looking at the rickety old truck bed.

"It's not hydraulic, so you have to empty most of it first before you can lift it."

"Where'd you get this piece of crap? Look at the tires on it. One of them is dry-rotted and the other one's bald!" Wally pointed at the tires. "You won't make it five miles with that load."

Dan laughed. "You just watch me. I could make it to the East Coast and back on those tires."

"That spare on the front doesn't look any better," Wally said, pointing at the spare. "You should stop in Bradley's Tire shop before you go anywhere."

"That's clear on the other side of town. I can make it. It's my friend's trailer, and I'll leave it there when I'm done."

"Well, if you're gonna be a dumbass, don't call me when they blow out." Wally shook his head as he walked over to his own truck. He watched in amusement as Dan pulled onto the street, with both tires bulging from being overloaded. He headed to the Otters clubhouse to do more research.

When he got there, Stan, who was the organizer and unofficial boss of the shop, argued with Tommy about the finer points of Edelbrock carburetors versus Holleys. Tommy's nickname was Tailpipe because he used to own a muffler shop.

"Why don't you two move to the twenty-first century and put those new fuel injection systems on your cars?" Wally teased.

"Ah, hell. Fuel injection is ruining hot rods if ya ask me," Tailpipe complained. "All those damned computers in cars now. What the hell happens when you break down in the middle of nowhere? Ya need a computer to fix 'em."

"I agree. Real hot rods have carburetors," Stan added.

"How many times have I tried to tell you two gearheads, there ain't no rules in hot rods." Wally enjoyed stirring the pot. Now that he got them all worked up, he continued on through to the office to use Stan's computer. A few minutes later the other two trooped in.

"What ya looking up?" Stan asked.

"I'm trying to find that guy named, Bob who I ran into near Phoenix at a truck stop. He owned a '68 F-100 truck. Said he lived in Henderson."

"Well, what's his last name?" Tailpipe added. "We can just find him in the phone book."

"Tailpipe, sometimes I think you breathed in too many exhaust fumes. If I knew Bob's last name, don't you think I would have done that already?" Wally threw a stern look at him.

"How in the world are you gonna find him?" Tailpipe threw a magazine across the room at Wally. "Don't get mad at me, 'cause ya don't have all the information."

"I know his name is Bob, and he drives an all blue F-100 with '1968' on the license plates." Wally glanced at both of them. "That should make it easier to narrow it down. I figured while we were in Vegas at the car show, I could go down and check on him, to be sure it wasn't him they found murdered."

Stan suddenly perked up. "Murdered! What the hell are you getting yourself into, Wally?"

"I told you about it. That detective called, and said they found my name and phone number in his jacket pocket."

"Well, what makes you think it ain't him?" Tailpipe asked.

"I'm just hopin' against hope that it wasn't," he frowned, then rubbed his hand across his face. "I was checking car club websites in the area and thought I might see pictures of the truck that would list his name."

"I'm sure all those local guys from Henderson will be in Vegas for the show," Stan assured him. "We can ask around when we get there."

"I have a cousin who is a member of the Desert Deuces from the area. He says a lot of their guys will be there." Tailpipe added.

"Next time you talk to your cousin, could you ask him if he knows of a Bob with a truck like that?" Wally shut down the computer and swiveled around in the chair. "Who wants a cold drink?" he said heading to the refrigerator.

"I better call him now, or I'll never remember." Tailpipe took out his cell phone and walked into the other room so he could talk. A few minutes later he came back into the kitchen area where Wally sat at the table.

"What'd ya find out?" Wally noticed there was a funny expression on Tailpipe's face.

"He thinks he knows the guy, based on the description. If it's who he thinks it is, the guy's name is Bob Foster."

"Why do you look like somebody kicked your dog?" Wally asked.

"Well, my cousin says this Bob Foster hasn't been heard from in a few weeks. It could be the guy you said they found."

"Crap on a cracker. The odds are not going in Bob's favor." Wally's phone rang. He looked at the display, answered, and laughed. "I told you, you dumbass." Disconnecting he shook his head and said to the others, "Excuse me, guys. I have to go rescue my idiot nephew whose worn-out tires blew out under a load of gravel."

"Tires? As in plural?" Stan asked.

"Yep. The dumbass was running with two bald tires and a dry-rotted spare."

Stan laughed. "Wait for me. I gotta see this. I'll follow you." They headed out to their trucks and left to rescue Dan.

~~ Detective Bartlett was up the next morning early even though she got in late. After a quick breakfast of black coffee, she went to security and introduced herself. They identified the room and left the office.

"He hasn't checked out yet, has he?" she asked the head of security.

"System indicates no additional charges and no checkout."

"Do you have someone monitoring the room?" Bartlett was surprised at how casual he acted.

"No. Detective, we were not apprised of a potential problem with one of our guests. We saw no flag on the card. It must have only gone to you, or it hasn't propagated through the system to our front desk computers." He didn't need this kind of attitude from some hayseed Arizona detective chick. "Did anyone from your department call here before you flew up?"

"I guess not," she sighed. Damn it, Verderosa! She hated looking unprofessional in front of other organizations. "I didn't mean to imply anything. I asked someone to call. Apparently, he didn't."

"No problem, Detective. Let's just get this guy." He smiled at her. They proceeded to the tenth floor, but upon entering the room found it empty except for a small bag sitting on a chair. It contained two pairs of jeans, a couple of T-shirts, underwear, and socks. The guy traveled light.

~~ Blackie woke early. He was hungry, so sauntered to one of the restaurants in the casino to eat breakfast. After grabbing a quick bite at a no-frills diner, he headed back to his room to shower and change. The waitresses flitting around downstairs made him think about Tammy, and he was lost in thought as the elevator doors opened. When he looked forward, he saw a man and a woman in suits stepping out of his room which was only one door to the right. A hotel clerk was closing his door. He stepped back into the elevator for lack of a better place to retreat to. When the three of them got on, the woman barely glanced at him. The man in the suit wore a badge with his name and 'Hotel Security Chief' below it.

"I'm trying to get to the lobby," Blackie said trying to explain his awkwardness. Embarrassment flushed his face. Fortunately, the man and woman were involved in a discussion and seemed not to notice his faux pas. He quickly pushed the button for the lobby before they could look.

"He's probably still in the casino," the man said.

"Do you have a picture of him?" she asked. "Maybe from when he checked in?"

"We should. I can get that when we go downstairs. Then I'll alert my staff to start searching."

Blackie noticed the man was holding the small gym bag containing Blackie's clothes. He tried to remember if he left anything else in the room. The money was still in the truck. He could buy new clothes.

"Oh, he was driving an old pickup with vanity plates. I don't have a picture of the exact truck, but it should look about like this." Blackie caught a glance as she handed the security chief a picture that looked as if she downloaded it from the internet. "They're Nevada plates that say '1968'. We should alert your parking staff, too."

"You know the color?"

"Registration says light blue. But the plates should be the giveaway. If he hasn't switched them or ditched the truck."

Blackie shrank back into the corner of the elevator. His fingers tapped the metal shell nervously. He was afraid he would throw up or hyperventilate. As the discussion went on, Blackie reminded himself he was not a scared little kid any longer. He felt as if destiny put him one step ahead of these stupid cops. They would never catch him unless he made a mistake or showed weakness.

When they arrived at the lobby, Blackie stepped forward and used his right arm to hold the elevator doors. He extended his left hand in a sweeping gesture. "Ladies first." He watched the couple exit, getting a close look at the woman who seemed to be in charge. She had a nice ass for a cop. He kind of liked the idea of being pursued by a hot woman.

Blackie quickly exited the casino on the street side, trying to avoid all the cameras in the parking lot. He walked into the lot from the far side, up a flight of steps in the corner closest to where he parked and got in his truck. Blackie calmly cruised out of the parking lot. He would stick to smaller hotel chains from now on. Too many cameras in the casinos. Man, Blackie, you are one lucky son of a bitch!

~~ "Damn it!" Bartlett was furious as soon as she saw the face on the surveillance tape.

"Here's a thumb drive with all the footage I can find of him, Detective." The video operator interrupted her thoughts, handing her the device. "Is there anything else I can do for you?"

"No, thanks," she said taking it. "Oh, can I get a couple prints of your best shot of the suspect's face? That would be great."

The operator hit a few keys, and the printer came to life. "There ya go," she said nodding at the printer right behind Bartlett.

The detective picked up the printout. "Thanks for all your help," she said, smiling at the young operator.

Bartlett headed back to the chief's office to exchange contact information. "Is the clerk who checked him in working now?" she asked.

He pulled up a screen with the schedule on it. "Yes, as a matter of fact. Do you wish to speak with him?"

"Couldn't hurt." They walked to the lobby and located the clerk. The card he used was Robert Foster's, and she wanted to know if they checked ID.

"Yes, Ma'am. We're required to ensure the identification of all of our guests matches the reservation," the clerk assured her. He pulled up the file with a photocopy of the license.

"You didn't notice the person appeared to be about twenty, and the date of birth said he was in his sixties?" Bartlett said, pointing to the screen.

The clerk looked embarrassed at having missed the age, but the chief jumped in, "We're not selling them alcohol, Detective. You mostly check to see the names on the credit card and license match, and the picture looks right."

The clerk nodded in agreement. "And we check in hundreds of people a day," he added. "It would waste time to look at irrelevant information."

"That makes sense. I didn't mean to imply anything," Bartlett backpedaled a bit. "I guess when you know the age difference ahead of time, it jumps right out at you. Did you notice anything else about the guy?"

"Not really. Seemed a bit nervous at first."

"Oh," the detective said remembering, "did the guy stutter at all?"

"No. Not that I remember," the clerk answered.

"Well, thanks for all your help. If you remember anything else, please let the chief know." Bartlett tilted her head toward the security boss. "He has my contact info."

"Will do."

The chief walked her to the exit promising to forward anything else they discovered. Leaving the casino, the detective noted all the surveillance cameras as she walked to her rental. This guy is either really good or very dumb and lucky.

Wednesday, June 15th (Late Afternoon)

Tammy slept in an all-night laundromat and called in sick the next morning. She was determined to do the right thing but unsure how to go about it. She called her lawyer's office and tried to get an appointment.

"I'm sorry, but the first available opening is four days from now," the receptionist informed her.

"You have nothing sooner?" she pleaded.

"Ms. Auer will be out of town the next three days at a seminar. That's the earliest I can squeeze you in."

"Okay. That's fine. I appreciate it." Tammy ended the call and pressed her forehead against the Corolla's steering wheel, trying to think of what to do and where to go.

She next called work but hung up before anyone answered. Better do this myself. Instead, she called her friend Donna who worked the graveyard shift at the diner. A groggy female voice mumbled hello. "This is Tammy. I'm sorry. Did I wake you?"

"I have to get up in a few hours anyway to make school lunches for the kids to take tomorrow, then go to work. What's up?" she tried to sound cheerful.

"How would you like to sleep in?" Tammy went into sales mode. "I was wondering if we could switch shifts for the next day or two."

"That would be great. My two-year-old was sick today, and I got no sleep."

"Oh, thank you!" The relief was apparently evident in Tammy's voice.

"Are you okay? You don't sound so good. Is everything alright?" Donna asked.

The dam burst and Tammy started crying and blubbering on the phone telling Donna how she met this kid at the diner, and how they were surprised by her ex while still in bed the next morning. She was careful not to indicate any complicity on her part. Donna said nothing during the whole explanation, and after the sobbing stopped, Tammy finally said, "I'm sorry."

"Oh, Honey. Do you need a place to stay?"

"I couldn't," was all Tammy answered.

"If you don't mind a cranky two-year-old in the same small apartment, you always have a place on the couch. I'm not kidding."

"Thanks, Darlin'. I might take you up on that." Tammy regained control. "Now you get to sleep, and I'll see you in the morning."

"Yep, I'll see you when I come in for your shift. Thanks!" Donna hung up.

Tammy first called the diner to let them know about the swap. The managers liked to think they controlled things. She still wore her uniform from yesterday, and it was four hours until she needed to be at work, so she decided to try to take a nap. But where? When she was a young girl, she spent time with her grandparents every chance she got. Her grandpa Harry was her favorite person in the world, and she would sit on the back porch and listen to him tell stories. He would be awake before her every morning, and she would quickly dress to go out to the back porch. It faced the morning sun and he would sit in his rocking chair with his cup of tea and a newspaper, or sometimes on the glider they kept out there.

"Well, look who finally woke up," he'd usually say. "I already milked the cows, and plowed the fields." Then his grumpy old face would break into a grin. He developed emphysema from a lifetime of smoking and could barely walk out to his car in the driveway without resting.

"Morning Grandpa." She would settle in for a story while waiting for breakfast to be served. Among the many stories, he told her was how he used to fall asleep in a graveyard.

"Won't nobody bother you in a graveyard. I used to get my best sleep ever there," Grandpa would declare.

"That's because you were usually sleeping off a drunk," Grandma said, coming out the screen door to round them up for breakfast. She winked at little Tammy. "I always told him not to come home drunk, or the door would be locked."

"Did she, Grandpa?"

"Heck. I used to prefer sleeping in the graveyard, to hearing some high-pitched caterwauling about your granny being woke up in the middle of the night," he said grinning at her. "Was peaceful out there. Nope, nobody will bother you in a graveyard." His voice echoed in her memory.

Tammy drove to the northern outskirts of town. Her grandparents lived in a small town back east, where there was far less crime. Thinking it was likely to be safer, she located a remote cemetery called the Desert Flower and found the gates open. After driving in, she parked behind a stone wall where her car could not be seen from the road. All sounds seemed to have been absorbed by the wall as she strained to hear the highway nearby. Even lowering her window a crack revealed nothing but one lone cricket calling for a mate. She was not sure if she could fall asleep out there as she set the alarm on her phone and placed it on the small car's dash.

Not even sure she'd closed her eyes yet, she was suddenly startled by a loud series of electronic tones. Her alarm. She double checked the time on the dash of the car as she started it. She slept for three hours. Perhaps Grandpa Harry was right.

Traffic was light at that time of the evening, and she made good time to the diner. As she pulled into the parking lot, she spotted Blackie's pickup. It sat in the corner of the lot, with him behind the wheel. He looked like he was dozing off. The truck seemed different somehow, but in the low light, she couldn't tell why. She slowly eased the Toyota to and out the exit. He didn't appear to see her car, and she hoped he hadn't noticed her.

"Shit! Now where?" she screamed at the windshield. She drove to her apartment and quickly changed out of her uniform but left in case Blackie came looking for her. Once back in her car, she drove aimlessly around the city trying to decide what to do next.

~~ When Dan saw both Wally and Stan rolled up in their respective trucks, he knew he was in for some relentless abuse. He looked over at his furry companion, whose blue eyes already detected the slight change in his mood.

"It's gonna get ugly, Syd," Dan said shaking his head. She nuzzled his forearm until he put it around her and gave her a hug. They were sitting on the tailgate of his big Dodge diesel pickup on a back road surrounded by fields of beans and peppers.

"Well, how we doing?" Wally asked dragging out the inevitable.

"You taking a rest before your delivery?" Stan chimed in. Syd stood and wagged her tail as the familiar figures approached the truck.

Dan made a half-hearted attempt to go on the offensive. "No, I was headed to Newman when Tailpipe called and asked me to come up with a reason to get you two out of the shop so he could get some work done."

"Always thinking of others, aren't ya," Wally went along with it for a second, knowing he had the ultimate advantage.

"Just say it," Dan said, bracing like a kid about to be punished.

"You're a dumbass," they answered in unison. Syd groaned and walked away from her owner as if to say he was on his own.

"Thank you. Now can we get on with fixing the darned thing?" Dan had already removed one of the wheels, and the trailer was on a jack stand.

"Give us the spare and the one you took off, and we'll head to Bradley's," Stan offered.

"Where you should have gone before you loaded this piece of crap," his uncle couldn't resist adding. "Do you think you can manage to stay here and watch the load without doing any further damage?"

"Hey Syd, do you want to come ride with some normal people for a change? Or do you prefer to always be the smartest one in the truck? Huh, girl?" Stan rubbed the soft fur on her ears as he insulted her owner. Both men laughed as Syd barked and put her paw out to give a high-five. Stan gently reciprocated.

Wally also slapped her paw and turned to go. "You want a cold drink?"

"Sure," Dan thought this finally signaled the end of the abuse.

"I was talking to Syd," came Wally's answer, with his back to them. He walked to the bed of his pickup and opened the cooler, coming back with some water for Syd and a Dr. Pepper for Dan. "Well, put those wheels in my truck," he tipped his head toward the bed of the Toyota he called his 'civilian' car, as opposed to his hot rod.

After Dan loaded the wheels, Wally handed him the soda.

Dan spent the next hour and a half alternating between sitting on the tailgate and throwing a tennis ball for Syd. Finally, Wally arrived with two brand new tires mounted on the rims.

"You're not gonna like the price of these," Wally said as he approached.

"What do you mean?" Dan was almost afraid to ask.

"Well, the tires were a hundred fifteen a piece."

"That's not bad. What's not to like?"

"Well, after I told Tony down at Bradley's about what happened," Wally looked over at Stan to draw out the punchline. "He slapped on a two hundred dollar dumbass mounting fee. So it came to four hundred and fifty with tax." Stan started chuckling, enjoying the show.

"Bullshit, Uncle. If he added a dumbass charge, it was because you were the one buying them."

"Ask Stan," Wally insisted, jerking his thumb toward his partner in crime. "I talked him out of charging you for the air in the tires, and the aggravation fee. Although, now that I think about it, the aggravation fee may have more to do with me." He scratched behind Syd's ears. "What do you think, girl? Is the guy sitting broke down by the road smarter, or the one that rescues him?" Syd barked and lifted her front leg again, and Wally slapped her paw. "Now let's get this show on the road."

Within fifteen minutes both tires were changed, and Dan was ready to hit the road again.

"When are you two leaving for the Las Vegas car show?" Dan asked as he wiped his hands on a rag.

"Eight o'clock in the morning," Stan answered. "If I can get your uncle moving that early."

"Do me a favor and keep him away from any trouble down there, will ya?" Dan shot his uncle a concerned look. "And do not let him near any murder investigations."

"I do not promise anything." Stan tossed the jack handle he was holding into the bed of Dan's truck. "Best I can do is bail him out or call you when he gets in trouble."

"I'm standing right here," Wally interrupted. "I can hear you two buttheads."

"Well, I better get this load delivered." Dan snapped his fingers and opened the truck's door. Syd immediately jumped in the cab followed by her owner. "Thanks for all the help guys."

Wally and Stan waved as he pulled out, then climbed into their trucks to head back to Modesto.

~~ Blackie cruised the city for a while after leaving the casino. He found the famous 'Welcome to Fabulous Las Vegas' sign and was surprised it was in the older part of town. Blackie was even more amazed to learn it was considered downtown. He decided to take a tour of the Mob Museum in the old courthouse on Stewart Avenue. That provided entertainment for most of the afternoon, and as he came out, the sun was painting a canvas of orange and reds as it set below the mountains to the west. Blackie decided to grab some fast food. Entering the restaurant, he noticed two patrolmen in uniform, sitting at a table by the door. At first, his heart raced a little, but they seemed to pay him no mind. Blackie sat near enough to them to try to hear their radios. He slid into the seat two tables away from the cops, who were busy talking about a new car one of them was considering.

One of the officers made eye contact with Blackie showing annoyance at his eavesdropping. "Oh, couldn't help but overhear. That new Challenger is a sweet ride." Blackie held his gaze refusing to look weak.

The patrolman smiled at the comment. "That's a pretty nice classic I saw you're driving. What year is that?"

Blackie realized the cop was facing directly at the space where he parked. "It's a '67. It was my uncle's, who passed last year." He saw the policeman's eyes go to the truck again and realized he'd made a mistake. It was too late to correct it now and look like he knew what he was saying.

"You sure?" The patrolman kept his eyes on the truck. "I didn't think they had side markers until 1968."

"Oh, he was in an accident in the nineties sometime, and all he could find was the front end from a '68, so he put those fenders on." Blackie was amazed at how quickly the lie came to him. The cop nodded his head but kept his eyes on the truck. Blackie concentrated on his dinner and said nothing else except to tell the officers to be safe out there as they left.

Once he could relax, Blackie thought about his situation. He wanted to find Tammy. He wasn't sure if he was more concerned about her or concerned she was arrested and was ratting him out. Blackie was never around someone with such class and stunning looks. He was attracted to her strength and decisiveness. She stepped right up when it came to disposing of the body. She was not a dependent little whiny bitch like his mother.

The thought of a strong woman made him think about the lady cop on the elevator. It was easy to tell she was in charge, firing one question after another at the hotel security boss. She had a pretty face with dark brown eyes that were visible the few times she glanced at him. They were cop eyes that showed little reaction but made sure she was aware of everything around her at all times. Blackie wondered what she would be like after a few drinks in a social setting. He couldn't tell much with the suit jacket on, but from the glimpse he got, she seemed hot to him. And with those dark eyes, she was what his friend Manuel called a smoldering beauty.

But that smoldering beauty was hot on his trail. He needed to stop daydreaming and devise a plan. Should he forget Tammy and just leave town, or try one last time? Maybe she changed shifts? Blackie decided to go watch the diner for a while. If she didn't show up this evening, or for the graveyard shift, he would leave without her. He pulled out of the fast food joint and headed to the diner. He chose a spot in the back corner of the parking lot with visual access to the entire lot and the front steps. He was also close enough to have a clear view of the waitresses moving around inside.

Several hours later he was sleepy and turned on the radio. It helped for a while, but near midnight he caught himself snapping awake as a small, gold-colored Toyota pulled out onto the street. He was too tired to drive tonight. Blackie went back to the older part of the city and found a motel that didn't look like there were cameras everywhere. Blackie cruised around the perimeter and confirmed there was no surveillance system. Satisfied, he went to the office to check in. He would start out in the morning.

Chapter Six - Thursday, June 16th

Bartlett woke early the next morning and dressed for a run. She was frustrated at how the suspect slipped through her fingers the day before and running at a hard pace was the only way to dissipate the pent-up energy. Glad she threw in her workout clothes at the last minute, she pushed hard both to punish herself for the screwup and to clear her head. After a breakfast of black coffee, toast, and yogurt, she began the mundane police work of tracking the old Ford.

She decided to stay in Las Vegas engaging with the LVPD to follow her only clue. They provided her a junior detective to help her comb through the DMV records for the late sixties Ford pickups in the area. Many of the registrations that old were not in the computer system, so they went to the basement to search through boxes of paper records. After ten hours of searching, she found two trucks with plates starting with thirty-five.

"You think that's the truck in the video?" the young detective asked. He was still gung-ho and had not even loosened his tie.

Bartlett, however, took her shoes off earlier and her feet were curled under her on a couch with a Diet Pepsi on the table beside her and a stack of files on the seat next to her. Her jacket hung over the back of the sofa, and the cuffs of her long sleeved blouse were rolled toward the elbows. As she looked up, he quickly diverted his eyes, and she realized he was standing over her trying to get a glimpse of her cleavage. Oh jeez, grow up. "Not sure, but it's a lead." She handed him the file. "Can I get copies of these?" Maybe she could keep the young pup's hands busy at least.

"No problem," he said taking the folder and heading for the copy room. When he came back, Bartlett was putting the last of her stack of files back in the cardboard carton and pointed at the shelf.

"It looks like that's about it for the files. I appreciate your help." She stood about three inches taller than him, and she noticed he took a step back. She was not exactly an Amazon at five feet ten and never felt physically intimidating.

"Glad to help." At least his smile came across as genuine. "So what are your next steps? You need anything else from us?"

"I'll probably follow up on these two leads first thing tomorrow." She thought for a few seconds and added, "Then I might go to Henderson to check out the victim's place to see if I can get a better feel for the guy."

"Well, yell if you need any assistance. I'd sure like to see this guy get caught." He accompanied her to the door of the station. "We put out a Be On the LookOut, or BOLO, for the guy, as a John Doe. But I'd sure like to have a real name to add to it. Keep in touch, Detective."

"We'll get him. Thank you." The sun was setting as she walked to her car.

Bartlett drove back to her hotel and decided to treat herself. After ordering room service, including a bottle of wine, she took a long hot bath. Even floating in the sea of bubbles with a slight buzz from the alcohol could not get the case out of her mind. She could have reached out and touched the smug bastard. Holding the elevator door open was like a slap in her face. Now it felt personally insulting. She decided to stick around Las Vegas for a couple of days to see if he turned up again, or if he left town. There were still a couple of leads to follow.

~~ Tammy had to resort to sleeping in the graveyard again, but this time she was awakened by the drone of the caretaker's mower as he got an early start before the heat set in. Disoriented, she managed to get the car started and exit the cemetery before he came over the small knoll that hid her from the maintenance building where he began his circuit on the lawn. Tammy fought her way through the Monday morning traffic across town to get to work. She wanted to get to the manager to explain what happened last night. As soon as she entered the diner, Donna rushed over to her.

"What happened last night? I caught all kinds of hell from Gustav because he was short-staffed."

"I was here, I swear. But when I pulled into the parking lot, that guy was sitting there in his truck. Thank God he was asleep, and I was able to get outta here before he saw me," Tammy explained. "Where is Gustav now?"

"He went to the bank to deposit yesterday's receipts. He —" Suddenly there was a commotion behind Tammy as Gustav stormed into the diner and slammed a bank bag on the checkout desk beside the register.

"You!" he shouted pointing at Tammy. "What you doing in my restaurant? Get out! You fired!'

Tammy spun to face the on-rushing bull. His chef's coat was open revealing a greasy, sweat-stained wifebeater underneath. Nobody knew for sure where he originated, but it was one of the Soviet eastern bloc countries. Dark hair covered every inch of exposed skin on his three hundred pound body. He looked like a brown bear in full attack mode. "I came in to explain."

"There is no explain. First, you call to switch shifts. Then you no-show," Gustav loomed over her only inches away. "Get out!" he screamed pointing at the door.

Tammy started to open her mouth, but his face bobbed closer, and his eyes bugged out as if daring her to speak. Tears flowed down her cheeks as she hung her head and slunk out the door, afraid to even look around at her colleagues for support. Tammy sat in her car crying for fifteen minutes before her hands would stop shaking enough to drive. She drove toward her apartment on autopilot, not even thinking about Blackie possibly being there.

When Tammy arrived at the older victorian house that was converted into apartments, she saw her roommate getting out of her car. She pulled the Corolla in behind Lisa's car.

"Hey, Lisa, where have you been already this morning? I figured you'd still be in bed."

"I ran a few errands," Lisa responded curtly. Tammy followed Lisa into the apartment. The place looked different, but she couldn't immediately put her finger on why. She walked into her bedroom, and it was empty.

"Where's all my stuff?" Lisa stood with her hands on her hips as if waiting for the question.

"Gone. I told you two weeks ago I needed the rent money." One of her eyelids drooped and her lips curled in a snarl expressing her disdain. "I haven't seen you in three days. You're a month late on rent. I took what I could to a consignment store and gave the rest of your junk to Goodwill."

Tammy was stunned. Already cried out at the loss of her job, she stood there, mouth open in disbelief. She did not even resist as Lisa placed her hand on her shoulder and guided her out the front door which promptly slammed behind her. On the large front porch, was a flower pot, with a small glass-blown bumble bee on the end of thin copper wire. The carnations that were planted were dry and brown, fried by the relentless sun. The bee was a gift from Freddie, her only remaining possession. She reached down and plucked it from the pot, hugging it to her chest as she zombie walked back to her car. She was jobless and homeless, without possessions or prospects. What next?

Thursday, June 16th (Evening)

Wally and Stan rolled into Las Vegas minutes before six o'clock that evening. Stan drove his '53 Chevy Belair, and Wally was in his '54 Ford F-100. The Chevy had an expensive paint job and perfect chrome. Wally's truck was covered in gray primer and heavily modified. Stan insisted on being in the lead so that the Ford's eighteen inch wide rear tires would not throw stones at his car. Wally solved it by racing ahead as they climbed out of Barstow until his temperature gauge started climbing also. They both managed to make the trip without any mechanical issues.

As they got out of their respective rides in the casino registration parking area, Stan couldn't resist a jab. "What? Did that thing start overheating on you during the climb? I noticed you slowed down pretty quick back there."

Wally, though indignant, tried to act casual. "No. It was running fine. I just didn't want to get too far ahead of you in case that piece of junk broke down."

"That'll be the day. The air conditioning was on all the way up the hill." Stan bragged.

"So was mine"

"Bullshit. I know it wasn't cause I saw your arm hanging out the window when you passed me.

"I rolled it down to wave goodbye," Wally lied.

"Uh-huh. Sure you did. Remember what tailpipe told you. FORD, fixed or repaired daily."

They managed to check into the casino and went to their rooms to stow their luggage. They agreed to meet back downstairs in ten minutes. When Stan walked into the lobby, Wally was sitting on one of the sofas intently studying a map spread out on the seat beside him.

"What are you doing?" Stan asked.

"I'm checking out the area. Henderson is a short ride south of here. I might go down there in the morning, to see what's what," Wally answered without looking up.

"Why don't you use your smartphone? They got apps for that nowadays." Stan took his phone out of its holster on his belt and held it up with the face toward Wally.

"Them dumbass phones might be okay for turn-by-turn directions, but you get no idea about the lay of the land," he complained. "It's part of the dumbing down of the whole world. People blindly follow some girl's voice on the phone right off a cliff." He tapped the map on the seat beside him. "They don't know if they're going north, south, or straight to hell. I'd bet half the kids today couldn't read a map if you handed it to 'em." He shook his head. "And I'll bet you a hundred dollars, ain't one of them at MIT that could fold one back. Sure, they could write a program to do it, but ain't one of them got the sense to function in the real world."

"Okay, okay," Stan held up his hands in surrender. "I'm sorry I even suggested it."

"Well, you know I'm right." He turned his attention back to the map. "You wanna run down there with me after breakfast?"

"Maybe, I just talked to Tailpipe. He was in his room and is coming down to meet us. Let's figure out what we want to eat for dinner and worry about tomorrow when we're all together."

"I'm going to Henderson, with or without you. You do what you want."

Tommy Tailpipe walked into the lobby and, seeing Stan and Wally, walked over to them. "I talked to my cousin. We're meetin' him for dinner."

"Where?" Wally asked.

"What does it matter?" he frowned because he knew where this was heading.

"Because last year in Reno you tried to take us to a seafood buffet," Wally grumbled. "I ain't eating no seafood or no damned dirty chicken."

"Don't worry, Wally," Tailpipe winked at Stan. "My cousin raves about this place. He said it's the best Ethiopian food in Nevada."

"Bullshit! You go on without me, then," Wally exploded. "What the hell is Ethiopian? I ain't eatin' nothin' I can't spell!"

"Cool your jets, Mr. Adventurous. He said it was a local Italian place that's really good. Sinatra used to eat there," Tailpipe said holding his hands up in front of him.

"I don't think he can spell Italian, either," Stan chimed in.

"Screw both of you." Wally stood and finished folding his map. "Man's got a right to eat what he wants."

Since Tailpipe brought his El Camino, Stan had the only car with a backseat, requiring him to drive. They met Tailpipe's cousin Frank at the restaurant and sat for dinner. "Nobody's heard from Bob for a couple weeks. The whole group's worried about him," Frank told them.

"Has anybody been by his place? Does he have any relatives in the area?' Wally asked.

"His only relative we know of is a brother in Alaska. Nobody has his number." Frank tore off a piece of Italian bread as he talked. "Bob lives outside of town. Had a guy who rents a small house out back of his. Guy named Jack. He takes care of the place when Bob was off working somewhere." Frank dipped the bread in a small bowl of olive oil and started to take a bite but stopped with the bread halfway to his mouth. "Last anybody from the club was out there was a week ago. Jack hadn't heard nothin' from him." He popped the bread in his mouth and chewed.

"Well, I think I'll head out there tomorrow," Wally announced again, "and have a look around."

"I have a club meeting, or I'd go with you," Frank said still chewing.

"I'm sleeping in," Tailpipe added. "That drive down here wore me out."

"I guess I'm stuck with you," Stan groaned. "I promised your nephew I'd look after you."

"I don't need a babysitter," Wally said looking at the menu. "What's a man got to do to get some butter for their bread around here?"

"Oh my god," Tailpipe exclaimed. "Use the olive oil. Bobbie's not here to butter it for you, anyway."

Chapter Seven - Friday, June 17th

Dan woke with a start. He dreamed he and his uncle were broke down on the side of the highway in a desert. No cars passed for hours, and the temperature was reaching well into triple digits. They drank all the water they brought, and Wally was becoming delirious and trying to drain the radiator to drink the antifreeze. Dan was caught in the molasses of time unable to get to his uncle to stop him before he poisoned himself. He was screaming that the antifreeze was poison as Wally raised the pan to his lips, the greenish liquid spilling out of the side of his mouth as he gulped.

"It's pois—." Syd raised her head as Dan sat up in bed, her ears up, on alert. As her owner looked around, realizing where he was, she stood and walked over to the bed to nuzzle his hand laying on top of the covers. He absentmindedly stroked her head, as he calmed himself. "Hey, Syd. Just a bad dream, girl. It's okay." Syd licked his hand, and relaxed her ears, though she kept a close eye on him.

Dan decided he might as well get up since he knew he would not be able to get back to sleep. He tried to call Wally a few times yesterday but figured the old Ford was so noisy he couldn't hear his phone if he were driving. "It's not like Wally can hear it when its quiet either, is it, girl?" he asked Syd. She answered with a short, low "uff" and put her paw on the edge of the bed as he swung his feet to the floor.

Dan grabbed his phone and tried again, but he got a busy signal. "That old goat better call me to let me know he made it to Vegas in that piece of crap." Syd stretched, and ran to her bed to grab a tennis ball, sensing everything was back to normal.

After Dan showered and dressed, he tried Wally's cell again. No answer again. He was glad his uncle convoyed with Stan in case either of them ran into trouble, but the lack of contact made him nervous. He went down to the shop and began his day, making a mental note to call at lunch.

~~ Detective Bartlett's morning was a bust. She tried to follow up the two leads on old Ford trucks registered in the area. The first address didn't seem to exist. The entire block was a giant construction site where they were building another strip mall. Just what the world needs. She tried the second address, but a woman answered the door speaking Spanish, sort of. Bartlett spoke decent Spanish, but could not follow this woman's dialect, or perhaps it was a speech impediment. After five minutes she decided to try later when someone else was home. The detective treated herself to a late breakfast at Starbucks, grabbing a yogurt parfait and a black coffee. Finally, she headed for Henderson. Once there she went to the local PD, to inform them she wanted to visit the Foster residence to see if she could find anything that could help. The desk sergeant told her there was a man stationed at the house, but he wanted to check with the detectives. She took a seat and scanned her email on her phone as she waited.

"Are you Detective Bartel?" She looked up to see what looked like a pair of the drugstore mustache, nose, and glasses on a short bald guy leaning over her. "I thought maybe a Playboy model was here to see me."

She stood and extended her hand. "It's Bartlett...like the pear?"

"Pair?" She noticed him glance at her chest. "Oh, I'm sorry. Damn! You're a tall drink of water, aren't you?" At least he had a firm grip. "My name's DeCicco, Detective Saul DeCicco." He removed his glasses, but the mustache and nose stayed. He was about five-foot-three with a genuine smile and easy manner she liked immediately.

"Hello. Hey, I know you're busy, but I wanted to let you know I plan to visit Bob Foster's house."

"Oh, right. Look, we're a little short on detectives right now. No pun intended. So I'd like to send one of our crime scene techs with you, to ensure integrity. You understand."

"Of course." She appreciated his self-deprecating humor.

"If something were to be missing later, I don't want any finger-pointing going on. This keeps it clean."

"I appreciate it and apologize for the distraction."

"Don't take this wrong, Detective. Heh, heh. But I could use more distractions like you around." He smiled and put his palm on the back of his neck. "When I heard a detective was here, I expected some crusty old dude with an attitude. You know, like me." A young Asian woman appeared through the door behind him. "Oh, here she is. Ling, this is Detective Bartlett, like the pear." She noticed him glance at her chest again. "Can you escort her to the Foster residence? Thank you."

"Ling?" Bartlett asked as they shook hands. "May I call you Ling?"

"Yes, Detective." They shook hands.

"Just tell Ling if you need anything else," DeCicco added walking back through the door.

When he was gone Ling gave her a slight frown, and asked, "What did you do to DeCicco? I've never seen him so flustered."

"He was having trouble with his eye-contact skills." Bartlett laughed.

"Yeah, he's a bit of a lech but completely harmless." Ling drove to the house with Bartlett who asked how she liked working in the lab. To Bartlett's surprise, she enjoyed field work the most, even the grisly crime scenes.

~~ Wally struggled to herd the cats the next morning. Tailpipe, true to his word, slept in and it was almost nine o'clock by the time he was able to rouse Stan down to breakfast. His reluctant companion tried to talk him into going for a pancake breakfast at Denny's. They finally agreed Wally would buy him a muffin at the Starbucks in the lobby of the casino. Wally approached the barista with Stan right behind him. "I'll take three dollars-worth."

"Excuse me, Sir," the confused employee said.

"Three dollars-worth. You sell coffee here, don't cha?"

"Yes, Sir, but…"

"Give him a grande of your Pike's Peak coffee, black," Stan interrupted.

"What he said," Wally pointed at his partner. "Sorry, I don't speak Starbucks." After Stan placed his order, he walked over to the other side and found Wally still chuckling to himself. "I always wanted to try that," he giggled. "Ever since I heard Click and Clack say it on that Car Talk radio program."

"Very funny," Stan added. "And don't think I didn't notice you walked off without paying."

"I'm sorry. Here." He handed over a ten-dollar bill. "I was having too much fun and forgot." They finished their breakfast as Wally sat cussing at his phone.

"What's the matter now?" Stan asked.

"This danged phone keeps dying on me. I put a new battery in it last year." He held the screen for Stan to see. "I charged it all night, and the silly thing's dead already. Good thing I brought a paper map with us."

"Did you buy some cheap aftermarket battery? Maybe you should take it back to the Apple store."

"They'll charge me twice as much. To hell with them."

"Well, you get what you pay for, dumbass. We can use my phone for directions." Wally drove, and using Stan's GPS program they got to Henderson and found the house without a problem.

As they arrived, Stan pointed at the house. "Is that yellow police tape?"

Wally sat looking at it for a minute. "Well, shit."

"Looks like we came down here for nothing."

"Now hold on. I learned from a deputy where we live that they post a guard at active crime scenes." He made a show of looking around. "I don't see no guard, so I think we're good."

"No! I'm staying right here. If you go in there and get arrested, I do not even know you. What the hell do you think you're gonna find anyway?" Stan was apoplectic.

"I won't know if I don't look. Besides, if it was still active, the cops would post a guard." Wally climbed out of the truck, strolled up the sidewalk and slipped under the yellow tape at the edge of the steps. He tried the front door, and to his surprise, it opened.

"Wally!" Stan stage-whispered to him. "Get back here."

He turned and gave Stan a little wave and raised his eyebrows twice to show how clever and unafraid he was. As Wally turned back around the door swung open, a Henderson Police officer stood on the other side with his hand on the handle. His nametag said he was Officer Gray.

"Oh, shit!" Wally managed to croak.

"Sir, are you feeling okay?" Officer Gray asked. "Everything alright?"

Puzzled by the question Wally shrugged his shoulders. "Uh, I, I guess."

"Cause you're on the wrong side of the tape unless you've got some kind of a badge," the cop answered pointing to his own badge and smirking.

Everybody's a smartass. Afraid at first, Wally was now pissed. "I've got my Vegas Car Show badge in the truck." He pointed his truck out with his thumb. "Wait, right here, and I'll be right back with it." He spun around to make a quick exit. The cop reached out and grabbed him by the back of the shirt collar forcing him to sit on the step. In one swift, practiced movement Wally's right wrist was cuffed, quickly followed by the left. "Hey! I thought you wanted to see my badge?"

"Where's your ID, Sir?"

"So. It's just dandy when you want to be a sarcastic prick, but when I joke around it gets physical, huh? And what's this Sir shit? I worked for a living all my life." Facing his truck as he sat on the steps, Wally saw Stan sink lower in the passenger seat, but the fuse was already lit. "I'll sue your ass for police brutality. This is elder abuse! That's a form of hate crime you know." He tried to look back over his shoulder to gauge the reaction. "They tack on extra for hate crimes."

"Sir! Is your wallet in your back pocket?"

"Possibly. I'm still dizzy and disoriented from being forced to the ground during the assault."

"Do you have any weapons, anything sharp, or anything else on you I should be aware of?" Gray walked around in front of Wally.

"Just a superior intellect, and rapier wit," Wally answered looking defiantly at the younger policeman.

The cop brought his hand up to act like he was rubbing his chin, but Wally could see the smile threatening to come out. "Sir, do I have your permission to remove your wallet from your pocket?"

"Are you planning on molesting me now?"

"No, Sir. And for your protection, this is all being caught on my body cam." He pointed to the device clipped to the front of his uniform. "Now, do I have permission to remove your wallet?"

"Sure, but could you move the camera a little to my right? That's my good side."

He turned Wally so he could access his back pocket, still smiling and shaking his head in disbelief. Carefully removing the wallet with two fingers, he dropped it into Wally's cuffed hands that were in front of him. "Here's your wallet. Please remove your ID for me, Sir." Wally did as he was told. "Mr. Williams, did you say you're in town for the car show in Vegas? Which show would that be, Sir?"

"It's a hot rod show. I think it's called the Desert Deuce Classic." He looked back over at his truck. "My friend made all the arrangements, and I simply tagged along. Pretty sure that's the name of it."

"Is that your truck?"

"Yes."

"Who's in the truck, Sir?" Officer Gray gestured toward the truck with Wally's driver's license.

"Nobody." He knew Stan would be pissed if he were dragged into this. The cop motioned for the person to come and join them. Stan hung his head.

"Sir!" He motioned again. "Please exit the vehicle and come here. And keep your hands where I can see them." Stan slowly opened the door and held his hands in front of him approaching them cautiously, glaring at Wally the whole way.

"Morning, Officer," Stan said.

"Good morning. That's close enough, Sir." Stan stopped. "Could I see some ID please?"

"I have to reach for my wallet, okay?"

"Slowly."

Stan took out his wallet, extracted his driver's license and handed it to the nice officer. "I tried to tell this dumbass —" Now it was Wally's turn to glare.

The cop looked up from reading the license. "Tell him what, Sir?" Wally's glare hardened.

"Uh, that, uh, it didn't look like Bob was home. That it looked like something was wrong, with the tape and all."

The officer looked at Wally. "Are you friends of the man who lives here?"

"I met Bob a little while back," Wally answered warily.

"I didn't know him at all," Stan quickly volunteered. "Never met him."

Gray looked from one to the other, saying nothing. The silence made Wally nervous causing him to add, "I've never been to his house. Wasn't even sure this was the right house. When I knocked the door was open. Then you came out." Wally thought he saw an opening.

Officer Gray spoke into the radio mike clipped to his epaulet, "Zalinsky, can you bring the car around?" He handed Stan's license back to him. Then he addressed Wally, "Mr. Williams, we're going to take a little ride downtown, long enough to check out your story a little better."

"What about me?" Stan asked.

"You're welcome to follow us to the station." After getting permission, Wally handed his keys to Stan and waited as a patrol car came around the corner.

"This ain't the first time I've eaten the State's bologna sandwiches." His bravado was lost on the officer. "I ain't scared."

"Nothin' to be proud of, Sir." Gray held Wally's arm as they moved toward the car.

"I told you to walk down and use the McDonalds bathroom," Zalinsky yelled out the car window as they approached.

"If I did that, I would have missed Dillinger here." Officer Gray nodded his head toward Wally.

"You were using a crime scene to take a piss?" Wally said turning to him.

"Yeah," he laughed. "Lucky you."

~~ Dan spent the morning putting final touches on a project and packing it to be shipped. He was going to lunch when his cell phone rang. He looked at the number on his phone with a puzzled look. "This can't be good." Syd raised her head from the edge of her bed.

"Dan, I told you I couldn't promise anything," Stan started immediately. "The damned fool wouldn't listen to me. You know how he gets. Don't be getting mad at me. I tried, believe me."

Dan held the phone away from his ear. "Stan. Stan! Listen! Slow down." There was a pause on the other end. "First, is he okay?" Syd walked over to Dan's side, worried at his tone of voice.

"Yes, I guess you could say he's okay. Okay, for an idiot. I —"

"Is the truck okay?"

"The truck's fine. I'm driving it now." Stan answered. "It steers for shit with that Watts link and those skinny tires on the front."

"Wait. Why are you driving Wally's truck?" Dan grew concerned again. "He doesn't let anybody drive that truck."

"That's what I'm trying to tell you," Stan acted as if Dan were the obtuse one. "The dumbass got himself arrested."

Wally's temper was legendary. If he thought he was right, he would stand toe-to-toe with a grizzly to prove a point. "What was he doing? Burnouts on 'The Strip' or something?"

"No. He crossed some police tape at Bob's place. If I drove, I would have left him there, but I was stuck. Then a cop came out as he was opening the door."

"Stan!" Dan needed to slow him down again. "Where exactly are you?"

"I told you. I'm in Wally's truck." He said as if talking to a three-year-old. "Following the cop to the police station."

"What police station?" Dan was losing his patience.

"I don't know. How many stations do they have in Henderson?"

"So you're in Henderson?" Dan tried to keep calm.

"Yes," Stan answered. "I told you. We were at Bob's."

"Stan, listen. I need to lock up here and deliver some packages to UPS, then I'm on my way. I'll be there as soon as I can."

"Okay, call me when you get here because Wally's phone doesn't work."

"Will do." Dan sighed and petted Syd's head, though his thoughts were elsewhere.

~~ Detective Bartlett and Ling had been to the Foster home and back earlier that morning. The only thing they found that would help was a DMV renewal notice for the truck with the serial number to help her confirm the vehicle if they located it even if the suspect changed the plates. She sat at Detective DeCicco's desk waiting for him to get out of a meeting. She reviewed her notes over and over, not sure where to go next.

Bartlett was always hard on herself. Being a woman, she knew she had to work harder than her male counterparts to be respected. The fact that men usually considered her good-looking only compounded the problem. When word got out about her standing in the same elevator as the suspect, her reputation would definitely take a hit. She felt if she went back to Phoenix now, it would be with her tail between her legs. She could find nothing in her notes that jumped out at her. No calls from the casino meant the suspect hadn't returned. Bartlett checked her email again hoping for a new lead, even though she didn't hear an incoming email tone and she'd checked it only five minutes ago. She waited for DeCicco to chat about the case, share any ideas, and coordinate on-going efforts. Her thoughts were suddenly interrupted by a uniformed officer leading an older man into the room approaching the desk where she sat.

"You must be new," the officer said, smiling and giving her the once over. "I was looking for DeCicco."

Flustered, she stood and began retrieving her things. "Oh, I uh … I was waiting for Detective DeCicco also." The contents of the files spilled out onto the desk. She managed to recover her composure enough to add, "I'm Detective Bartlett. I'm with the Phoenix PD, here on a case." She extended her hand.

He released the old man's arm and shook her hand. "Officer Gray. You're a hell of a lot better looking than DeCicco." Seeing the look on her face he added, "Sorry, umm …" He looked over at Wally, suddenly remembering why he was there. "I caught this guy trying to get into the Foster house. I figured DeCicco would want to talk to him."

Glad for the change of subject, the detective turned her attention to Wally. "Really?"

"Hey, I know you," Wally spoke. "We talked on the phone. I'm Wally Williams. You're that detective who called me."

"Ah, yes, Mr. Williams but, uh, I thought you lived in California."

"I do. I came to Las Vegas for a hot rod show," he explained. "I thought I'd take a chance and come down to where Bob lived, hoping maybe it wasn't him that you found."

"So you knew the victim from before?" the detective was confused.

"No. I told you I met him at the truck stop." Wally suddenly realized where she was going with this. Putting him back on the suspect list. "I met some of his friends who are hosting the car show. They told me where he lived."

"Why were you in his house then?" She didn't look like she was removing him from the list yet.

"I wasn't in his house." He stiffened his back, indignant now. "I was at the front door." The detective looked at the patrolman for an explanation.

"He was inside the crime scene tape," Officer Gray added.

"Of course, I was inside the tape." He gave the officer a derisive look. "You had the damned tape out on the post by the steps. How the hell else could I knock on the door? I was trying to see if anyone was home. What'd ya expect me to do? Stand on the lawn and throw pebbles at the windows?"

Gray shoved him gently down into the visitor's chair beside DeCicco's desk. He looked at Bartlett. "Would you mind watching him for a minute, while I check in? I'm gonna let our detectives figure out what to do with this guy."

"Sure. I'm still waiting to talk to DeCicco anyway." She looked at Wally. "You going to behave?"

"Yeah, you seem like a lot better company than this one." He tilted his head toward the policeman. "A lot smarter anyway." The patrolman rolled his eyes and walked away shaking his head.

Bartlett gathered the contents splayed across the desk and organized it back into the folder. She was hoping the old guy would sit there and keep quiet as she concentrated on getting things back in order. She hated disorder.

"My nephew was right about you," Wally blurted after a few minutes. She didn't take the bait, and he continued, "He said you sounded good-looking when we talked to you." She gave him a stern sideways glance to indicate she wasn't amused. "What's the term the kids use now? Hot! He said you sounded hot."

It was time for the detective to roll her eyes. She was tired of all the labels. Tired of men never getting past the packaging to look at the person underneath. She wasn't the detective, she was the hot detective. Even the badge didn't gain her enough respect to be treated as a professional first. What made this guy think he could broach such a subject with a perfect stranger? Even when she was married, wearing a wedding ring did not prevent it from happening. Boundaries people! She was told by her counselor coming out of the marriage that she needed to work on defining boundaries. She had a history of trusting too soon and letting people run all over her. So she stopped dating. Put up a brick wall the shrink said was too rigid. When she bristled, he assured her the process of learning boundaries was like anything else. At first, she'd go too far and overreact, make mistakes, but eventually, she would learn.

Her thoughts were interrupted once again by Wally. He looked down watching what she was doing. The picture of the truck from the casino was clipped on top of the registration sheet she received from the LVPD, with a yellow post-it note that said, possible owner. "That's not a '67."

"Excuse me?" She was still angry about the boundaries, and now the interruption was not helping.

"The truck in the picture is not a '67. It's a '68. That can't be the registration, or they got it wrong at the DMV," Wally said. He seemed so damned sure of himself, but she calmed herself.

"How do you know?"

Since his hands were cuffed, he jutted his chin toward the picture. "See those side markers? The little reflectors on the side of the fenders."

Christ, now he was mansplaining. "I'm aware of what side markers are," Bartlett couldn't stop herself from saying.

"Well, they weren't required until '68. So that has to be a '68." He looked at her matter-of-factly. "That can't be the correct registration. They gave you the wrong one."

"Are you some sort of expert?"

"I owned one. So I'm pretty familiar with them."

"Oh. Okay." Her voice softened a bit. "Thanks." She remembered she had the registration renewal from the Foster house and checked the VIN. Sure enough, it didn't match. She mumbled to herself, "Damn it. That was my last lead." She might as well head back to Phoenix after she talked to DeCicco. This guy was gone, like a dust devil that materializes in the desert, disappears, and suddenly pops up somewhere else. All she could do was bide her time until he surfaced again.

"Sorry. Just trying to help." The look on his face made it clear he felt bad. "I do know of a case where a guy bought a '58 Ford late in 1957. The DMV automatically put '57 on the title, but the car companies used to put out the next year model in September of the previous year. Technically, it was a '58 model. But that guy would argue until he was blue in the face, that it was a '58." He paused until he saw she understood. "World's full of dumbasses." She smiled slightly at that.

"Well, thank you for your help." She decided to have some fun with him. "So, is your nephew hot?"

Surprise registered on his face. "Well, I uh, I don't know. He's alright, I guess."

"Does he look much like you?" She decided to push his boundaries. "I mean, is he well hung?" She tried to not smile.

"I, uh. I don't know that I..." He looked down at the floor and turned a bit pink in the face.

"You know, we hot women have pretty high standards." She shrugged. "We can't waste our time with average." He turned his head away and grunted.

~~ Blackie peeked between the curtains of his motel window, squinting at the burst of sunlight illuminating the room. Blinking until his eyes adjusted, he saw a breakfast place across the street. He would be able to keep an eye on his truck while eating to see if it was attracting attention before he approached it. Blackie congratulated himself on how wily he was getting as his confidence grew. Exiting his room, he walked in the opposite direction of his truck, crossed the street and entered the café. The smell of bacon hit him as soon as he walked in the door. Bacon, and coffee. Morning smells.

He found a booth and sat facing the motel to keep an eye on the Ford. The table in front of him had two girls who looked to be in their early twenties and were overdressed for the place. The one with her back to him had big hair blocking his view of the other girl, but the brief glance he got showed she was cute. The girls were laughing and sharing stories about something. From snippets he could hear, it was clear they had been out partying all night and decided to grab breakfast before heading home.

An older waitress suddenly appeared at his table. With bleached hair and tired eyes that had seen it all, she rocked back on her heels appraising him. "Have you been seated, Sir?"

Blackie looked around. "Me?"

"Yeah, you." A look of disapproval crossed her face.

"I'm sitting, ain't I?" Blackie was annoyed.

"The sign says, wait to be seated," the sing-songy tone of her voice made him want to reach up and grab the ornate pin that hung over her nametag, and shove it down her throat.

"I musta missed it." He saw that Big Hair had left, but the cute brunette was watching him. "There was a fat guy in front of me when I came in," he added as he smiled at the girl.

A heavy sigh. "Let me get you a menu, Sir." The impatience in the air was thicker than the pancake syrup sitting on the table. She turned and walked away.

"Ooooh. You got in trouble." It was the brunette flashing a smile and raising her eyebrows. He grinned and glanced at his truck. After a few seconds. "Are you a bad boy?" The last two words came out of pouting, teasing lips, as she winked.

Keeping his face toward the window, he glanced at her sideways. A playful smile formed as he turned to face her. "Maybe." He tilted his head to the side trying to look disinterested.

It seemed to work. The brunette slid out of her booth and into Blackie's, facing him.

"I'm Britney." At the same time, the grumpy waitress came back and tossed the menu on the table. Blackie glared at her causing her to suddenly realize she was needed elsewhere. Britney laughed as the older woman glanced back once she was at a safe distance. "You're kinda cute, for a Mexican." Blackie's jaw tensed at the comment. He actually had only about one-eighth Hispanic blood in him and even had a blond-haired half-brother. The remainder was mostly Texas redneck, and his mother's maiden name had been Travis. He had endured relentless teasing as a kid for his Hispanic looks.

He glanced around, and said," What happened to your friend?"

"Oh, you greedy boy! You do want to party." Britney touched his hand. "She went home to crash. Party-pooper." She looked around to see who was within earshot. "But I just did a line in the bathroom." Her high-pitched giggle filled the room. "I'm good for another couple hours."

A different waitress came. Blackie tried to think of the quickest thing to order to get on the road, so settled for scrambled eggs and hash browns. The food was on the table in a few minutes. He suspected the waitress was trying to get rid of them, but at this point, it was in his best interest. "I have a room right across the street. Want to go back there?" he asked as he threw some bills on the table.

"Let's go," she said and giggled again. They walked across the street. Blackie kept a wary eye as a police cruiser went by.

"Hold on a second," Blackie said and trotted over to his truck to retrieve some condoms out of the glove box.

"Is that yours?" She gestured toward the Ford.

"Yeah. It's a sweet ride." He steered her up the concrete steps toward the second floor of the motel.

As she turned and climbed ahead of him, she giggled, then said, "That's a first. A Mexican with an old pickup." She laughed at her own wit. Behind her, Blackie's face grew dark, and his eyes bored into the back of her skull. How dare her! He unlocked the motel door and held it open for her. Britney was trim. A little too thin for his taste, but she had a pixie face and a quick smile.

Blackie grabbed her before she took two steps into the room. He had his right hand on her chin, and his left on the back of her skull where he had been staring moments ago. With a quick snap, he broke her neck like his grandmother used to do to the chickens for Sunday dinner on the farm. His grandmother didn't spin the chicken around like some people. A quick snap and it was over. No fooling around or showmanship. The chicken would be strutting around with the others one second, then bam, gone, plucked and in the pot. The break didn't completely sever the spinal cord so she was still breathing as he laid her back on the bed.

He feigned a thick Mexican accent as he spun her around and positioned her body. "So, you want to party with a Mexican? Let's party, Mamacita!" Still conscious, the look of surprise on her face now turned to terror, as Blackie lifted her skirt and climbed on top of her. Even though he knew she couldn't feel anything, he wanted her last fleeting glimpse of the world to be of him. The movement must have further injured the spinal cord because she began to struggle for breath. He watched as life left her eyes, the terror replaced by oblivion.

When he finished, he sat on the edge of the bed, full of remorse. Suddenly, the comment about Mexicans and old trucks came back to him, and he grew angry again. How dare the skinny bitch! Blackie thought about what to do next. He went through her purse and took all the money. Then he calmly walked back across the street and threw the empty bag in the dumpster behind the restaurant, along with her cell phone. Back at the motel, he went to the alley behind his room to see if he could drop the body out the bathroom window. It was a sliding window with a bar in the middle that was too small even for a skinny person to fit. His luck held, however, because as he walked past the dumpster, he noticed a large discarded suitcase with a broken handle and two missing wheels off the bottom.

Blackie took the suitcase back to the room. Her body would fit into it, but it would be hard to carry with a broken handle. Once he had the luggage zipped and ready to carry down to his truck, he took a quick look around. There was no blood. No evidence that a murder had taken place there. He smiled. In the bed of the truck, it looked like any other suitcase. He was simply a guy on a trip.

~~ After spending another night in her car, Tammy was tired and wanted a shower and a change of clothes. She had no money to buy new ones and only managed to scrape three dollars in coins out of her center console and ashtray. As she sat in McDonald's with a small coffee and a breakfast sandwich, she tried to think of what to do next. There were not a lot of options. She dropped out of high school in her senior year and worked at waitressing ever since. Looking at the sign in McDonald's that said they were taking applications, she remembered the measly wages and lack of tips which caused her to leave the fast food industry after a stint in high school. She had no skills and a spotty employment record. With a quarter tank of gas, she couldn't get far even if she had somewhere to go.

Back in her Toyota, she sat facing the street watching the cars whiz by. She wondered where in the world all these people were going. It seemed everyone had somewhere to go but her. They had jobs and homes and families. It almost brought her to tears thinking about where her life was heading. She sipped the last of her coffee and was about to toss it into a trash can she was parked beside when she noticed an older looking truck coming down the street. At first, she was sure it was Blackie, but the color looked wrong. She kept an eye on the pickup, and as it got closer, she saw it was definitely him. He must have had it painted, which explained why it looked different the other night in the parking lot.

Seeing the truck and Blackie so close suddenly turned her depression to anger. He was the one who destroyed her life in a few short days. One day really. She thought about the money he flashed at the diner, and how she was only trying to prevent the poor kid from getting rolled by some low life. Well, to be completely honest, she had some designs on the money herself but would never hurt the kid. The money! That little asshole screwed up her whole life, and now she deserved to have some of the cash to get her through this rough patch. She tossed the cup out the window, short of the trashcan because she was focused on a different target now. Starting her Toyota, she quickly took off after the truck.

Blackie seemed to be moseying along, and she had no trouble catching him. Fortunately, the streets in the area were four lanes wide. She pulled beside him in the left lane and blew the horn. She watched him jerk his head in her direction, and the truck veered to the right as he reacted to being startled. It took a second beep and a wave before he recognized who she was. He gave her a tentative smile and waved but made no effort to pull over. After motioning to him for several blocks, she finally got him to pull to the curb. Tammy moved over to his lane and stopped about twenty yards ahead of the truck. Watching in her mirror, she saw he made no effort to get out of the pickup. She exited the Toyota and sauntered back, giving him yet another wave and her best fake smile. She noticed he had a large suitcase in the bed of the truck which she had not seen before.

"Hey, I've been looking for you," he said sticking his head out the window.

"It's been a rough couple days." He sat looking at her as she continued. "I got fired from my job, and my roommate sold all my stuff to pay the back rent." She was suddenly self-conscious realizing she had slept in her car for a few days and probably looked a mess. "I've been living out of my car."

"I thought you were avoiding me," he complained. He stared at her hair.

She was sure it was a bird's nest. She looked away, feeling embarrassed, and noticed the broken handle on the bag. "Whose luggage?" she found herself saying before she could rethink it. She wondered if he was already with someone else.

Blackie quickly exited the truck and stepped between her and the bed of the pickup. "M-m-mine." She had never heard him stutter before. He put his arm around her and began to steer her toward her car, but she could feel his arm shaking as if he were afraid. "I got it at a Salvation Army Store. It was cheap because of the broken handle." He was speaking rapidly now. She glanced at him and stiffened at his touch. "Why don't we find someplace where we can talk and get lunch?" He gave her shoulders a squeeze. "I was really worried about you."

"Sure," she said, but her voice betrayed her lack of conviction. They were beside her car now, and he opened her door. "I'll follow you."

He glanced nervously back at the truck. "I'll tell you what. I have one small errand to run, and then I'll meet you..." He glanced around. "At that Chili's Restaurant over there." He reached into his pocket and came out with a twenty. "Here. Buy yourself a coke or something until I get there."

Tammy wondered what he was really up to. "Okay. But don't take long."

"Well, here's another twenty in case I get delayed." He handed her the bill. "Go ahead and eat if you need to."

"Are you okay?"

"Yeah, I'm good. I promise I'll see you in a bit." He trotted back to his truck but sat there until she pulled out and cut across the street

Friday, June 17th (Afternoon)

Syd loved car trips. She would sit in the passenger seat and watch the world go by, happy to be with Dan. Dan would occasionally sing along with the radio, and on rare occasions, Syd would join in. She liked Willy Nelson songs the best. When he hit one of his twangy high notes where his vibrato kicked in, Syd would tilt her head back and howl. At first, Dan thought she did it out of dislike, but when he reached to turn it off, she put her paw on his hand as if to stop him. When he tried to get her to do it on her own, she wouldn't. Only when Dan and Willy were singing did Syd join in.

"You are something else, girl," he said when he could catch his breath, then tousled her ears.

Other times for entertainment, he would put sunglasses on Syd. She would sit and look out as if she wore them every day. He watched people in other cars react to the show. They would usually laugh or point her out for others to see. Kids especially seemed to enjoy Syd's antics. He worked on teaching her to wave, merely a high-five from Syd's point of view, but reserved it only for the kids who squealed with delight and returned the gesture. He would give her the command, and she would put her paw on the window. After the first few times, she did it without prompting.

Dan stopped at a rest stop along Route 99 to take a break after two hours on the road. Sitting in the parking lot made him think of Bob and how this whole adventure first started. When it came time to stop again, he found a fast food place to save time, eating in the parking lot for Syd to take another break, stretch her legs and eat her dinner in the bed of the truck. Dan had been pushing the speed limits hard trying to get to Las Vegas to check on Wally. While watching Syd and eating his burger, he called Stan again to see if there were any updates. Stan had not been able to find out much and sounded annoyed because he was forced to waste most of the day in Henderson instead of the car show. In the end, the police told Stan they were going to hold Wally at least overnight, causing him to decide to go back to his room at the casino and try to meet his friends for dinner. Dan and Syd climbed back in the Dodge and hit the interstate again.

~~ After leaving Tammy, Blackie didn't have time to bury the suitcase in the desert. He drove to a light industrial area that looked like it was on the decline. He was looking for one with a dumpster but no cameras which seemed to be everywhere now. It took almost forty-five minutes of driving around, but Blackie finally saw what was needed. Parking the truck on the far side of the dumpster, he was able to stand in the bed of the pickup and lift the case to the edge of the trash bin, and push it in. The dumpster was only half full, and his deposit dropped out of sight. He managed to dispose of the body and pull away in less than a minute. He drove away slowly, checking once more for any signs of surveillance. Satisfied he found a safe spot, he headed back to meet Tammy. He hoped she would still be waiting at the restaurant.

Blackie walked into Chili's to find her sitting at the bar. She had a plate of nachos in front of her, and some sort of drink. He walked up to her and reached to hug her. "Hey," he said. "sorry that took so long."

She spun on the stool to face him. "Where the hell have you been?" She looked a bit unsteady and had a nacho in her right hand that she thrust at him like an accusing finger. He'd not seen this side of her and took a step back as cheese dripped between them onto the floor though she was oblivious to it. Flashes of his mother drunk and feeling sorry for herself crossed his mind. His jaw set and his eyes hardened but he said nothing while deciding what to do next.

"Oh, sorry. I hadn't eaten much since lunch yesterday, and that Margarita hit me pretty hard." She smiled weakly, gesturing toward the plate in front of her. "Need to get something on my stomach. I was getting worried, Darlin'." Her smile seemed to radiate genuine concern.

Blackie relaxed, there was the class that won him over. They hugged each other, and he sat on a stool beside her. "No sweat. It's what I get for being a nice guy." His eyes did a half-roll and sneered a derisive smile. Blackie tried to explain the suitcase's disappearance from the back of the truck. "The motel manager asked me to deliver that suitcase to the bus station for a guest who forgot it, but he gave me the wrong address." He saw her frown slightly at his explanation and felt a bit of panic not remembering what he'd told her about the case before. The frown cleared like passing cloud, and she turned to smile at him. Even without makeup, he loved the curve of her upper lip and lost himself thinking of kissing it. When she reached out to touch his face, he forgot ever hearing the harsh words she'd said. He never had anyone act so tender toward him, and he could have sat there with her hand gently touching his face forever.

~~ Tammy congratulated herself for recovering so quickly since she was feeling a little buzzed from the drinks. When she saw the look on his face, she was afraid she went too far. With all her other options crumbling around her, this guy was her meal ticket until she could separate him from the cash he seemed to always be carrying. Her quick apology and change of tactics made him melt in her hands. Men were so easy to manipulate. She vowed to make quick work of him so she cooed about how great it was to see him. She didn't like to be so calculating, but she was backed into a corner, and he was an easy target.

Blackie's excuse for being gone so long and about doing a favor for the motel manager was bogus. Something about taking the suitcase to the bus station. That was different from what he said before. She tried to remember exactly what he said earlier. She wondered what he was up to. Whose was it, really?

"I was worried you were arrested," Blackie told her.

"I haven't heard a thing from the cops, but I was afraid to go to work or my apartment," Tammy lied. "Then the diner manager got mad and fired me. When I went back to my apartment, my roommate had sold my stuff to pay the back rent." She started crying thinking about it. Blackie put his arm around her as the bartender came to check on them.

"I think we'll move to a table now," Blackie told the bartender, who signaled for the hostess to seat them.

"I'll transfer the check to your table," the hostess said as she escorted them to a booth.

Once they were seated and Tammy regained her composure, she reached across and took his hand. "Sorry for being so emotional, but I was worried about you and with everything that was going on…."

"No sweat. I did have a close call with some cops and had pretty much decided that if I didn't find you this morning, I was gonna leave town today."

"Where would you go?" Tammy asked.

"I don't know. I was thinking maybe California. Maybe LA." He squeezed her hand enjoying the contact. "What do you think? It might be good to get outta town for a while."

"So you're coming back here?" Tammy wondered if she should risk going along with him, or if she should stay where she knew at least a few people. He didn't seem that dangerous and only hurt Freddie because he considered it self-defense.

"I might." He seemed to mull it over. "Depends on how it goes."

"It would be like a road trip!" she said, suddenly enthusiastic. "I've always wanted to drive the Pacific Coast Highway."

"Road trip!" Blackie shouted enthusiastically and hugged her. She stiffened in his grasp at first but forced herself to relax.

"Sorry, you startled me." She smiled and hugged him back. "What should we do with my car? Should we take two cars?"

Blackie considered it. "We should sell it. Do you have the title?"

"It's all I have left in the world!" She was suddenly emotional. "And it gets better mileage than your truck. Maybe we should sell the truck."

"I can't sell my truck. My uncle gave it to me. It has a lot of sentimental value," he lied.

"Maybe I can leave the Toyota at my friend Donna's place."

"Whatever." He seemed to tire of the details. "Give her a call, and then let's eat. I can't wait to start our road trip!"

Tammy called and made the arrangements. Donna was at the diner still covering Tammy's shift. She ended up taking it permanently after Tammy's firing and was glad for the money. Donna agreed to take the car anytime, but Tammy did not share that information with Blackie. Tammy wanted to stall long enough to do a few things before she left with him.

Tammy hung up. "She won't be home until after five. She'll meet us then."

"Can't we just leave the key somewhere?" he looked over at the clock above the counter which indicated it was only one-fifteen. "I'd really like to get going."

The two things Tammy needed to do would require ditching Blackie. First, she wanted to write a note saying she was leaving with him, then give it along with a description of him and the truck to her lawyer. Second, Tammy planned to access her safety deposit box, to get her birth certificate, and also leave a copy of the same letter there along with a picture of Blackie she had taken with her phone while he was sleeping the first night. She already copied it to a thumb drive she would include with the letter. Tammy knew this wouldn't keep her alive, but if something happened to her, they would be sure to get him for it. She couldn't believe she was playing such a high stakes game, but she felt there were no other prospects. If she could get his money, and get away from him, she could start over. Maybe even pay for a beauty school course.

"Donna said she didn't trust the neighborhood. If anyone saw me leave a key, the car would be long gone." Tammy wasn't sure he was buying it because he frowned. "Look, that car is all I have left. I don't want it to disappear. If we could stick around long enough to sell it, then maybe ...." She paused hoping he would take the bait.

Blackie looked around. "Okay, we can wait until five. But the cops almost grabbed me a couple days ago. I took a big risk waiting this long to find you."

Tammy had a sudden thought of how to slip away from him. "Okay, we leave this evening. In the meantime, I need to get some clothes. I've been wearing these for two days now. My roommate gave all of mine to Goodwill or someplace." She smiled as he reached into his pocket and took out a wad of bills. She didn't even need to ask.

"Here," he said. "You'll need some cash." She took the money. "Where do you want to go shopping?"

She started to answer, but she realized something was off. "Wait, I haven't heard anything about Freddie's body being found. Why would the police even be interested in you?"

Blackie suddenly seemed very nervous. "I, uh, I don't know," he lied. "I guess I'm just getting paranoid. Y-y-y-you know." His face turned red, and he closed his eyes and took a deep breath. His shoulders relaxed, and his eyes hardened seeming to stare at her mouth. "You were gone," he continued. "I thought maybe you'd been arrested. Suddenly I was in an elevator surrounded by cops."

He rolled his wrist as if to say etcetera, etcetera. She realized he might be wondering why she was asking such questions.

"Oh, yeah. That makes sense," Tammy said recovering. "You poor thing. You must have been really spooked." Tammy reached across and took his hand, smiling again.

He relaxed and smiled at her. "I was." He shook his head as if to clear it. "Okay. Shopping. Where to?"

Oh crap! Back to this. "Well, we still have two cars, so why don't I head to the mall, and meet you at Donna's at five." He frowned, as if not liking the plan, causing her to add, "I might even have a few surprises for you in my new wardrobe."

She watched his eyes move down her body, then back to her face. A sly smile came to his mouth and eyes. "Ooh, I like that idea. Maybe I'll get the oil changed in the truck for the trip." She quickly gave him Donna's address and a general idea of how to get there before he paid for lunch and they went their separate ways.

~~ Wally was not happy being forced to sit and wait for the detective to escape from his meetings to determine Wally's fate. After the hot detective had asked about his nephew's penis size, Wally sat next to the desk in silence for thirty minutes. She busied herself with her notes and email. Finally, Officer Gray reappeared after wandering off for a while.

"Okay, Mr. Williams," Officer Gray said, walking up to him from behind. "Looks like the detective is going to be busy for a while, so I'm gonna put you in an interrogation room for now."

"Isn't there anybody else I can talk to?" Wally asked. "Is this Detective Desoto the only one around here with a brain that can follow a simple explanation of why I was looking for Bob?"

"It's DeCicco's case, Sir. He'll want to speak with you himself."

"Then drag his ass out here, so I can straighten him out, and be on my way," Wally's voice was starting to show some strain. "He's not the only person in the world with things to do, damn it. I'm a busy, busy man."

He tried to stand, but the officer put his hand on Wally's shoulder and pushed him back down. "Please remain seated Mr. Williams and try to stay calm."

"Just because you call me Mister don't mean you have the right to manhandle me, damn it!" Wally shook his shoulders violently to escape from the grasp of the officer. "That's twice now, and don't think I'll forget it. What's your badge number, Tough Guy? I'm filing a complaint."

"Please lower your voice, Mr. Williams," Gray was starting to get annoyed too. "I'm gonna take you to the interrogation room. I'll give you the forms you need to file a complaint and my badge number once you're inside." He started to grab Wally's arm to pull him to his feet but stopped. "Would you please stand, Sir?" Wally stood looking around the room at the other officers staring at him now.

"That's better, thank you." He heard the hussy detective groan and saw her shake her head and saw her roll her eyes.

"This way, please." Officer Gray pointed in the direction of the interrogation room, and Wally started walking. His hands were still cuffed, but he held his head up as if he owned the place.

Once in the room, the officer agreed not to cuff him to the table. He brought Wally a cup of coffee and the promised forms. Wally glanced over the papers. A yellow Post-It note was stuck to the top with Gray's name and badge number written on it. "Thank you," Wally said as he set the forms on the table. Suddenly he added, "Hey, I'm gonna need a pen."

"Sorry, but if you're not cuffed to the table, I can't give you anything that could be used as a weapon."

"Well, what makes you think, I couldn't roll up these papers real tight, and drive it through your chest cavity?" Wally said attempting to be sarcastic. "Maybe they taught me that in Navy SEAL training."

Tired of wasting time on the old geezer, Officer Gray snatched the papers off the table and said flatly, "Good point. Can't take any chances with a highly-trained, ex-SEAL." He spun and walked out the door leaving the prisoner staring with his mouth open.

~~ Blackie stood at the counter of the Speed-Pit Oil Changers listening to the employee explain all the service options to the woman in front of him. She seemed to have no idea what she was doing and was getting more confused by the moment. At first, he was annoyed but soon realized he would have been in the same boat if he did not pay attention. His ego wanted him to look like an old pro when he told them what he wanted. Blackie acted as if he was reading a brochure he picked up as he listened. When it was finally his turn, he recited the line he had been practicing in his head.

"I want the Deluxe Oil change with 10W-30 weight." Adding to impress the clerk, "and check all the fluid levels while you're at it."

"That's part of our basic service for all vehicles, Sir." The kid across the counter was about the same age as him.

"Well, uh, at the last place I had to remind them."

"Not here at Speed-Pit, Sir. We follow our twenty-eight point checklist for all vehicles that pass through our station," the clerk added a little too cheerfully. "That's a cool old Ford you have there. I'm surprised a guy like you doesn't change it himself."

"Normally I would," Blackie lied. "But I'm traveling."

The clerk's forehead wrinkled, "Traveling? When I entered the license plate number, it says you're from the area."

"Oh, uh, yeah. I am." The nosy little prick. "I'm getting ready to travel," Blackie congratulated himself mentally for recovering, "and I didn't have time before I leave."

The clerk seemed satisfied. "We'll get right on it."

"Thanks." Blackie took a seat where he could watch the street for any police cars and could also see the work being done in the bays. It worried him that they entered the license plate number. The encounter with the cop in the elevator left him spooked. They were definitely looking for him because they were in his room. But they hadn't known what he looked like, making it likely that the use of the credit card in the Casino had triggered it. He would have to use cash from now on. Can the cops track license numbers like they do credit cards? Blackie had seen shows on TV where they could find anybody with any information the way the computers were all tied together now.

He stood and looked out the front window. A police car cruised by, causing him to turn quickly away from the glass. He started to tell the clerk he changed his mind, right as they pulled his truck into the bay. He was committed now.

"Everything okay, Sir?" The pesky clerk asked.

"Yes. Thinking about all the things I need to get done before leaving," Blackie added keeping to his storyline. He suddenly realized he was slipping back into being a scared punk again, like Frankie. He must show confidence. Fake it until you make it! He need not worry about the cops. They were too stupid to catch him. It was fate that he would end up with a cool ride and a hot chick to share it. Otherwise, he would have been caught on the elevator. Screw the cops! His whole stance changed as his shoulders dropped down and back. A sneer came to his face as he walked to the seats and then sat with his back to the windows. He picked up a car magazine and flipped aimlessly through it. Within minutes, the clerk called him to the counter. Blackie paid in cash and sauntered out to his truck. Next, he treated the Ford to a car wash, then headed to meet Tammy at Donna's address.

Friday, June 17th (Evening)

When Stan informed him the Henderson PD was going to hold Wally, Dan decided to increase his effort to get there. He pushed hard for the last three hours of the trip and made it to the city limits of Las Vegas by early evening. Rather than trying to find Stan and the others he decided to head down to Henderson so he could go directly to the police station the next day.

When Dan hit the city limits, he called Stan again and learned Wally was at the West Police Station on Green Valley Parkway. Dan went to the area and found a Marriott Courtyard not far away. He unloaded his suitcase and a backpack he used as a briefcase from his truck. Dan needed to get a proposal out by the following Monday and tried to distract himself by working on it at the small desk in the room. Syd was a bit restless until he took her for a short walk and fed her dinner. After getting Syd situated, he went to the bar to grab a late snack. Plus, a beer or two might help him sleep. He figured the bar would be faster than the restaurant so he could get back to his proposal. Sitting at the bar, he noticed a tall, athletic brunette walk in and sit a few stools away from him.

~~ At four o'clock, Detective Bartlett gave up waiting for DeCicco. She decided to go back to her hotel and work out. After sitting around all day, she needed some activity. Bartlett had checked out of the casino in Las Vegas and had her things in the car. After searching on her phone to find which hotels in the area had the best gyms, she settled on the Courtyard located a few blocks away from the police station on Green Valley Parkway. It was still too warm to go for a run, so she spent ninety minutes in their small, but basically equipped fitness room, ending with a brisk forty-five-minute stint on the treadmill.

She showered and found a small place with a decent menu, thanks to the desk clerk, and had a light dinner of salmon and a salad. Feeling refreshed and nourished, she stopped in the bar and ordered a glass of chardonnay. The bartender was busy getting food for a table of customers, and she sat on a stool to wait for the barkeep to return. There were only a few people around. The courtyard bar opened to the lobby, designed specifically for women not to feel like they were walking into a dark male dominated place. There were a few people at one table, another table with two suited businessmen, probably chatting about some deal they were making, and an attractive casually dressed man a few stools down from her. He glanced her way, but went back to his cell phone, probably checking his email or messages. Finally, the bartender came back and asked what she would like. "A glass of chardonnay to take to my room please," she answered. The man to her left looked away from his cell phone and glanced over.

"Sure, no problem." The bartender started to pour a glass but noticed the bottle was almost empty. "Let me get a fresh one. I'm not sure how long this was open."

"I can taste it if you like," Bartlett said.

"I don't think there's enough for a glass anyway. I'll just get a new bottle," the young blonde behind the bar said. She spun and disappeared into the stockroom.

Bartlett noticed the guy looking at her, and said, "Now that's a young lady who believes in service." He smiled at her but said nothing, still looking her way. Suddenly uncomfortable, she glanced down at her blouse. Nothing spilled from dinner. "I'm sorry, do I have something in my teeth?" she asked.

"Oh, I'm sorry." He shook his head. "I was trying to come up with an excuse to keep you talking."

"Talking?"

"Yes, I love your voice," he said looking even more embarrassed. "It's uh, what my friend Wayne would call sultry."

She had been told similar things before, and he wasn't bad looking. "Well, you could try talking to me. You know, like a conversation. You ask me something. I answer. Then we talk." She liked the vulnerability he was showing, not trying to be a player.

"You're obviously better at this than I am." An awkward smile appeared. "Best I could come up with was to ask you to read me the menu."

"Oh man, that's lame." She laughed and saw the wrinkles around his eyes soften, and the smile relax. "And what would your excuse be for needing me to read it?"

"I was still working that out," he admitted.

"You are one smooth devil there, uh, what's your name?"

"Oh, Dan." An open smile this time. "Nice to meet you …"

"Angie," she answered. "Nice to meet you, too." Since her divorce eight years ago, she'd not been in what she considered a decent relationship. The guys at work were just trying to score with the hot detective for bragging rights to boast to their buddies. Most guys outside of work tended to be intimidated when they found out she was a cop, except for the few who made sophomoric references to her owning handcuffs. There was a brief silence as she was trying to decide if she wanted to continue this conversation or cut it off.

"Honestly, I wasn't trying to hit on you." He looked uncomfortable again. "I think you have a great voice."

This was getting fun all of a sudden. "Why? What's wrong with me?" she asked feigning a pout.

A look of panic crossed his face, then a broad smile. "Oh, you're good." He laughed, and she knew he'd recovered his footing. "Besides, I don't like to use women for their voice." He wrinkled his nose dismissively. "Feels cheap, you know."

Angie tossed her head back and laughed openly. Now that they were on equal ground, she was much more interested. She was in a strange city and had not been with a man for a while. What would be wrong with having a little fling, then going on her way? She had done it once before on vacation in Cancun. The guy claimed he was a lawyer from Denver, and she said she was a flight attendant from Dallas. It was simply harmless recreational sex.

The Detective and Dan talked for a while until she began to wonder if this guy was really interested since he didn't seem to be making any kind of move. The bartender came back and poured her a glass of wine, and he ordered a beer. After her second glass, she began to get a bit impatient. "Well, it's getting late," she said glancing at her phone. It was only a quarter after nine. "Would the gentleman care to escort the lady to her room?" No more time for subtlety.

"I, uh, sure!" He looked taken aback. "Look, I, uh. I really had no ulterior motives." He looked unsure of what to do. "I really do love your voice." He stared at the napkin that his hands were shredding.

"That's the only reason it worked, Mr. Smooth," She used the term mockingly. It suddenly seemed to dawn on Dan she was hitting on him. He jumped off the barstool and offered his arm, which she took, holding her third glass of wine in her hand. Now that he got it, his confidence seemed to rise.

"If you don't mind, I'd like to stop by my room first," he glanced at her, judging her response, and continued, "I have to see if my dog approves of you. I consult her on all matters of character."

"Dogs and old men love me," she said with assurance. She thought about the old guy at the police station today that said she was 'hot,' or something like that. They entered his room one floor down from hers. Syd was immediately at the door, greeting them both. Dan quickly checked the dog's water and gave Syd a bit of food to momentarily distract her. Angie laid her purse on the bed and sat on its edge watching the interaction and smiling at the affection shown by both animals. Syd downed her snack and came over to investigate the welcome stranger until she went near the purse. Her excitement level dropped significantly, and she moved between Dan and the stranger. Angie suddenly realized that her badge and gun were in the purse, and the dog was probably able to smell the gun's oil or powder residue.

Dan, however, was enamored with his guest and did not notice the change. "I apologize for the mess," he started, indicating an array of papers and files on the small desk in the room. "I was working on a bid for a job and didn't expect company."

"No worries." She waved her hand. "My room looks the same. I had only gone down to grab a glass of wine and then continue." She suddenly remembered she had files of the crime scene spread out all over the extra bed. She didn't want to scare this guy off with gruesome photos as soon as they walked in the door, so her room was out of play. "Does Syd help you with the bids?" She reached out to the dog. She was glad when Syd nuzzled her hand and lifted her paw to shake.

"She helps me with the math mostly," he said smiling.

"Really?"

"Yes, she's a math whiz, watch." He snapped his fingers to get the dog's attention. "Syd, ready for some math?" The dog assumed a sitting position in front of him. "Okay, Syd. What's three minus two?" Syd immediately barked once. "Good girl."

"That's impressive," Angie said giving her eyes a little roll.

"Now hold on, she's got to warm up." He focused his attention on Syd, "Okay, girl. What's fourteen divided by seven?" Syd tilted her head sideways as if she was thinking for a few seconds, then barked twice. "Very good, Syd!" Dan praised her as he patted her neck. Angie clapped and smiled.

"Division was my downfall in grade school," Angie admitted.

"Ready for more of a challenge, Syd?" Dan asked. The dog spun in a circle, then sat facing him again. "Now, how much is three thousand, eight hundred and twenty-one, divided by thirteen?" Syd laid down on the floor, rolled onto her back, and raised both front paws up to the sides of her face as if thinking hard. "You can do it, girl!" Dan encouraged. Suddenly the dog stood back up, looked around the room, and ran to the desk where Dan had been working. She put her front paws on the desktop and grabbed the calculator in her mouth, bringing it back to Dan and dropping it at his feet. She used her nose to push it toward her master.

Angie burst out into laughter at the dog's antics. "Syd, you are a riot."

Dan shook his head in mock disappointment. "Ever since I let her read Einstein's biography, she refused to memorize anything she can look up." Angie laughed until she had tears in her eyes. She grabbed Dan and kissed him as they both fell back on the bed. The next few hours were a whirlwind of passion, and laughter, with periods of rest, or simply cuddling.

They fell asleep in each other's arms.

~~ Tammy spent the afternoon first hitting a library where she drafted the letter describing Blackie, what had happened, and slanting it as if she were being forced to go with him. She indicated that her lawyer was retaining a copy of everything including a picture of her 'captor.' Tammy stored it on the same thumb drive in her purse, which contained the photo of Blackie. Leaving the library, she went to a copy center to copy the letter for her safe deposit box and the lawyer. Tammy retrieved her birth certificate from the safe deposit box, barely getting to the bank before they locked the vault for the day. She did some quick shopping at her favorite store and picked out a few outfits. Her last stop was the lawyer's office, even though she knew Ms. Auer was still out of town.

"Can I help you?" the receptionist asked.

"I know she's still not in, but I want to leave this for her to put in my file." Tammy handed her the letter she had written. On the outside, the envelope said Do Not Open Until June 30th. Tammy wanted to give herself some cushion, in case she could take care of things faster. "Could you be a Darlin' and put it in my file?"

The receptionist took the envelope glancing at the instructions, "I'll leave it on her desk. Ms. Auer can decide if she wants to file it."

"Uh, okay." Tammy struggled for an explanation. "It's just for insurance," she added hoping the receptionist would think it was insurance papers or something mundane.

"That's fine. I'll take care of it."

Tammy looked at her cell phone. She was already an hour late for meeting Blackie, and she decided to take her chances. "Thank you." Then added, "Tell her, I'll see her soon," hoping to erase any lingering suspicions.

She drove the short distance to Donna's and saw Blackie's truck sitting across the street. She expected him to be mad, but he gave her a big smile and waved as he got out. "We need to get you a cell phone," she said as he came to the car. "I had so much fun shopping I lost track of time. I'm sorry, Darlin'." She could see his eyes taking in the tight, V-neck sweater she wore.

"Looks like it was worth the wait," he said admiring the view.

Men were so easy. "What say we drop off the key, and then I have an idea?" She opened the door and took out the overnight bag she bought for the trip. She patted the luggage as she handed it to him. "I have a few surprises for you." She could practically see his mind racing. "You put these in the truck, and I'll be right back." Tammy hurried to the front door that opened as soon as she approached it.

"I almost called the cops on your friend," Donna said as she approached. "He's been sitting there almost two hours."

"I don't have much time. Here are the keys, and I want you to take this." She handed Donna a copy of the letter and the picture of Blackie. "It's information about him, in case he gives me any trouble."

"Why would you go with him if you're worried about that?" Donna asked. "He looks kinda young for you, don't you think?"

"I'll be fine, but I want someone to have information about who I'm with." She glanced over her shoulder and waved at him. "He's pretty harmless, but you can't be too careful. If you don't hear from me in a week or two, then use this."

"Okay. But I'm not sure about this." They hugged, and Tammy trotted across the street and climbed into the truck as Blackie held the door.

As soon as they were in the truck, Blackie asked, "What was the idea that you mentioned?"

Writing the letter and going through the machinations to get it to people had made her a little nervous. Tammy thought she would try to keep him in the area for another day or two to see how things were going before actually taking off. She thought of the idea as she drove to Donna's place. "I'm so excited to be with you again, that I don't want to wait. Why don't we find a place on the edge of town, and have us a little reunion before we do all that driving?" As she said it, she pulled a skimpy red teddy out of her luggage and roped it between her hands, and let it brush his arm as he tried to drive. The results were as she suspected, almost causing him to rear-end a car at a stop light.

"Sounds good to me! I'm in!" He had trouble keeping his eyes on the road, so she put the negligee away.

Tammy used her phone to find a motel on the west side of town that looked like it would do. After stopping at a liquor store, they pulled into the motel. She went to the front desk and booked the room because he was not in a state to be seen in public. She wasn't sure she would be able to get enough alcohol in him this time before he called her bluff. He followed her up the staircase holding the shopping bag in front of himself to hide his excitement. Once inside he threw the package on a chair and immediately grabbed her.

"Whoa, whoa, whoa, there, Cowboy." She pushed his hands away.

"What'd I do wrong?" He stood there with his hands raised in a surrender position.

"Nothing exactly. A lady just likes a little romance. That's all." She pushed him to a seated position on the bed. "A little anticipation. A little build-up, to get the juices flowing."

"Okay. What would you like me to do?"

She couldn't help but roll her eyes, then looking in the nightstand, saw a deck of cards in the drawer. "Ah. Perfect. Let's play strip poker." She gave him a seductive side-ways glance.

"Sure. I'm in."

"Now, that's what I'm talking about. You need to slow down and make me want you so bad that I will beg for it, not jump on me like a dog in heat." She grabbed the bottle of tequila they purchased and sat opposite him. 'Now here are the rules. We play a hand, and whoever loses, has to take a slug of tequila, and take off a piece of clothing." She smiled. "And make a real show of it, don't just rip it off. You're my male stripper for the evening. Got it?"

"Sure, but I've never seen those guys. I don't know what they do."

"C'mon, take it off slowly, and tease me." She leaned forward and kissed him.

"Got it."

Tammy dealt the first hand and intentionally lost. When she was trying to get a job with the casinos, she had gone to dealer school and got to know the instructor, who taught her the kinds of card tricks you're not allowed to use in the business. Tammy could deal a card from anywhere in the deck. When he won, she made a show of taking a big swig of tequila, but in reality, she held her tongue against the opening. She stood and slowly unbuttoned her blouse, swaying and twirling. She dropped the garment off her shoulders with her back to him, and then to the floor. Even though she was still wearing a bra, he looked like he might lose it right there, causing her to decide not to tease him anymore and to sit back down.

"I like this game!" He hardly paid attention to the cards after that. Within thirty minutes, he was naked and passed out on the bed.

Tammy laughed as she rolled him to one side of the bed and threw the covers over him. After extracting the keys from his pocket, she spent the next hour searching the truck for his stash of money. She had no flashlight and had to use the light from her cell phone. There was nothing under the seat, behind it, or in the glove box. She sat frantically looking around for other places he could have hidden it but thought of nothing. How in the world was she going to get out of this?

~~ Wally was pissed. He'd been sitting at the detective's desk for almost two hours, then was moved to an interrogation room and left to stew for several more.

"Hey, you assholes! When do I get my phone call?" he shouted at the mirror, convinced they were just making him wait. "This is how you treat senior citizens? What if I needed my medications? Did ya think of that?" They hadn't handcuffed him to the table, allowing him to pace around the room. He walked over and checked the door. Locked. Wally kicked it, and shouted, "Hey! Do you jerks even know how often an old man with an enlarged prostate has to take a piss?" Still no answer. He banged on the chicken-wire reinforced glass. "I need to use the bathroom." He was clearly being ignored.

Wally was nothing if not resourceful. He walked over to the metal trash can and lifted it. He looked at the mirror. "If you think I'm gonna give you sick bastards a show, you got another think coming." He carried the trash can to the corner along the mirror wall and placed it on the floor. Wally relieved himself in the trash can, picked it up again, and put it on the chair meant for the detectives to use. Then he sat across the table with a self-satisfied smirk on his face.

Twenty minutes later, a young patrolman walked in. "Mr. Williams, we're gonna move you to .... " The patrolman paused and sniffed. "Jesus, it smells like urine in here." Looking around the room he spotted the trash can on the chair. "Did you—?" He pointed at the trash can and looked at Wally.

"Hell, yes I did. You bastards ignored me when I banged on the door and told you I had to go." He gestured to the chair. "You can't leave an old man with a bad prostate locked in a room for hours. That's cruel and unusual punishment. Now when do I get my phone call?"

"That's disgusting!" A look of distaste crossed the officer's face.

"Well, I guess you're lucky I didn't have to go number two, aren't you? I'm building me a hell of a case for elder abuse by you bastards."

"I came in to tell you the detective is still in meetings, and we're moving you to a holding cell where you have a cot and a toilet. We can also get you some dinner since it's getting late." He motioned for Wally to come with him, eyeing the makeshift urinal warily. "I'll get this taken care of. Uh, sorry about that Mr. Williams. It was probably the shift change when you were lost in the shuffle." Wally was escorted downstairs to a holding cell.

He walked into the cell and looked around appraising it. "I've been in worse."

"You should be more comfortable here, Sir. I'll have them bring your dinner."

"Thank you." Wally leaned closer to look at his name tag. "Officer Taylor, is it?"

"Yes, Sir"

"I'll make sure to exclude you from my lawsuit." He walked over and laid on the cot, after testing it first with his hands.

"Thank you, Sir."

Michael L. Patton

Chapter Eight - Saturday, June 18th (Morning)

As Dan woke the next morning, still in the afterglow of the end of his long dry spell, he rolled over and reached across the bed to gently stroke her hair, as much to make sure she was real as to show affection. Dan was sure he would be wracked with guilt having not made love since his loss of Janet in a car wreck, but he was at peace. He knew she would want him to move on. The touch of his hand caused her to stir, and right as Dan was about to open his eyes and say good morning, he felt a tongue move across his face from his chin to his eyebrow. "Wait!"

"Syd! What the hell are you doing in my bed?" Dan sat up looking around the room. Syd, ears back, slinked down to the floor and sat looking at him, trying to figure out what she did wrong." Dan didn't notice. He was too distracted wondering where and when Angie went. "Angie?" he called as he climbed out of bed. Don't tell me she left without saying goodbye. He'd call the front desk to ask them to connect him. Suddenly, it occurred to him, and he said aloud, "I don't even know her last name." Realizing that Syd was the only other being in the room, he looked over at her. "Oh, I'm sorry, girl. You surprised me." He reached down, and she immediately came to him. He hugged her and patted her side. "No doggies in the bed. You got that?" His voice was now soft and pleasant, and she again licked his face. "Good girl."

Suddenly, the warm, peaceful feeling he felt earlier was gone. He never had a one-night stand, and it was never his goal. What was a wonderful fun evening, suddenly felt cheap. But Angie did say something about an early meeting at one point. Maybe he would see her later. He focused on the real reason he was there and would check on Uncle Wally. He'd worry about Angie later that evening when she was likely to be back at the hotel. He rose, showered, and dressed. He fed Syd and took her for a walk before phoning Stan.

"I haven't heard a thing," Stan said in response to his question.

"Well, I'm only a few blocks away from the police station. Were you planning on coming down this way?"

"Not 'til this afternoon, why?"

"Oh, I have Syd with me and was trying to figure out what to do with her while I'm there."

"You can't leave her in the room and put the 'do not disturb' sign on the doorknob?" Stan asked.

"I guess, but I don't know how long I'll be. It's not a good solution."

"I'll get down there as soon as I can, but it won't be until after lunch."

"Don't worry, it's my problem. Syd'll be fine." Dan tousled her ears as he talked. He ended the call with Stan and walked down to the front desk. A woman who looked to be in her early twenties was working. "Hi, I wanted to remind you that I have my dog with me in room 153. I don't want any of the staff to go in and be frightened. I put the Do Not Disturb sign on the door, but if maintenance or someone went in, I also don't want her getting out. She won't hurt anyone."

"Not a problem, Sir. We deal with that all the time," she smiled as she answered. "As a matter of fact, I'm about to go off shift and start my day job is as a dog walker. I could take her out if you need it."

"That would be great. If I'm not back, could you do it around lunch?"

"I'd love to! I have an arrangement with the hotel to do it for a number of guests." She took out a pad and wrote the room number and lunchtime and paused. "What's your dog's name?"

"Syd, that's S-Y-D, she's a girl."

"That's a cute name." She wrote it down. "What kind of dog is she?"

"Mostly Australian Shepherd."

"Great! I can even add the cost to your room bill if you want."

"That will work. Gee, if you're the night clerk, and do this during the day, when do you sleep?" He was amazed she could be so energetic after working all night.

"Oh, I catch a few naps during the day, and get about four or five hours in the evening." She gave him a crooked little smile that showed it wasn't easy, and said, "Gotta pay for college!" Boom, the enthusiasm was back again.

"She's been fed and walked already, so she just needs a quick break. Syd's a great dog and won't give you any trouble."

"Well, don't worry. I'll take good care of Syd."

He read the name off her nametag. "Thanks, Lisa!" Dan headed back to the room, to double-check that the sign was on the door, and to say goodbye to Syd. He told her he had made arrangements for her and made sure the room was safe, and nothing embarrassing was left out from last night. It looked okay, so he headed for the police station.

When he got there, he was directed to a desk sergeant. Dan walked up and said, "I was told that Wally Williams was brought here yesterday."

The sergeant stopped his paperwork and looked over the top of his half-glasses. "Old guy who's threatening to sue everybody?"

"That sounds like him."

"You his lawyer?"

"No, Sir. I'm his nephew." Dan rolled his eyes playing to the cop's annoyance.

"God help you." He typed into the terminal on his desk. "He should still be in holding. With his attitude, he's lucky he didn't get sent to the downtown Detention Center. I'll call to see if he's finished his breakfast in bed." Dan thought he detected a sarcastic smile. "I'll have him brought to a conference room where you can see him." He typed again. "I'll put you in Room 3."

"Thank you, Sergeant."

"You sure you're related to him?' he said, apparently referring to Dan's polite manner. He handed Dan a visitor's badge. "Hey, Minoli! Show this guy to Room 3, will ya?" The sergeant looked back at Dan. "Good luck."

The small conference room had a window looking into the squad room, and one facing outside the building onto a parking lot. Dan glanced around the squad room and observed the usual bustle of a police station. He sat at the table and occupied himself with his email, trying to keep himself distracted from the night before. Damn it! He had really liked her.

Finally, after close to an hour, a uniformed officer came into the room. "Mr. Williams?"

"Yes."

"I was told to escort you to Detective DeCicco's desk."

"Detective? I'm here to see my uncle. Wally Williams?"

"Just following orders, Sir." He stood by the door waiting for Dan and guided him to the other side of a partition which seemed to be where the detectives were housed. Dan saw Wally sitting in front of one of the desks. Behind it, facing Dan was a short man with glasses and a mustache in an ill-fitting sport coat.

As they got close, Dan said, "Hey, Uncle."

Wally turned his head toward the voice. "Dan! Am I glad to see you. These assholes—"

The short man was out of his seat and placed his hand on Dan's arm. "Please come with me, Mr. Williams." He turned Dan around and shuttled him toward a nearby office.

"Don't you tell these bastards nothing," Wally shouted behind him. "I'm gonna be a rich man by the time I'm through with them."

The detective closed the door. "Mr. Williams, we want to ask you about your encounter with a murder victim, Robert Foster, on the night he died. We've managed to get bits and pieces out of your uncle, in between threats of lawsuits and claims of elder abuse."

"Sure, what do you want to know?"

"Just tell me, in your own words, what happened. If it corroborates your Uncle's whereabouts, we can let the pain in the ass go. Excuse my language." He glanced out the office door window at Wally, who was still talking and gesturing animatedly.

Dan chuckled. "We were headed from California to the observatory at Mt. Hopkins and stopped at the Eloy TA truck stop. When I came out of the restroom, Wally was talking to a guy, who turned out to be Bob. We chatted for a few minutes, mostly about Bob's old truck, and then we left and drove on."

"So your uncle was with you the whole time after that on the trip?"

"Yes, Sir. We only took one truck, and we were together 24/7 until we got back to California. We stopped at the same truck stop on the way back the next night and saw a lot of police activity. A trucker told us they found a body, but we had no idea it was Bob until the Detective from Phoenix called Wally."

"And why did she put the two together?"

"Oh, because Wally had given him his phone number on a scrap of paper. Bob said he had a friend who might want to sell a similar truck. Wally had one like it years ago, and was kinda interested." Dan shrugged his shoulders. "That was it."

"Thank you, and God bless you." The detective turned toward the door but spun back around. "Any idea why he would go to the Foster house since they didn't really know each other?"

"I think he went there to check on Bob, hoping that it really wasn't him. You know, wasn't the same Bob."

"But why would he cross police tape?"

Dan laughed. "You might not have noticed, but he can be a stubborn old cuss sometimes."

DeCicco raised one eyebrow at the joke but didn't laugh. "If I turn him over to you, do you promise to keep him out of Henderson?"

Dan rubbed the back of his neck and looked down at the floor considering the offer. "I promise I won't bring him back here, but I can't always control what he does on his own."

"Good enough." They walked from the office back to where Wally sat. "Mr. Williams, you're free to go."

Wally snapped his head around to look at the detective. "Why the hell wouldn't he be? He ain't done nothin'."

"I was talking to you," DeCicco said, shaking his head. "You're free to go. We're not going to press charges since you didn't actually go inside the house. But I hope you learned not to cross police tape again."

Wally looked around and stood. "Oh, well that's different. I tried to tell that dumb cop."

The detective warned, "If I were you, Mr. Williams, I would shut up, and leave before I change my mind."

"I think I'm owed an apology," Wally said indignantly. "I got you guys on elderly abuse, cruel and unusual punishment, and false imprisonment."

The exasperated DeCicco looked at the ceiling and clenched his jaw. "On behalf of the Henderson Police Department, I apologize, Mr. Williams," he said trying to hold his temper. "Now, please, get out of my precinct and out of my city."

"Well, now that's better. Thank you," Wally said as he started walking toward the door. Dan quickly turned and put his hand on Wally's shoulder to keep him from stopping or turning around. Wally continued to mutter loudly. "Not much of a city anyway, if you ask me. More like an overgrown suburb of Las Vegas."

"Shut up and keep walking." Dan tried to hurry him. When they were about ten feet from the detective's desk, Dan stopped in his tracks. So did his uncle. Walking toward them was the woman Dan had met at the bar the night before. It took a few seconds before he regained enough control to speak. "Hey!"

Angie closed the remaining gap quickly and grabbed the hand Dan lifted from Wally's shoulder. "Hello, I'm Detective Bartlett, Phoenix PD. Nice to meet you, Mr. …"

Dan stood there with his mouth open. Wally jumped in, "Williams. He's my nephew, Dan."

"Mr. Williams, nice to meet you." Angie let go of his hand and stepped back.

Dan was frozen with a confused look on his face. Wally added. "Dan, this is the detective we talked to on the phone. I was gonna tell you she was here and that she was hot, but I can see you've already noticed." He waited a second. "Close your mouth, boy, before you step on your tongue."

Dan finally managed to speak, "Nice, uh, to meet you, uh, Detective."

Angie looked past him at DeCicco, and said, "Well, I can see you're busy, Detective DeCicco, so I'll come back later." She spun on her heel and started to make her escape, but the detective stopped her.

"No, they were just leaving. Now's as good a time as any, before I get pulled into another meeting." There was an awkward moment as she and Dan brushed shoulders passing in the narrow aisle. Dan threw quick sideways glances at her, but Angie stared at the floor.

"What the hell was that about?" Wally was on him before they were out of the squad room.

"What was what?"

"Don't give me that shit, Son. I mighta been born on a Friday, but I wasn't born yesterday." Wally pointed with his thumb back over his shoulder. "That woman spooked the shit outta you."

"Shhh! Damn it! Keep your voice down," Dan pleaded as they finally reached the door.

"Well, I wasn't sure if you saw a ghost, or if you were gonna hump her leg right there in the middle of the police station," Wally answered in a loud whisper.

"I'll tell you in the truck, could ya keep it down?'

Wally reluctantly kept quiet until he and Dan were outside the police station. As they approached the truck, Wally asked, "Hey, where's Syd?"

"She's back at the hotel. I didn't know how long this was gonna take, and I didn't want to leave her in the truck."

"Good move. You'd better take good care of that dog. Syd's the only female that gives a damn about you."

"I'm quickly learning that," Dan said shaking his head.

"What the hell's that mean?" Wally gave him an inquiring look. "You been holding out on me?"

"Nope. That's why I was trying to get you to shut the hell up, so you didn't make it worse," Dan climbed into the driver's side. He waited for Wally to get in before continuing. "I met a woman last night that I thought I hit it off with." He blew out a sigh. "But I guess I was wrong."

"What's that got to do with ..." A look of recognition came over his face, "that Detective?"

Dan looked at the roof of the truck and sighed. "I was tired when I got in last night, and I went down to the bar to get a burger. This brunette came in, and we started talking. The first thing I noticed was her voice. I thought I'd heard it before." He stared out the windshield recalling. "She only said her name was Angie. I had no idea who she was, and she never said what she did."

"You need to slow the hell down, Son. Just because she talked to you in a bar, doesn't mean she's ready to get married." Wally chuckled. "No wonder you haven't found someone else yet. With an attitude like that, you'll scare 'em all off."

"Well, we had a good time. So when I saw Angie just now, I was gonna give her a hug, but she was stone cold." Dan looked at his uncle with a pained expression.

"Hell, it's different for women in a job like hers. She was probably trying to keep it professional in front of the other cops."

"Yeah, you're probably right. We did surprise her." Dan started the truck and drove toward the hotel. "I only want to get Syd, and then I can take you back to where you're staying." He looked at the clock on the dashboard. "Since I found a good dog sitter, I'll stay here again tonight."

"This doesn't have anything to do with hoping to run into that detective again, does it?" Wally smirked as Dan looked over.

"Screw you, Papi." When they got to the hotel, Syd was not in the room. Wally was concerned, but Dan walked calmly to the desk with his uncle in tow. "Hello. I'm a guest here at the hotel, room 153. Do you know where Lisa might be? She's dog-sitting for me, and I want to pick up my dog."

"I think she's out at the pool, sir," the cheery clerk answered.

"Thanks." They walked out to the pool area, and at first, Dan didn't see anyone. All the chairs were empty. He started to turn around but saw Syd's tail in the corner, in a shaded grassy area. As he walked to where his view was not obstructed by the chairs, he noticed Lisa lying on a towel in the grass, reading a book. She was wearing a bright yellow bikini, and Syd had her head on Lisa's stomach. The girl was absentmindedly stroking the dog as she read. Dan would never have recognized Lisa after seeing her in the frumpy hotel blazer and skirt. When she was at the front desk, she was helpful and girl next door cute. In the bikini, she was a knockout.

"Damned, lucky dog," Dan heard Wally whisper as they approached. He gave his uncle a stern keep quiet look.

"Hi, Lisa!" Dan said to announce themselves.

She looked up and smiled. "Hi, Mr. Williams." Syd looked at them and wagged her tail but made no effort to get up. "I hope this is okay. I took her for a walk earlier and couldn't stand the thought of her being cooped up in that room, so I brought her out here with me."

"That's fine. It was very nice of you." He chuckled as he looked down at Syd. "Doesn't look like she minds at all." Then to Syd, "You ready to go, girl?" Syd laid her head back down on Lisa's stomach and nudged the hand that was petting her.

Wally laughed. "Smart girl."

"Oh, Lisa, this is my Uncle Wally."

"He just sprung me from the pokey," Wally added, making Dan give him a quizzical look.

"Uh, hi, Uncle Wally." Lisa looked from Wally to Dan unsure of what to say. "Hope it wasn't anything serious."

"Murder One," Wally answered. "Dan here broke me out, and we gotta get across the state line real quick, so c'mon, Syd, let's hustle." Lisa's eyes grew wide, wondering if she was an accessory to a crime. Syd looked up because Wally was using a strange voice.

"Ignore him." Dan pointed at Wally using his thumb. "He always tries to impress pretty young girls, because he's old and senile." Lisa laughed nervously. "He got picked up for crossing police tape. Basically, for being stupid."

"Who you callin' stupid?" Wally protested. "I'm a dangerous man." Wally winked at Lisa, and she smiled realizing he was kidding. She sat up, forcing Syd to stand after losing her pillow.

"Syd's a great dog," Lisa said, patting her on the shoulder. "I'd be happy to hang out with her anytime."

"She's smart too!" Wally added.

"Syd, what do you do when Uncle Wally takes his shoes off?" Dan asked her. "Huh, girl?"

Syd did the classic roll over and play dead move. Lisa burst out laughing and rubbed the dog's stomach.

Wally laughed too. "And that after I gave you a compliment. Shame on you, Syd." Syd rolled over and stood but drooped her head and kept her tail down as if she had been scolded.

"Come on, ya big ham," Dan called to Syd. "Should I pay you or will you add it to the hotel bill when I leave?"

"Either way. Whatever is easier," Lisa answered. "It was only ten dollars for the walk. Hanging out with Syd by the pool was fun for both of us."

Dan handed Lisa a twenty. "Thanks for taking such good care of her. Maybe I'll see you before I leave tomorrow."

"Sure thing, and thanks!" she added when she glanced at the bill. "Bye, Syd."

Dan, Syd, and Wally walked out to the truck to go to the Las Vegas casino where Wally was staying.

"Shame you didn't check out, so you could stay at the casino with us tonight, Lover?" Wally elbowed Dan's arm once they were far enough away from Lisa. "If you do get her to take off her protective vest, make sure you wear some protection."

Dan blushed. "Thanks."

~~ Detective Bartlett sat in a darkened conference room when the door opened, and DeCicco stuck in his head. "There you are. I've been looking all over for you." He looked around the room. "Why are you sitting in the dark?"

"Oh, I had a couple of calls to make. I was just talking on the phone, no need for lights," she lied.

"I'm free now if you want to talk." He looked at his watch. "Shit! Got another conference call in fifteen though, so you'd better hurry."

"Sure. I only have a few issues. Do you want to talk here, or at your desk?"

"Here's fine," he said turning on the lights before sitting. "People might get the wrong impression if they see us coming out of a dark conference room. Heh, heh," DeCicco said as he turned a shade pinker.

"Yeah, sure," she answered dismissively. "Look, I need to get back to Phoenix. Do you have any new leads on the suspect?"

"Not really. Hey, what's going on with the young guy back at my desk? He looked like he saw a ghost." DeCicco watched her closely.

"Beats me. Maybe I look like one of his ex's." Bartlett's face was impassive. "Look. I need to get going but let me know if you hear anything. I left my card and a copy of my notes on your desk."

"Yeah, I saw those. Thanks."

"And if I make any progress, I'll also let you know. We need to get this guy."

A uniformed cop poked her head in the door. "DeCicco, we got a call about a body found in a suitcase over on our side of Sunset."

"Well, there goes my day," DeCicco said standing. They shook hands. "Good luck, Detective."

"You too. Are you always this busy?"

"We're a couple detectives short right now. If this moron had left the suitcase on the other side of Sunset, it wouldn't be ours." He shrugged his shoulders. "When it rains, it pours."

Bartlett went back to the hotel, checked out, and headed for the airport. She thought about leaving a note for Dan … make an attempt to explain things. But she decided against it. Better to make a clean break. She really enjoyed their time together, but he lived in California so there was no future. Plus, if word got back that she had slept with a potential witness, everything she had worked for regarding her professional image would be shattered. No, it was best to let him remain a pleasant memory and both go on with their lives. She threw her bag in the trunk and headed to the airport.

~~ Tammy awoke before six to the sound of Blackie snoring. She lay there staring at the ceiling going over her search the night before. When Tammy went through his wallet and jeans, she only found a few hundred dollars. She knew he had more, so it had to be in the truck, but she couldn't think of anywhere he could have hidden it she'd not already checked. Tammy even laid the seatback down and looked for any part of the cover that seemed to be disturbed. There was a headliner in the truck, but it too looked intact, and she wasn't sure how to remove it to look behind it. Even if she managed to get it open, it was unlikely she would be able to put it back without signs of a search.

She thought about checking the engine compartment. She knew there were all sorts of gadgets and cubby holes in there. She felt under the dash, but there was no button or lever to open the hood. How did they open them back in the old days? She was afraid to mess with anything under there anyway and would use her feminine wiles to find out where the money was hidden.

Throwing back the covers, Tammy crawled out of bed and padded to the bathroom. After using the toilet, she looked in the mirror. She wasn't bad looking. She wasn't stupid. How in the world did she end up like this? Well, standing around feeling sorry for herself wouldn't help. Tammy shook her head to snap out of it, undressed and stepped into the shower. The soap at the cheap motel was small and the heavily-bleached washcloth felt like sandpaper on her skin. Tammy was startled by the cheap plastic curtain blowing against her when Blackie opened the door and stepped into the small room.

"I'm sorry. I tried to wait, but I really have to pee," he apologized. Tammy listened as he used the toilet and washed his hands. "You need any help in there?"

"No, thanks. You need to give a girl a rest." She knew she would run out of excuses soon and either have to have sex with him or leave. "I'll bet you worked up an appetite after last night," Tammy smiled knowingly. "Let's get some breakfast." Coffee was all she really wanted. The crap from the in room machine was weak and tasted of chlorine.

"Sounds great! Then we can finally get on the road." They dressed and threw their things in their respective bags. Tammy put on one of her new blouses with a low neckline that sparked Blackie's interest. Hmmm. Maybe she should wear a sweatshirt.

"If you like this, maybe I should go shopping again," Tammy teased. She was running out of ways to stall.

"You've got my vote, but there will be plenty of time to shop along the way." They walked to the truck and climbed in. A few minutes later they pulled into a restaurant parking lot.

"You still okay for cash, or do you need to get some more?" Tammy asked casually.

"I'm good," he answered.

As she sat in the restaurant eating her eggs and enjoying some decent coffee. Tammy thought of ways to diminish the amount of money he was carrying so he'd have to go to his stash. Spending a couple hundred dollars was not typically a problem for her, but she wasn't usually under so much pressure.

"Don't you like your breakfast?" Blackie asked, bringing her out of her reflection.

"Just enjoying the coffee. The breakfast is fine." She smiled at him and took an enthusiastic bite of her eggs. She saw his eyes slide down from her face to the low-cut blouse. Tammy stared blankly out the restaurant's window until she realized the answer was right in front of her. Across the street was a store specializing in leather clothing. She could drop a few hundred there, easily.

"You ready to hit the road?" Blackie was anxious to get moving.

"Sure. Let me finish this cup. This is the best coffee I've had in weeks." Again, his eyes drifted south. "Hey, you know what would really set this top off?" She paused for effect, and finally, his eyes came back up. "A black leather skirt! There's a leather store right across the street."

Blackie's eyes lit up like a kid coming down the stairs at Christmas. "Let's go!" He quickly paid the bill, and they hurried across the street, leaving the truck in the restaurant parking lot. Tammy took her time wandering around looking at the jackets and purses before trying on the skirts. She made sure to model everything for him to keep his attention. He was enthusiastic about a pair of leather pants she tried on, but when she came out in a tight black mini-skirt, she thought he might blow a fuse right there in the store.

"Which one should I get, Honey?" she teased, knowing what his answer would be. Tammy loved the skirt, but the pants cost more, which would better serve her purpose.

"Get 'em both. What the hell."

Bingo! "You sure, Darlin'? That would be a lot."

"Let's do it!"

Tammy shot back to the dressing room and picked up the leather pants, and her jeans. "I think I'll wear the skirt if you don't mind," she added with a demure bat of the eyes. Her answer was handed to her when he grabbed her ass as they walked to the counter. Tammy noticed he used all the money in his pants pocket and emptied out several different folds from his wallet. Mission accomplished!

"Damn, you look hot!" Blackie said as he held the door of the truck for her like a gentleman. Tammy pretended to primp in the cab while she watched him fiddling with one of the holes in the top side wall of the pickup bed. She remembered her dad had called them stake pockets and said that people used them to put boards in to make the sides higher when they carried larger loads than wouldn't fit in the bed. The stake pockets of the Ford had aftermarket tie-downs installed in them. She watched as he turned the eye hook which extended out of one of the stake pockets. It loosened a thing that had a plate covering the hole. Underneath was basically a molly bolt that spread out to hold the tie-down in the hole by pressing against the lip of the pocket. When it was cinched down, bungees or straps were used to secure the load in the pickup. Blackie took the tie-down out of the hole and reached inside. He pulled out a large wad of bills, and peeled a few off, careful to block his actions. From behind, it would look like he was tightening or fooling around with the tie-down.

"Everything okay?" she asked while pretending to finish her primping. She noticed there were six pockets in the truck bed. That's where the cash was! She never would have found it because she had no idea how those silly things worked. Now all she had to do was wait for a chance to make her move.

"Oh, yeah. Just checking something." Blackie quickly shoved the tie-down back in and screwed it tight with one hand while stashing the cash in his jeans with the other. Climbing into the cab, he asked, "Ready to start our road trip?" He looked over and smiled at her. "We have fresh oil, a full tank of gas, and we're ready to roll."

Confident she could pull the theft off, Tammy slid over close to him on the bench seat. She tossed her overnight bag on the passenger side floor. "Let's go!"

Blackie started the truck, and they were outside the Las Vegas city limits within a few minutes, heading west on Interstate 15. Tammy glanced at her watch. It was a little after 1:00 PM when they finally hit the road. The ride through the afternoon was uneventful with Tammy trying to plot how to distract him long enough to get at the money, and Blackie driving and humming along with the radio. He looked over at her and asked, "Are you okay? You're awfully quiet today."

"Oh, sorry. I'm lost in my own world, thinking about the past week." She reached over and patted his leg. "A lot has happened in a short amount of time."

"That's for sure." It was his turn to pause and consider all the changes in the last week and a half. He could never have imagined them.

"Can we stop soon? I probably shouldn't have drunk so much coffee."

"Sure," he agreed. "We're in no hurry." He smiled and reached over to take her hand. They turned off at the next exit that indicated it had services and found a gas station. Blackie pulled the truck to the pumps even though the gauge read half a tank. "It's good to get gas while you can. So I'll just top off the tank."

"Good idea." Tammy climbed out of the truck and headed to the restroom, leaving him to take care of the vehicle. She hurried out of the bathroom and went into the small convenience store all modern stations seemed to have. She was not able to see him from the restroom and wanted to be ready if he decided to use the men's room. Pretending to pick out a drink, and glancing at snacks, Tammy kept an eye on him. After filling the tank, and checking the oil, he headed into the store to pay, a downside of using cash.

"Ready to hit the road?" She jumped when he approached her from behind. "Didn't mean to scare you."

Tammy laughed nervously. "No worries. Probably the caffeine." She turned to face him. "Did you already hit the restroom?"

"No need. I'm good."

Damn! He steered her toward the counter and paid for her drink. They headed back out to the Ford. "California, here we come!" she said as he started the truck. He's got to go sometime. I'll have to be patient.

~~ Dan pulled into the parking lot of the casino where Wally was booked. He drove around the multi-floored structure until he came to the area reserved for the hot rods to park. To Wally's relief, his precious '54 sat in the far corner near where Stan and his friend's cars sat.

Dan parked as close as he could to the restricted area, and they walked over to Wally's pickup. Wally immediately circled it looking for any damage. Syd followed him around the truck, thinking it was some kind of game.

"Give it a rest, Uncle. Your baby is fine. Stan didn't hurt it."

"Screw you. I ain't never let anyone else drive it before." He gave Dan a dirty look. "Wouldn't have this time if I hadn't been in a bind."

"Yeah, a bind of your own making, dumbass. Crossing a police tape." Dan shook his head. "Sheesh."

Wally knew better than to expect sympathy for pulling a boneheaded stunt like that, but he still didn't care what Dan thought. He opened the door of the truck and looked inside. "Damn his fat ass. Stan readjusted my seat and mirrors. Now it will take me a week to get 'em right again." Syd jumped through the open passenger-side window and came over to nuzzle Wally thinking he was upset. "Syd, you're the only dog I'll let in my truck. And do you know why?" Wally's voice going up at the end of the question caused Syd to bark and put her paw on his arm. Wally continued, "Because you don't mess with my damned seat. Do you, girl?" Another woof was his answer.

"So, what are you planning to do now?" Dan asked.

"I'm going to grab something quick to eat and take a nap. I didn't get any rest in that noisy jail."

"Well, if you don't need me, I think I'll head back to my room and work on the proposal that's due Monday."

"When are you leaving for home?"

"Probably early in the morning," Dan answered.

"I might go with you. I've had about enough of this damned town already." Wally gestured toward the casinos and glitter assaulting them from every direction.

"I plan on being on the road by six, and I don't want any whining from some cranky old goat about how early it is."

"I'll be in my own truck, and if you hear any whining, it will likely be your Dodge straining to keep up."

Dan laughed. "That'll be the day." He slapped his leg, and Syd trotted over to him. Dan gave his uncle a quick nod and turned to leave. "Try not to get arrested tonight, okay? See ya at six."

On his way back to his hotel, Dan decided he would take a chance and try to find Angie. Earlier, he had not known her last name to place a call to her room. But now that he knew she was Detective Bartlett, he could at least call and ask to be connected.

"Can I help you, Mr. Williams?" the young clerk asked, as he approached the desk. Dan was surprised she used his name.

"How did you —"

"Actually, I recognized Syd. Hey, girl." The clerk looked down at Syd who wagged her tail. "I took my break out by the pool earlier when Lisa was watching her. What a great dog."

"Yep, she's a rock star, alright. I didn't know she was a local celebrity though." He scratched the top of Syd's head. "Say, can you tell me which room Detective Bartlett is in? I have some information for her."

"I can't give you a room number, but it doesn't matter anyway. Ms. Bartlett checked out about a half an hour ago." She must have seen the disappointed look on his face. "I don't have any information I can provide you. Sorry."

"Oh, I have her number." He knew her phone number was still on Wally's cell. "I was just hoping to catch her in person." Dan forced a smile. "Thanks." He turned away, feeling disappointed. Changing his mind, he spun around and went back to the desk.

"Yes, Sir?"

"Is it too late for me to get a late checkout? I think I'll hit the road too."

"Well, technically you're a half an hour past the cutoff, but I think we can accommodate you, Mr. Williams. Do you want to leave the charges on your card?"

"Yes." Quickly, the printer spit his receipt out, and she handed it to Dan.

"Just drop your key off here, or you can leave it in your room."

"Thank you." Dan hurried back to his room and packed their things. He loaded the truck and pulled under the awning by the lobby, leaving Syd sitting in the driver's seat. When he came back out from dropping off the key, the shuttle driver was reaching through the window to pet Syd.

"Is Syd driving you home?" the driver asked.

"We trade off every couple of hours. She has a bad habit of wanting to stop and pee everywhere. You know how girls are." They both laughed, and Syd moved over to the passenger side as Dan slid in. "C'mon, Rock Star. Let's get outta here before your head gets too big to fit in the truck." Syd barked and laid her head on the window sill as they pulled away from the lot.

Once they were driving, Dan called Uncle Wally's cell. After several rings, a sleepy voice answered. "This better be damned important!"

"Sorry, Uncle. I've decided to head home early."

"You already told me that, dumbass. We're meeting at 6:00 AM."

"No, I've decided to leave today. Now." He paused to let it sink in. "You still interested in going with me?"

"Now? What the hell? Did that Detective Hottie Pants run you out of town?"

"Kinda." Dan didn't want to go into it. "You in or you out?"

"Can a fella get about an hour's sleep before I have to drive five hundred miles?"

"Sure. I'll eat lunch and call you in an hour to wake your lazy old ass up." The line went dead as Wally hung up. Dan checked the screen to make sure it wasn't the battery. "I guess that's the plan, Syd. Where do you want to eat, girl?" Syd sat up and started looking around. By the time Dan ate lunch and went to collect his uncle, it was close to two PM when they left the city limits of Las Vegas heading west on Interstate 15.

~~ By four o'clock in the afternoon, Tammy was worried about the distance they were getting from Las Vegas. It finally sank in that she was taking a huge risk. Tammy knew she couldn't keep asking him to stop for restroom breaks without him becoming suspicious. She wondered how he could go so long without needing a break himself. He must have a bladder made of steel. They had not made a lunch stop because of the late breakfast, so she was hungry. They passed several signs for places along the way. However, most were not visible from the highway, so they were only names on a billboard. There was one place advertising a 1950's theme, Buddy's Burgers. The pictures showed vintage cars with promises of juicy burgers and shakes. As they entered Barstow, one sign said it was two miles ahead. Since they were within the city limits, things were not as far from the interstate as they were in rural areas. As they came around the corner, Buddy's sat off to the right. The place was surrounded by old hot rods mixed in with modern cars. Most were probably headed to the car show they saw happening in Las Vegas before they left.

"Hey, look at those old cars." She pointed at the exit ramp ahead of them. "Do you want to stop for a bite to eat?"

"Sure. I could eat, and we could check out the cars too." Blackie exited and pulled into the lot. It was a madhouse with cars parked everywhere. He smiled as some of the crowd turned to check out his truck, and an old guy in a Mustang waved. They were lucky to find a spot not far from the door of the restaurant where Blackie could keep an eye on the truck. Blackie and Tammy climbed out of the Ford and headed for the restaurant checking out the old cars along the way. They took their time wandering around the lot, hoping the line to be seated would go down. Many of the vehicles had flawless paint jobs that made Blackie self-conscious about his rattle can disguise work. There was a long line to get a table, but the excitement of the place made the wait less annoying. Cars cruised in or out, and everyone turned to see and hear the tricked-out rides. Once seated, it took a while for the waitress to arrive, but neither of them minded because they were not in a hurry and had no specific destination for the day.

"Oh, crap. I left my hairbrush in the truck. I must look a mess." Tammy said as the waitress finally walked away with their order. "I'll just run out and get it."

"No, I'll get it," Blackie answered, trying to show her he was a gentleman. He stood.

"You've been driving all day. You're probably tired." She tried again to get time alone with the truck.

'I'll do it" He started away from the table but turned back. "You know, your hair is fine. I think you're the prettiest woman in here."

"Thank you." She gave him a quick smile.

"Here you go," Blackie said as he returned a few minutes later. He noticed she only gave her hair a few quick strokes and stuck it absentmindedly into her purse. Their food arrived a few minutes later, and they ate as they looked out the window at the scene in the parking lot.

~~ After their late start, Dan and Wally were finally in high gear rolling along Interstate 15. Dan watched his uncle closely because he knew Wally had not gotten much sleep. Syd was settled in the passenger seat, occasionally sitting up to look out the window or sniff the air. Dan was glad Wally decided to go back with him so he could keep an eye on the cranky old goat. Much of the afternoon went by without incident as they pushed hard to get home at a decent hour.

However, when they reached the edge of Barstow, Wally suddenly accelerated and passed Dan. This usually meant he needed gas or wanted to stop. If it were anything more important, he would have called on the cell phone.

Sure enough, Wally pulled off at the next exit. It looked like he was going to turn left at the end of the ramp to hit the gas station which could be seen on the other side of the overpass. Instead, he turned right and headed for the crowded burger joint with old cars. Dan followed him into the parking lot of the diner, and they both searched for a place to park. They weren't able to stay together, with Wally taking the first spot closer to the front of the lot. Dan had to park a short distance down in the same row, but could still see Wally's truck. By the time Dan walked back to his Uncle Wally, he was standing beside a different truck, inspecting it closely.

"I thought you needed gas," Dan watched his uncle walking around the truck.

"No. I need a restroom. I am also getting sleepy, so figured we should eat."

"What's so danged interesting?" Dan nodded at the truck. "Looks dead stock to me." He knew Wally would only usually be interested in cars that were in the pro-stock style or customized in some unusual way.

"Yeah, it is," Wally answered still focusing on what looked like a late sixties Ford pickup.

"So, what's the big deal?" Dan was annoyed at having to pry information out of him.

"Does this truck look familiar to you?"

"No. You've seen one stinking Ford pickup, you've seen 'em all."

That got him an annoyed glance, but Wally went back to paying attention to the truck, as he walked around to the driver's side. When he got to the wing window of the driver's door

Wally shouted, "I knew it! Quick. Come here." Wally waved him to the other side of the truck. "See this?" He pointed to a small sticker on the window.

"Yeah. So?"

"You remember Bob's truck that we saw in Eloy at the truck stop?"

Dan was lost. "Bob who?"

"Bob. Damn it! Bob Foster. The guy who was murdered."

"I remember it was '68, but I didn't look that close. Why?"

"Well, I did. And this is it." Wally pointed at the truck beside them. "While you were still in the restroom. I went over to look at it? It had this sticker."

Dan looked at the sticker his uncle was pointing at. "So? Lots of people probably have those." It was a car club sticker with a coiled snake that said, 'Desert Rattlers.'

"No. Listen, damn it." He pointed at the truck again. "This is a '68 F-100. Most of it is the same color as the one we saw, and you can see somebody did a cheap assed rattle can job on the bottom of the side to try to change the color. So that means the kid's here."

"But you didn't see the kid?"

Wally shook his head. "Just the back of his head. The sticker was reflective, and I didn't pay it much attention then, but that club changed its name about fifteen years ago from the Rattlers to the Desert Aces. Bob told me he left the old sticker on it because he was a founding member, and also to piss off the president of the new club. That's why I remember it."

"Really?"

"Yes." The gnarled finger was now pointed at him. "Now, how many '68 F-100s do you think are still around, and have that exact sticker, in the same place?"

"I don't know…uh…two?"

"Bullshit. This is Bob's truck. Plus, he welded a plate over the bottom of his stake pockets. See. Those are supposed to be open at the bottom." Wally looked toward the restaurant. "Which means the bastard who killed him is in there now."

Dan eyed the restaurant which was packed with people and had a line backed up out the door.

"What do you think we should do?"

Wally was already taking his phone out of his pocket. "Call the damned cops!" Dan watched him dial nine one one and put the phone to his hear. He turned his back and put his finger in the opposite ear as a '67 Camaro with a blower and loud exhaust drove by. Dan ignored the car and kept looking from the restaurant to his uncle. Finally, Wally walked back over to him. "They're on their way."

"Do you remember what he looks like?"

"I saw a picture your girlfriend had."

"So, what does he look like?"

"A Mexican kid." Wally thought for a second.

"Well, that helps a lot. Do you see him?" Dan scanned the restaurant again.

"No. But I'm staying right here until the cops come. This truck ain't going nowhere." Dan could almost see the lightbulb go off in Wally's head. His uncle turned and walked over to the front of the truck, opened the hood and removed the coil wire. "That'll fix his ass."

Dan laughed at his uncle and turned to see a police car pull into the lot. He stuck his hand in the air and waved trying to get the driver's attention. The lot was so crowded it took long seconds for the officer to notice Wally jumping up and down in the bed of his Ford. Finally, the police officer stopped near the truck. "Good afternoon, officer," Dan said as his uncle carefully climbed down from the pickup bed.

"What seems to be the problem?" The policeman reached to turn down his radio. He was bigger than both Dan and Wally and looked to have some experience under his belt. The cop unfolded himself from the front seat of the cruiser and towered over them.

~~ Blackie had his burger halfway to his mouth when he noticed Tammy watching a police car pull into the driveway. It passed their window with the lights on but no siren and stopped near the back of his truck. He leaned closer to the window to get a better view.

"Shit," he said under his breath. "Great."

Tammy didn't appreciate him practically shoving her over in the seat and gave him a dirty look. The policeman got out of his car and approached the two other men in the parking lot. One was younger, and kinda cute she thought. Definitely her type. The other was an older man, who began talking and pointing at Blackie's truck.

"Shit is right. What cha think is going on?" Tammy asked. All at once the old man pointed at the restaurant, and the cop and the young guy looked right toward them. She jerked away from the window reflexively. "We gotta go." She shoved him with her shoulder, trying to get him to move.

"Relax. The windows reflect on the outside." Blackie put his hand on her leg to calm her. It did help a little she had to admit. She couldn't believe how calm he looked with the police standing right outside. "Hey. I've seen those two before ... somewhere." His forehead creased as he searched his memory.

"Well, I've got to go to the restroom before we leave." She bumped him with her shoulder again. This time he got up and let her out but slid back onto the seat and watched. Tammy grabbed her bag and started for the bathroom.

"Don't take long." He grabbed her wrist to get her attention. "We might need to move quickly."

Tammy pulled her wrist away and increased the distance between them. She'd take as long as she wanted. Tammy felt her face flush and was suddenly nauseous. Should she scream now and pretend she was a hostage? No, the police were still too far away. She decided to hide in the bathroom and listen until they caught him and took him away. She walked in, went into the first empty stall, closed and locked the door, and sat on the commode listening.

~~ Blackie watched for several more minutes. It wasn't until he saw the dog that he remembered the two men from the truck stop the night he killed Bob. Were they friends of Bob's? What the heck were they doing here?

The cop walked around Bob's truck. He peered into the driver's window and then went behind it writing down the license plate number. He spoke into a microphone clipped to his shirt. Blackie hoped since he was now in California, it would take a while to figure out the switched plates. The officer cringed at the noise of an early seventies Dodge starting right behind him. He turned and walked to his patrol car, got in and closed the door. After a minute he climbed out and stepped over to talk to Bob's friends, then he looked toward the diner.

Blackie was amazed at how quickly his mind worked and how a stillness settled over him. It was similar to when Tammy's ex-boyfriend barged into the room and challenged him. He loved the danger. He walked up to the hostess. "Hi. I noticed that you were giving away hats like the busboys wear to the kids." He waited until she nodded yes. "Could I have one for my nephew?"

"Sure," the hostess said smiling. She handed him a paper hat with the restaurant logo on it.

"Thanks." Blackie walked through the doors and out to the parking lot. He put the hat on hoping he would look like an employee sent out to empty trash cans or something. Walking to the far side of the lot, he circled around and casually joined the small crowd checking out the old Dodge that annoyed the policeman. The owner had the hood open to show off his engine.

"Hemi my ass. That's a 440 wedge right there," the driver was explaining.

Blackie positioned himself so he was part of the crowd admiring the engine but could see his truck. He watched as the old guy turned and walked over to a 1950's era Ford pickup. The old guy leaned in the window and opened the glove box. When he did a cluster of papers slid out of it and fell onto the seat and floor. Blackie heard the man cursing as he opened the door and scrambled to pick them up and find what he needed. He piled most of it on the seat and returned to the cop, handing him what looked like the registration and his license. The younger guy was also showing his ID, and the officer was writing down the information.

While they were occupied, Blackie eased away from the group and went over to the old man's truck. He froze when a dog started barking a few cars down from the cop and the two men showing their IDs. The dog was looking straight at Blackie from the bed of a Dodge 2500 diesel. Fortunately, the animal was on a leash. Since the men looked over at the noise instead of him, Blackie relaxed and moved again. He picked up a discarded cup to keep his employee image going. Reaching the passenger door, he glanced to see if it was unlocked but noticed the window was down. Blackie grabbed the first two documents off the top of the pile the old guy left on the seat. The longhaired dog in the Dodge was raising such a fuss the two men walked over to settle her down. He looked back to see if they noticed him. They were occupied with moving the dog to the cab and didn't even look his way, so he casually walked away looking down as if he were searching for more trash.

"Now, I gotcha," he said as he opened the first document to see an entry form for a car show in Las Vegas. It had the man's name and address in California. The second document was a coupon for a speed shop near the event. He stuffed the registration in his pocket and the coupon along with the other trash he collected in a receptacle in the parking lot. Blackie continued walking around between the cars. He watched as the cop walked into the diner with the older man, searching for the suspect, him. When they exited and looked in his general direction, Blackie bent down behind an SUV and grabbed a discarded bag. He was just another Hispanic-looking kid doing the job no one else would take. They both scanned right past him.

Once the entrance to the restaurant was clear, he walked to the door removing his hat and stuffing it in his back pocket. Blackie walked toward the restrooms, and almost bumped into Tammy as she came out of the lady's room.

"Jesus, you scared me." Her voice quivered, and her hand went to her throat.

"Relax, Babe," Blackie put an arm around her shoulder. "I think we're in the clear, but we need to get out of here, and we can't go back to the truck." They both returned to the table.

"Oh, there you are," their waitress said as she placed their drinks back down. "I was beginning to think you stiffed me."

"No. It was a long stretch on the highway," Blackie tried to sound assuring. "We both needed to hit the restroom."

"I hear that." She smiled. "Can I get you anything else?"

He nodded toward the glasses she had put back on the table. "Maybe a refill."

"Sure thing." They sat on the same side of the booth and watched the waitress leave.

Blackie noticed Tammy's hands were shaking and put his arm around her. "It's gonna be okay," he added, as he watched an older lady park in the handicapped spot by the door and totter into the restaurant. Her friend of equal age followed behind. The hostess recognized them and seated them immediately near the door, chatting on the way to the table. Blackie watched as the old woman placed her bag and keys on the table. She started to sit, but instead turned and moved toward the restroom, remembering at the last moment to grab her purse. Her companion followed suit.

"Here ya go," the waitress chirped, clearly relieved she hadn't been stiffed. She placed the refills on the table along with their check. Blackie noticed she stayed where she could keep an eye on them.

"Let's go," Blackie said as he stood.

Tammy looked at him, eyebrows raised and palms up. "How?" she implored.

"Just follow my lead." He threw cash on the table, then took her hand and moved toward the door. As he passed the old lady's table, he swiped the keys in a casual motion, never turning his head to look at them. Taking Tammy's right arm by his left hand, he guided her out the door, and toward the white Camry in the handicapped space. The whole time she kept glancing at him questioningly.

He found the fob, and the doors chirped and unlocked. Success. Blackie closed her door and walked quickly to the driver's side and got in.

"Where did you – "

"Buckle in." He started the car and exited the parking lot. Since the police and the truck were behind them, no one even noticed them leave.

"What about our stuff?"

Blackie gave her a stern glance. "We have to leave it."

"Shit."

"The rest of my money is back there too," he added, his jaw clenched. "I've only got about a hundred bucks on me. I'm gonna get that old bastard."

"What old bastard?"

"That guy who called the cops." He banged his open palm on the steering wheel. "I got his address." He was quiet for a few minutes, then added, "Damn it. I liked that truck."

"Let's just go back to Las Vegas."

"No. We're still taking our trip along the coast that I promised you. Nobody will even notice us in this old granny car. Then I'm gonna find that bastard and kill him."

Tammy stared intently at him but sat in silence.

~~ Wally was quickly losing patience. He shoved his cold plate of French fries away and slumped back in the booth. "This is what you get for being a good citizen," he grumbled. "We coulda been fifty miles on the other side of Bakersfield by now."

"At least they recovered Bob's truck. It should be easier to track the killer now. He can't get far." Dan picked up the butter knife from the table and out of boredom was using it to look behind him at the sudden commotion near the door.

There were two older ladies frantically looking around and under their table. One was almost hysterical, yelling something about her car keys. Wally leaned to his right to see around Dan.

"What's going on?" Dan asked trying to resist turning around and staring.

"Some old lady has got her tail all twisted in a knot. Somebody probably put too much salt on her fries." Wally continued to watch the show, and Dan turned to take a quick peek.

"Who you callin' old?" He turned back to face his uncle. "She could be your younger sister."

His uncle's head snapped back to look directly at Dan with daggers in his eyes, he caught himself, returned his attention to the spectacle and said, "Screw you, punk."

Dan laughed. Suddenly the yelling behind him became shrieking as the ladies discovered their car was gone too. Dan turned to watch as the hostess ran out to the police car that was still in the lot. "Well, at least we got some entertainment."

"Shit," Wally muttered as it dawned on him who might have taken the car.

As soon as he heard Wally, Dan realized what probably happened. He dropped his head back staring at the ceiling showing his frustration. "He's probably halfway to LA by now."

"We shoulda skipped the cops, and just come in here, grabbed him and kicked the shit out of him." Wally was disgusted. While they were sitting around filling out forms and asking questions the bastard was getting away. He looked around the room and spotted security cameras in each corner. Up and out of his seat, he walked over to the manager who was working to calm the old lady. "Do you have security cameras in your parking lot?"

Still focused on the hysterical guest, the young manager didn't respond.

"Excuse me, I asked a question," Wally insisted, tapping her on the shoulder.

She slowly turned to face him. "And you are?"

"I'm a concerned, goddamned citizen … whose trying to help. That's who I am." Wally was instantly hot at being challenged by the young manager.

As she opened her mouth to answer, the police officer walked in the door and up to the manager. "I need to see your security footage, both inside and out, for the last hour."

"Right this way officer." She smiled at the policeman but turned and glared at Wally. The manager spun on her heels and headed toward the employee-only door. Wally walked directly behind the cop following the manager. As she held the door, she looked back. "Whoa. Whoa. Where do you think you're going?"

"I'm a witness." Wally gave her a Cheshire smile.

Turning to look back the CHP interrupted, "I need him to determine if the man we were looking for, is the man who took the car." He hooked his thumb at Wally.

The manager glared at Wally as he slipped past her. "Why thank you," he taunted. She took them back to her office in a little cubbyhole tucked away near the back door. Next to tall shelves was a locked cabinet and on her desk a monitor. The screen was divided into four parts, showing camera feeds that changed every ten seconds to a different camera. She hit a few keys and the time jumped back an hour.

"That's weird," the manager said as she toggled to zoom in on a figure in street clothes and a restaurant hat. "He's not an employee."

As soon as the screen zoomed in enough for Wally to see the face clearly, he shouted, "That's the guy!"

"Are you sure?" The policeman turned to face him. "You told me you hardly noticed him slouched on the seat of the pickup truck."

"Right, but I also saw a picture of him that the detective from Phoenix had."

"How did he get a picture of the guy?" the cop asked.

"She. She had a picture from a casino. The dirtbag used Bob's card to get a room."

"And that's the guy?"

"I just said it was, didn't I? What the hell is wrong with you people?" Wally turned to the manager. "Pull up the camera on the old lady's car."

The manager looked at the CHP, who nodded. She reluctantly complied with Wally's direction. "Same guy," she added as she zoomed in on Blackie holding the door for Tammy. "But there's a woman with him."

"Can you print pictures of both, please?" the officer asked.

"Certainly." There was that syrup again. Another glare at Wally. "Since you asked so nicely."

Wally had enough. He rose to his full height, towering over the short brunette in the chair. "Lady, while you're going around trying to piss in people's cornflakes, we're ... " he pointed at the cop and himself, "trying to catch a killer."

The CHP officer stepped in between them. "Calm down, Mr. Williams." He put his hand on Wally's shoulder.

Wally continued to stare at the woman. "I am calm, Sir. This is me trying as politely as I can to tolerate someone else's unhelpful attitude." He took a step back and shook his head.

"My God. I didn't realize the guy was a murderer. Really?" She looked at the patrolman.

"We think so."

"You can have whatever you like then. I'll print those photos now." She hit a few keys, and the printer came alive. "Would you like a copy of the files too?" The manager hit some more keys and handed a thumb drive to the cop. "It was bad enough when it was just a car theft. Thank God, no one in the restaurant was hurt."

"Thank you." The officer guided Wally back toward the door. "And thank you again, Mr. Williams. We'll get this guy."

"So, are you done with me?" Wally asked.

"Yes, Sir. I have all your contact information if we need anything else. We've kept you long enough." The patrolman shook his hand.

Wally watched as a flatbed tow truck drove by the door of the restaurant with Bob's truck on it. He turned back to the CHP cop. "Hey, can you let me know if nobody comes to claim that truck? I'd sure hate to see it go to a scrapyard, and I don't know if Bob had any relatives who'd want it."

"I'll sure try, Mr. Williams, and I'll put a note in the record." He pointed at the notebook in his hand with the pictures.

"Thank you." Wally walked back to the table where Dan waited impatiently.

As Wally sat to explain what happened, Dan spoke first. "I swear to God, Uncle. Your bathroom trips take longer every day. I was getting ready to form a search party."

"You always gotta go there, huh?" Wally shook his head. "Just for that, I'm not gonna take you with me to the citizen of the year award ceremony when I win it."

"You'd probably spend the whole time in the bathroom there too and miss the presentation," he goaded his uncle. "What do they give you for senior citizen of the year? A plaque shaped like a toilet seat?"

"Kiss my wrinkled old ass, kid." Wally laughed. "The nice officer said we could leave finally. You think you can get that Dodge started again?"

They both stood, and Dan scooped up the small piece of meat wrapped in a napkin he saved for Syd. "Shoot, you better be nice to that Dodge. You're likely to need it to tow you home." The exchange continued until they separated to go to their respective vehicles. Syd popped up and stuck her head out of the window as soon as she detected their voices. After a quick bathroom break for her, they were finally back on the road.

Saturday, June 18ᵗʰ (Afternoon)

Tammy moved the sun visor down on the passenger side and watched in the mirror for any police cars behind them. She tried to calm herself by fiddling with the radio on the pretext of finding a good station instead of the old lady's talk shows. How could people listen to that crap? But nothing helped. After having tried to outwait him in the ladie's room, she walked out right as he came for her, and he practically forced her into the stolen car. She hoped it looked that way to any witnesses anyway.

She no longer had any reason to be with him now that the money was gone. He already admitted he only kept a little cash on him. The rest was in the truck, and once she knew where it was hidden, the stupid cops impounded it. Of all the bad luck.

Blackie brooded as he wound his way through the streets of Barstow, apparently looking for something. His face lit up suddenly. "There!"

"What is it?" Tammy was freaked out. She turned and looked in the direction he pointed expecting to see the cops.

"California uses paper license plates with only the dealer name on them. No way to trace them, and there's one over there." He pulled into a strip mall parking lot, around the first row of cars, parked in front of a late model Chevy and got out. Blackie popped the hood of the Camry and acted as if he was checking something. Tammy watched him bend down and spin to face the Chevy. After a few minutes, he closed the hood of their car, and climbed back into the driver's seat, tossing a paper license plate that said, 'Bradley Buick Gently Used Cars,' with a phone number and website listed.

"What good is this?" Tammy asked.

"Its harder to trace a recently sold car that is not in the computer systems yet. We'll put this on our car, and it makes us more anonymous." He gestured toward the cardboard plague. "I'll put it on somewhere else." He started the car and left the parking lot. "Now we need money," Blackie added as he scanned the area.

"What are you looking for, an ATM? Won't they be monitoring your cards?"

"Sort of an ATM. As good as one anyway," he laughed, as Tammy wondered what he was planning. He pulled into another shopping center. "How about some tequila for our trip?"

Tammy looked up to see a liquor store in front of them. Maybe this would be her chance to escape while he was looking around the store. To her surprise, Blackie came around the car and took her by the arm, escorting her in the door. The cash register was to the right, and as they walked past the end of the first aisle, Blackie grabbed a bottle of tequila and moved them toward the clerk. She saw a sign for the ladies room to the right. "I need –"

"Damn, it's fate." Blackie interrupted her when he noticed the clerk counting his receipts and stuffing it into an open bank bag. To the clerk, he demanded, "Give me the money." Setting the bottle of liquor on the counter, Blackie produced Bob's gun from behind his back.

Tammy wasn't sure where it came from. The clerk, who looked to be middle eastern, turned paler than Tammy thought possible.

His right hand went back toward the drawer, possibly to get more money, she wasn't sure. Out of the corner of her eye, she saw Blackie swing the pistol and catch the clerk on the side of the head. He cried out in pain and fell back against the wall knocking down a container with lottery tickets.

Blackie steered her around to the side of the counter where they could see the employee cowering under a shower of scratchers and lotto entry cards. "Please, sir!' His hands were held up in front of him defensively.

"Hold this." Blackie handed her the gun. Her hands shook so badly, she was barely able to take it. Her eyes were as wide as the clerks. Blackie moved to the register causing the man behind the counter to curl his legs into a sitting fetal position, hands covering the back of his head. Blackie grabbed the bank bag and lifted the divider insert out of the drawer. "Well, hello." He scooped up several fifty and hundred-dollar bills that were stashed under the tray. Once satisfied, he spun and reached to take the gun back. Tammy's trembling was so severe the gun fired as soon as he touched her, striking the clerk in the chest. Blackie quickly stepped in front of her as she screamed, then escorted her back toward the door. He paused only to grab several large bottles of vodka and tequila on the way out.

Tammy was so stunned she complied with his directions, climbing back into the passenger's side. They were out of the parking lot and down the block within seconds. She began to hyperventilate and covered her face with her hands sobbing.

"C'mon now. It was an accident," he said rubbing her back. "Everything's fine now." Blackie tried to soothe her. She saw him smiling at her. Suddenly he seemed to notice the paper license laying on the seat. "Oh, yeah." Blackie pulled to the curb and jumped out to put the plate on the back of the Camry. Once back in the car, he added, "Now we're completely anonymous. They'll never catch us." Tammy continued to sob, eventually calming to an occasional sniffle.

Back on the interstate, they continued at a moderate pace so as not to draw attention. Blackie donned oversized sunglasses he found in the console. While not particularly masculine, they definitely changed his appearance. When they got near Victorville, California, he stopped to regroup. Blackie found a cheap motel, and as they entered the room, Tammy collapsed on the bed, her legs so wobbly she needed to sit or fall down. "I'm not cut out for this."

She lay back on the bed and stared at the ceiling as he closed the blinds and fiddled with the air conditioning. "Let's go back to Las Vegas."

"No way. You said you wanted to drive up the coast." He sat on the bed beside her. "We'll be fine. We've changed the plates on the car, and we have money now." He emptied the bank bag containing the money onto the bed and sorted the bills. She wasn't sure how much time passed before he continued. "We've got a little over four thousand dollars. That should be plenty for our trip."

"I just want to go home."

"You don't even have a home anymore. Remember? Your roommate kicked you out and sold your stuff."

The matter-of-fact manner in which he said it hit Tammy very hard and she started bawling. She didn't want to come on this trip but felt compelled by the possibility of getting some of his money. Now that was gone, and she was involved in at least two crimes in less than four hours. She was homeless, penniless, and on the run. All because of this boy who walked into her life only a few days ago. Hopefully, she could get away from him soon. Right now she wanted to sleep. Maybe after a hot bath and sleep she could make her escape. That was it. She needed to plan.

Blackie put his arm around her shoulder to comfort her, a clumsy effort from beside her which ended up as more of a grope. He was so close, she could hear him breathing through his mouth. How did she get mixed up with a mouth-breather? "I'll take care of you," the boy tried to comfort her.

"Could you run me a bath?" she asked meekly. Anything to get him away from her.

"Sure." He jumped up like an obedient little servant and walked into the bathroom. She heard water running. Finally managing to stand, she went over to the sink just outside the toilet door. Blackie left the tequila there. She unwrapped a plastic cup and poured two fingers of the amber liquid. Tammy gulped the first shot, poured another and downed that one too. As the third hit her throat, it clenched around the burning liquid. Tears filled her eyes, and she coughed as the burn moved down her esophagus causing her to grab the side of the counter. As Blackie exited the tiny bathroom, she entered carrying her cup and poured a small bottle of bubble bath into the tub. Tammy sat down on the side. The tequila kicked in causing her vision to blur around the edges. She was transfixed by the growing mound of bubbles, watching them act as prisms from the single lightbulb fixture in the bleak industrial green bathroom. Even in the destitute surroundings, she found beauty in the rainbows reflected by each tiny world the bubbles created.

She heard his voice in the other room, sounding distant. She pushed the door closed at the same time he tried to re-enter the tiny space. Privacy. That's what she needed now most of all. She dropped her clothing, letting it lay where it fell and stepped into the sudsy water. Sitting, then gradually reclining, she sipped the tequila, feeling it warm her from the inside, as the hot bath colored her skin to a pink hue. She was lost in her own little bubble. Private and safe and warm.

Suddenly the door burst open. "Are you okay?"

"Get out!" she screamed at the intrusion. How dare he? She threw the cup with its remaining dregs of the liquor at Blackie. It bounced off the doorframe with a dissatisfying clunk of plastic against metal, not nearly as dramatic as a shattering glass tumbler would have been to demonstrate her indignation. But it had the desired effect. He ducked out of the room and closed the door.

"Sorry, you were so quiet. I was worried you'd drowned."

"If only," she whimpered, more to herself than to him. She woke hours later, shivering in the cold tub. She forgot to move a towel close enough to reach so had to step over the clothes she previously discarded. Quickly drying herself, she dashed for the bed and slid under the covers.

He was far from her dream man, but at least the bed was warm. Lying with her back to him, listening to his raspy breathing, she fell asleep.

Saturday, June 18ᵗʰ (Evening)

Because of the delays dealing with the police reports, Dan and Wally would not get home before midnight. At a gas stop near Chowchilla Dan walked over to check on his uncle as Wally pumped gas. "How ya feeling, Uncle?"

"Like I've been rode hard and put away wet."

"Maybe we should grab you a cup of coffee before we move on?"

"I wouldn't say no to a cup. What about you?"

Dan gestured toward himself with his open hand. "My body's a temple. I don't drink coffee."

"Well, maybe we can find some Dr. Pepper for that finely tuned machine. That's got caffeine in it, doesn't it?"

"Now you're talking my language," Dan answered.

Wally finished pumping his gas, and they both walked into the mini-mart part of the station. They each grabbed their drinks and sat in one of the small booths at the end of the room. "Here. I got these for you." Dan tossed a bag of pretzels at his uncle. "It'll keep you awake if you're munching on something. It might keep up the blood sugar in that old body of yours."

Wally got up, took the pretzels and exchanged them for a bag of Frito's. "My blood sugar's fine, but you can keep your pretzels."

"Fine. Ingrate." They both laughed. "I know you didn't get any sleep last night, so I thought they might help you stay awake. You really okay to keep going?"

"I can make it another couple hours." Wally sipped his coffee. "You hear anything from your girlfriend yet?"

"Nope." Dan's brow creased. "I don't think she has my number. Just yours."

Wally gave Dan a concerned look. "I thought I taught you better than that. Letting her get away without even a number. You want hers?"

"Wouldn't hurt, I guess." Dan tossed his empty cup into a nearby trash can. "You need to hit the bathroom, old man? I'm not stopping for you again."

"I got my own brake, Bud. I don't give a damn if you stop or not. If I have to go, I'm stopping." They both laughed and headed for the restroom.

By the time Wally got out to his truck, Dan was standing there with Syd beside him. "Syd wants to ride with you."

"What for?"

"She says you're a better driver." Syd barked and put her paw up for Wally to high-five her, which he did.

"Well, I'm definitely a better conversationalist than you." He opened the passenger door of the Ford. "C'mon Syd. Saddle up." Syd jumped into the front seat and stuck her head out the open window.

As Wally walked around to his side of the truck, Dan said to Syd. "You keep the old guy awake, Syd. Okay?" Syd woofed a positive response as he rubbed her ears, then Dan walked to his Dodge, and climbed in.

~~ The dog sat in the passenger seat of the old Ford, but instead of looking out the window, she was focused on Wally. He drove along fine for a while, occasionally reaching over to pet her.

"How do you like riding in a real truck, Syd?" She gave an enthusiastic bark. "It's probably good to get away from that knucklehead for a while, I'll bet." Syd remained non-committal to that one.

After a while, Wally turned on the radio. "What kind of music do you like, kid?" He dialed in an oldies station and settled back into driving. Syd noticed his blinking became more frequent, so she used her nose to push the bag of Fritos on the seat, toward Wally.

"What? You want a Frito, Syd?" Wally opened the bag, reached in and put one on the seat. Syd sniffed it, then licked some of the salt off, but left the chip laying where it was. "You're a smart dog. Them things aren't good for ya." Wally munched on a few mindlessly as he continued down the interstate. Forty-five minutes later he was shaking his head and rolling down the window to bring his concentration back. The lack of sleep was taking its toll.

Syd would occasionally put her paw lightly on his arm, causing him to reach over and give her a few pets. "You sure are high maintenance," Wally said, as he petted her for the third time in ten minutes. "Don't you know that you're not supposed to distract the driver?" He laughed and ruffled her ears.

"Rooow, rooow, rooow," Syd made her argument.

"Okay, point taken." Wally laughed at how the dog scolded him rather than the other way around.

When a Willy Nelson song came on the station, Syd started singing along with the warbles. Wally never heard her singing act and laughed so hard there were tears in his eyes. Once he discovered her talent, he put in one of Willy's CDs, and they both spent the rest of the trip singing along without a care in the world.

When they pulled into his driveway at home, Wally left the garage door open and walked her back to Dan's truck. The big diesel idled as he opened the door.

"I've got to tell you that Syd's a helluva lot better company than you," Wally said holding the door open as she jumped into the Dodge.

"That's because she hasn't heard all your dumb stories and jokes a million times."

"She's a better singer than you too." Wally gave the dog a hug. "She sure likes Willy."

"She's something else." Dan patted the dog. "Well get your wrinkled old butt to bed before you fall down." He glanced to see his Aunt Bobbie open the garage door to the kitchen to welcome Wally home. Dan waved at her.

"Uh oh. That crazy old married woman, I'm living with is still up."

Dan laughed at his uncle and drove away as Syd watched Wally totter toward the kitchen door. "Good job, girl. Sounds like you kept him entertained." Syd laid across the seat and put her head on his thigh, letting out a heavy sigh. "Poor thing. You must be dog tired." Syd groaned as Dan laughed at his own joke.

Chapter Nine - Sunday, June 19th

When Blackie woke the next morning, Tammy was cuddled tightly to him, and her face was against his chest with an arm curled lightly on his stomach. He stayed there enjoying the closeness. Last night Blackie went to bed not sure if she wanted him around anymore. This woman sure did run hot and cold, so he resigned himself to enjoy the good times while they lasted. She was devastated after the shooting yesterday. What did it matter? It was an accident. They didn't even stick around to see if the store clerk was dead.

But he guessed he wouldn't like a woman who could shoot someone and walk away without a second thought. He would have to train her better with the gun. That was it. She needed more practice to get comfortable. He held her as he watched a small sliver of sunlight knife through the crack in the curtains and widen on the sheets of the bed, moving up her arm to her shoulder and finally bursting into shades of red in her hair. He followed it along each strand noting the slight variations in color. Listening to her breathe and feeling her warmth he felt suddenly empowered, wanting to protect her. She shifted slightly giving him a glimpse of her cleavage, one breast falling heavy against his upper arm. This caused a stirring in him that grew as he enjoyed the shape of her left leg which protruded from the covers. He was a man now. She needed him to be strong and lead the way.

Blackie quietly slipped out of bed. He would surprise her with coffee and breakfast. He would plot a course of action so she'd know he was in charge. Yes, he could both comfort her and guide her so she would be glad she was with such a man. And after they ate, and he shared his plan, they could make love to show their enthusiasm for it. He quietly got dressed and eased out the door.

He walked down the street to a bakery the motel manager recommended.

As Blackie came back into the motel room, he heard the shower running. "I brought you some coffee and a croissant," he yelled through the bathroom door. Blackie set the coffee and bag of pastries on the small table in the corner of the room and absentmindedly turned on the TV. Grabbing a croissant, he tore off a bite when his hand stopped halfway.

"Locals are calling them Bonnie and the Bandito, as a couple goes on a daring crime spree in the Barstow area," the cheery blonde news anchor announced. On the screen was a security video of Blackie and Tammy stealing the keys from the table and exiting Buddy's Burgers. The video switched to an outside view showing them getting into the Camry and driving off.

"Shit," Blackie muttered as Tammy came out of the bathroom.

~~ "What's wrong?" Tammy asked. One towel was wrapped around her body as she used another to dry her hair. She stopped and looked to see why he wasn't responding. There on the television was a video of Blackie and her in the liquor store. Her back was to the camera, and she saw the clerk cowering behind the counter. The gun was in her right hand but the camera didn't clearly show Blackie reach across and jar her hand because her body was blocking the camera. In the video, all she saw was the gun in her hand go off and shoot the clerk.

"As you can see, the woman in the picture kills the clerk in cold blood for no reason at all," the male news anchor added. "Police are saying it is one of the most senseless crimes they have witnessed in years."

The room became fuzzy as Tammy sunk to her knees at the foot of the bed. "Oh my God! I'm on the news as a murderer." She felt Blackie's arms grab her, and he lifted her and placed her on the bed.

"Just breathe," he whispered. "The camera in the liquor store doesn't get a good shot of your face. It'll be okay."

She sat in disbelief, focusing on the news again, as they concluded the segment with close up pictures of both of their faces from the restaurant. "If you see these suspects, do not approach them. Call the police. They are both considered armed and dangerous." It was the blonde anchor again, shaking her head with a mock concerned look on her face. "That's terrible, you don't usually see women commit such horrendous crimes. I hope they catch her and put her away for a long time." The male announcer nodded in agreement. His face brightened as he moved on to a feel-good piece about a local woman helping needy cats.

Tammy dropped the towel used to dry her hair and fell back on the bed, feeling dizzy. "We need to turn ourselves in. We have no other choice."

"Sure we do," he tried to assure her. "We already switched the plates on the car, and there must be a million white Camrys out there," he waved his arm in the general direction of the parking lot. "And I didn't shave this morning. I'll grow a beard."

"What the hell am I supposed to do? Grow a beard too?"

"Uh, uh, no. You could dye your hair. Or, or wear a hat and glasses." He wracked his brain for other ideas. "We can get another car."

Tammy wanted to choke him. She wanted to scream. She wanted to run away and hide somewhere safe. But there was no safe place anymore. Her life was over, ruined by this maniac in front of her. "They think I'm a dangerous killer for Christ sake!" She sat on the bed shaking from both fear and rage. She buried her face in her hands and sobbed. "How in the world did I end up like this?"

"Baby, I love you, and I won't let anything happen to you."

The bawling stopped, and she turned on him. "Won't let anything happen to me. Who in the hell do you think got me into this mess? A week ago, I had a job, an apartment, and a life." She looked at him with disgust. "Then you came along. Won't let anything happen to me. Ha! You're the cause of it all." Suddenly propelled by anger, she stood and pulled on her clothes. She felt caged with him in the small room. She wheeled around and grabbed the car keys as she opened the door.

"Where are you going?" Blackie asked

"Out."

~~ Wally's cellphone rang at seven o'clock on Sunday morning. He fumbled for the offending device on his nightstand. Hitting the button to answer the call, he growled into it, "Somebody better be dead or bleeding."

A few seconds of silence, then, "Uh, excuse me? Hello?" It was an unfamiliar female voice.

"Who the hell is this?" Wally asked as he shook the cobwebs loose.

"Mr. Williams?" The voice was distinctive, but he still couldn't place it.

"Do you know what damned time it is?" Wally didn't care if it was the Queen of England.

"Well, it's eight o'clock here, so it must be seven there. I'm sorry. Did I wake you, Mr. Williams?"

"No, dumbass. This is just my sexy morning voice." Wally hung up wishing he could slam down the receiver like in the old days. Suddenly it occurred to him to look at the phone to see who it was. Detective Bartlett. "Shit!"

He padded to the bathroom to empty his bladder, splashed some water in his face, and walked into the kitchen to sit at the counter. He stared at the infernal coffeemaker wishing he had learned to master the thing. His wife Bobbie always made the coffee by the time he woke up. She was a ball of energy that rarely stopped moving from the time she bounced out of bed until she went to sleep at night. When she did sit, she was always reading, or knitting or doing something productive.

He reached for the pot, determined to get something going. At that same instant, the machine came to life and started popping and groaning, startling him to the point of almost dropping the flask. Suddenly a small stream of coffee poured out of the filter and onto the heating plate below. Wally scrambled to get the glass container back in place causing drops of hot coffee to land on his hands and the counter.

He was standing at the sink cussing with his hand in a stream of cold water from the faucet, and brown coffee stains down the front of his tidy whities when Bobbie came around the corner.

"What are you doing in the kitchen, at this time of day?"

"I was just walking through, and that miserable machine attacked me," he said nodding at his spewing nemesis.

"Looks like it got the better of you. Maybe you should let the grownups make the coffee from now on." She snickered at him, making him even angrier.

"Well, thanks a lot for the goddamned sympathy. I was just trying to fire it up when it came alive and started spitting."

"You know I've had the coffee pot on a timer for the last fifteen years, Dear," she clucked her tongue at him. "You watch me add the water and coffee every night before we go to bed."

"I don't pay no attention to what a crazy old woman does in the kitchen." He frowned at her as if she were deranged to suggest such a thing. "You're always running around the house like an untrained bird dog most of the time anyway."

The machine went through its final death moans, and Bobbie adeptly poured Wally a cup and placed it in front of him. "Here's your coffee, Helpless." She looked him up and down. "Did you burn your little pee-pee?"

"Don't you worry about my pee-pee. Just keep that damned thing away from me." His hand stopped burning enough that he picked up his cup and gave a wide berth to the now silent machine.

After changing shorts and putting on jeans for protection, he sat on the couch and grabbed his phone. Hitting redial, he sipped his coffee while he waited for it to connect.

"Detective Bartlett."

"Hello. Detective?" He didn't know where to start. "Uh, this is Wally Williams. You called me a bit ago."

"Mr. Williams. Nice of you to call me back. I'm sorry if I woke you."

"No problem, Detective." A nervous chuckle. "I've got a cup of coffee now, so I think all the brain cells are firing. What can I do for ya?"

"I'm on my second pot. Sorry again about waking you. I received an email that said you ran into our killer yesterday in Barstow."

"Well, I didn't see the son of a bitch, but I recognized Bob's truck and called the police."

"That's fantastic Mr. Williams!" Bartlett actually sounded like she meant it. "I understand they managed to get video of him and the car he stole from there. That should help greatly, too."

"Yep, they got it all over the news here in California. That and the liquor store robbery." Wally wondered if she knew about that.

"I saw that too. So the suspect has a female accomplice, did you see her by any chance?"

"Nope, not that I recall. I guess she's as crazy as he is since she shot that clerk. Might be a good thing I didn't see her."

"So can you tell me what happened at the burger joint? I know you told the local folks, but I just want to go over it so I can get this killer." The detective picked up her coffee as Wally went into his explanation.

Wally ended the description by saying, "The thing that made me sure was the car club sticker on the driver's window. The club has changed its name, but Bob told me he left the old one on there."

"You would have made a good detective, Mr. Williams."

"Not me. I don't have the patience."

"It does take patience," she had to admit. "Well, thank you, Mr. Williams. If you think of anything else—"

"Detective, I know it's none of my business." Wally wanted to say something before she wrapped up. "My nephew seemed to really like you, and he was pretty butthurt about you kinda disappearing on him."

She was silent for a few seconds. "That was unfortunate. I would not have spent time with him if I'd known he was involved in the investigation." She struggled for how to put it. "It could really complicate the case and my job. I hope you understand."

"Well, he's a good guy. Don't ever tell him I said that though." Wally laughed, and it seemed to relieve a bit of the tension. "He just really seemed to like you."

"Thanks for understanding, Mr. Williams." She quickly ended the call.

~~ At first, Blackie sat on the bed, his mouth dropped open at the level of wrath being directed at him. But the memory of her last sentence triggered his own anger. 'You're the cause of it all.' His mother frequently used those very words, ruing the day he was born, and how he had tied her down. Blackie had ruined her life. He was the cause of it all. Blackie closed his eyes and tried to control his temper. He didn't ask to be born. It wasn't his fault his mother got pregnant. Blackie thought of Tammy's beautiful face contorted with fear and anger and hardly recognized it.

She'd stormed out of the room. Blackie listened as she started the car, wondering where she would go. Would she just leave him?

He hoped she wouldn't go to the police and turn herself in. He wanted to run out and tell her how sorry he was. He never meant for her to get in trouble. She was the best thing that happened to him in his short life. He paced around the room wondering if he should leave in case she went to the cops, or if he should wait for her. If he stayed how long should he hang around?

He looked at the new leather skirt hanging on the rack across the room. Man, she looked good in that thing. Blackie felt sure he would never meet another woman like Tammy again. He reached out and touched the soft black leather, remembering how firm her ass felt underneath its suppleness. He walked over to the window at the front of the room and pulled the curtain back a little to peek out. The Camry was still sitting there!

Blackie wondered if he should go to her. He opened the door and stepped out on the sidewalk separating the motel from the parking lot. Two metal chairs sat by their front window in case they wanted to relax and enjoy the view of the cars. The Toyota was three spots down to the left. It was running, and Tammy sat in the driver's seat. She was staring at something she held in her right hand.

~~ Dan was awake by six trying to recover the time he lost on his projects by going to Nevada. He opened the shop and was busy using a bead roller to add a few lines to strengthen a panel for an equipment box he was making. Syd busied herself with herding some cats, literally. A mother cat adopted the shop and recently delivered a litter of kittens under a rack where Dan kept his recycled oil outside. Having discovered them, Dan made a box inside the shop the mother found acceptable now that the brood was old enough to move around.

Syd had made friends with the mother, and Dan was surprised when he found both licking the kittens to clean them. Syd was like a second mom. She would use her nose to nudge them in the direction she wanted. Once they became more mobile and playful, it became a game for the kittens. They'd take off in different directions, and Syd would nuzzle and bark, trying to direct them back to their nest. Often that resulted in one of them pouncing on her head. Dan watched them play for a few minutes, but duty called and back to work he went.

He was shocked to see the number on his cell phone when it rang. His Uncle Wally was actually awake before nine on a Sunday. "What the hell are you doing up this early? After driving all day, I thought you'd sleep until noon."

"Well, you thought wrong, Einstein. I likely woulda done that, but your girlfriend called and woke me at seven in the AM. You need to straighten her out."

"Did she call to ask you about your handsome nephew?"

"Wrong again. I guess she got wind of us finding Bob's truck."

"That figures." Dan couldn't keep the disappointment out of his voice. "Did she give you anything new?"

"No. She just wanted to hear my version of things."

"Hey. Can you do me a favor and send me Angie's phone number?" Dan decided to take a chance.

"Sure, but don't go telling her where you got it." Wally laughed and added, "She really didn't call you, huh?"

"Nope. I'm just working in the shop, trying to get caught up from all the time I lost going to Las Vegas to save my dumbass uncle." Dan knew he'd better go on the attack before Wally detected any weakness. "Besides, if she'd called me I wouldn't need to ask you for her number, you senile old goat."

"Just because your girlfriend would rather talk to me is no reason to go getting mad. It ain't my fault I got a natural charm that women flock to." They both laughed. "You need any help down there?"

"No, you just keep your charm at home today. But be ready to go at it hard tomorrow," Dan warned.

"See ya in the morning."

~~ Detective DeCicco was on about his twentieth cup of coffee for the day. He made the short trip to Barstow before dawn and spent most of his day waiting for information from the other agencies. Just as he thought he was making progress with the locals, the FBI appeared and started throwing their weight around. They barged in and interrupted his meeting with the local detective named Walker.

Kristoff, the arrogant Special Agent in Charge, asked him, "Who are you again?" The punk was about half DeCicco's age with a lot to learn.

"DeCicco. Henderson Police Department." He saw no look of recognition in Kristoff's eyes. "Listen. I think we have a serial murderer on the loose here. Now that we have those videos of the guy, we can place him at the scene where a body was disposed of in a suitcase." The SAC at least looked up from his papers now. "And that is in addition to him being the prime suspect in the truck stop murder in Arizona."

"All the more reason for the FBI to be handling it."

Man, this guy did not know how to play nice. "I'm not trying to steal your cupcake, Junior. I'm just saying we need to share information and work together before someone else gets hurt." DeCicco pushed his coffee away because he was starting to lose his patience. "The suspect was seen leaving a restaurant with the woman whose body we found in the luggage. Her neck was snapped, and she had been raped. We're not sure in what order. This guy is unpredictable."

"The FBI will work up a full psychological profile, Detective."

The attitude was thick enough to walk on.

DeCicco glanced at the local detective hoping he would jump in. The guy just shrugged and rolled his eyes. "Have you identified the woman who is with him? She could be in grave danger."

"No we haven't, but I think we are close." Kristoff gave them both a little smirk. "We withheld some critical information we think will make her come forward, and turn herself in."

"What kind of information?" both DeCicco and the local detective named Walker asked in unison.

"Pay attention to the video on the screen on the left." Kristoff pointed at a bank of video monitors on one end of the conference room. "That is the one the news programs are running." He paused for effect. "See in that one it appears the woman shot the clerk because the camera was behind her." He clicked a remote, and a second video appeared on a different screen. "Now, in this one, you can clearly see the male suspect first forcing her to take the gun. She is obviously afraid and has no training at all because you can see she rests her finger on the trigger. When he is in the process of taking the gun away from her, it goes off." He points at the screen. "You can see how surprised and terrified she is. The whole time she held the gun, she was shaking like a leaf."

"So you want this woman to think she's a murderer?" DeCicco was confused.

"If we put pressure on her, we think she will likely break before he will." Kristoff seemed to have all the answers.

"You're assuming he hasn't stuffed her into a suitcase by now," Walker finally spoke.

"And you're assuming he isn't controlling her every move," DeCicco insisted. "What if she's a hostage?"

"It's the only play we have at the moment." Kristoff dismissed them with a wave of his hand. "Just let us handle it."

"You don't know this woman's motives. You could be jeopardizing her life with this game you're playing."

"That's a chance I'm willing to take," Kristoff shot back as he left the conference room.

~~ Tammy left the room intending to go to the police station and turn herself in. The thought of having taken another life was more than she could bear. Sure, she helped Blackie bury her ex-boyfriend in the desert, but that was after he was killed in self-defense while trying to rob the kid. Even though she helped plan the robbery she did not tell Freddie to bring a loaded gun. Once things got out of hand she was forced to act. If it came out that she was in on the robbery attempt, she would go to jail. But actually shooting another person to death was way over the line.

She got in the car and started it. When she realized she didn't even know where a police station was located, she just broke into sobs and sat there, picturing her life in jail. No, not jail, prison. Oh, God! Tammy was certain she couldn't handle prison. She could barely stand having a roommate, let alone living in a small cell with other women. She immediately lost her resolve to drive to a police station.

Tammy sat looking at the room. There was as much repulsion to going back in there as spending her life in prison. She couldn't stand the thought of continuing with Blackie. He caused so much damage to her life in such a short time that she wanted to run. But where? Her instincts told her to go back to Las Vegas; she at least knew a few people there. However, with no job or place to live, Vegas could be a pretty tough town. She had no real family to speak of. How in the world did she live for more than thirty years on this earth with so few connections? A wave of self-pity swept over her and further dampened her spirit.

From of the corner of her eye, she saw movement in the window of their room. Oh geez, he would see her. She couldn't stand the thought of being near him again. The money was gone. He was nothing but trouble. The one thing she was clear about was getting away from him. Remembering where he put the pistol, she quickly opened the glove box and grabbed it. Sure enough, the motel door opened, and he peered around the door frame.

As soon as he saw the car, he stepped out onto the sidewalk. He tentatively sauntered toward her.

As Blackie took a step toward the car, Tammy focused intently on him. Her hand moved toward the window and pointed the gun in his direction.

Suddenly, Blackie realized she was holding the pistol that killed the clerk. He'd put it in the glove box after they left the liquor store, and now it was pointing at him.

Tammy held the gun in Blackie's general direction. Her hand trembled so severely, she had little control. Panic struck her as she realized she was aiming a weapon at another human being again. Her breath caught. Perhaps she was a natural killer. Self-disgust raised in her throat like bile making her want to throw up. Tammy moved the gun under her chin like she was going to shoot herself.

"Tammy! No!" Blackie shouted and waved both arms as he sprinted toward the car.

The end of barrel steadied under her chin. Maybe it would be better to end her pain and failure right now before she hurt someone else. But she wasn't sure she could do that.

Her tormentor stood a few feet away with a goofy grimace on his face. Tammy's hand quivered as she stared at Blackie. Perhaps she could get him to back off by threatening to kill herself. She closed her eyes and tried to tighten her grip to gain control.

She heard Blackie suddenly yell loudly. He was coming for her; he wouldn't let her escape. Fear caused her to flinch and her muscles contracted. The last sound she heard was a terrible roar as the gun fired; then Tammy was enveloped in peaceful blackness.

~~ Blackie was barely four feet away when he heard the blast and saw the driver's window was obscured in a splash of red. He heard a metallic ping as the bullet exited the roof of the Camry. Blackie stopped, stunned. His frown faded. It took a few seconds to comprehend what Tammy did. Fortunately, the blood on the glass was so opaque he couldn't see into the car. He turned his head, unwilling to look at the woman who was so beautiful only seconds ago.

Blackie spun on the balls of his feet and jogged in the opposite direction. He continued past the room and kept going. The more distance he could put between himself and Tammy's death the better. Panic flooded his brain like a blinding white light. Only functioning on a feral level, his focus was on three basic needs. Breathe. Walk. Escape.

~~ DeCicco and Detective Walker still sat in the conference room grousing about the Special Agent in Charge, when Walker's cellphone rang.

"Walker," he answered flatly. "Yeah? When?"

Walker looked at DeCicco, his eyes widening. "What is it?" DeCicco asked.

"What makes you think that?" Walker started scribbling on a pad with DeCicco leaning over trying to read it. He wrote 'Victorville' 'gunshot' and 'white Camry,' and finally 'female victim.'

"Holy shit," DeCicco said as Walker ended the call. "Is that what I think it is?"

"Cop friend of mine from Victorville. Too soon to tell for sure. The plates don't match, but the victim could be our female accomplice."

"They can't ID her?"

"Unfortunately, she was shot in the face, but it could be her," Walker answered. "Looks like he might be cleaning house."

"This guy is a savage." DeCiccos face tightened thinking of the brutality. "You gonna tell the special agent?"

"What? And waste his time with something we're not even sure about?" Walker smiled. "I wouldn't dream of it. But since you've got nothing else to do, I wouldn't mind if you tagged along."

"Heh, heh. Don't mind if I do. After you, Detective."

By the time they arrived at the crime scene and talked to Walker's local detective-buddy the uniformed officers had already traced the serial number from the car, identifying it as the stolen Camry. The inside of the car was a mess with the blood, and what looked like part of a tooth on the dashboard. Walker pointed to an exit hole where the bullet exited through the edge of the roof. One of the crime scene technicians was gathering evidence from the seat, and door of the Toyota.

Walker stopped short, causing the CSI to look at him. "Did they remove the body already? I thought you needed to wait for the coroner?"

"She wasn't dead," the female technician answered matter-of-factly.

"I thought they said she got shot in the face?" DeCicco asked.

"The bullet entered under the chin and exited just below the left eye. She should make it," she answered pointing at her own face to show the entrance and egress points. "Lost a couple of teeth though. Gonna leave some nasty scars."

"Was she conscious?" It was Walker asking this time.

"Not while I was here. EMTs were wheeling the victim out as I arrived."

Walker and DeCicco walked over to a table under a pop-up tent to look at what evidence was collected so far. Seeing nothing definitive, they turned to go. "They didn't have this vehicle very long," DeCicco explained. "They stole it just yesterday. We found a lot more stuff in the truck."

"Let's stop by the hospital to see if she's gonna make it," Walker suggested. "Once we've personally, positively identified her as the shooter, we should inform the FBI."

"Oh. Of course, Detective. After we have done the positive ID." DeCicco winked and slapped his co-conspirator on the back as they walked toward Walker's car.

When they got to the hospital, the patient was still unconscious. Her face was heavily bandaged, but the EMTs grabbed her purse on the way out to take with her, so they were able to not only identify her as the woman on the video from her driver's license picture, but they were also able to get her real name and address. However, when they called the number listed as her home number, a woman said she no longer lived there and was rather abrupt with DeCicco.

"I threw that deadbeat bitch out last week," her ex-roommate declared.

"Well, I'm from the Henderson police department. She's been in an accident. Do you mind if I stop by this week sometime to see her room and ask you a few questions?"

"Look. I don't care if you are the head of the CIA. I told you I threw her out. And I sold off all her stuff to pay for her back rent, and I already have a new girl who's moved in. There's nothing more to say." She hung up on him. He would still follow up when he got back to Vegas.

"Did she say anything about who Tammy left with?" Walker asked him when he hung up.

"No. Obviously, they didn't part on the best of terms." DeCicco stuck his cell phone in his pocket. "It doesn't get us any closer to finding out who this guy is."

"Well, maybe you should start sharing the video from the liquor store on the Vegas news stations and see if anyone comes forward."

"That's a good idea. Although, I may have to get permission from His Highness to do it."

~~ Dan sat at the small table in the corner of his shop that served as a lunch area. It included a sink, a small refrigerator, and a microwave on the counter. Syd's food bowl and a dish of water were on a rubber mat in the corner. He stared at his phone. More accurately, he stared at Angie's number on the screen of his phone trying to gather enough nerve to call her while planning what he would say if he did manage to find the strength to press the call button.

Syd stood from her bed near the shop door and walked toward him. She was focused on his face because he was acting so nervous, and she did not see the kitten sitting on the stool. As she walked past it, the furry kamikaze leaped from its perch onto Syd's tail. The kitten was attracted by the white fur on the tip that was moving when Syd started wagging her tail as a greeting when approaching Dan. What the kitten didn't calculate was Syd's tail not being substantial enough to support his weight. The attacker soon found himself grabbing for purchase as he sailed past the intended target. Syd gave a quick look back when she felt a light brush of her fur and saw only an orange ball of fluff rolling off in the other direction. The activity stirred the interest of one of the attacker's brothers, who pounced on him before he could regain composure. To Syd, it was karmic justice.

Syd turned her attention back to Dan, who didn't even notice the treachery taking place a few feet away. She reached Dan just as he summoned the nerve to hit the call button on his phone screen. The volume on the phone was loud enough for her to hear both sides of the conversation.

"Detective Bartlett here."

"Wow. That's how you answer your phone on a Sunday?" Dan was thrown by the formality.

"Excuse me? Who is this?"

"Sorry, Angie. It's Dan." Dan struggled, feeling like he had blown it already. "Dan Williams."

"Oh, Mr. Williams. How are you?"

The call felt like a huge mistake already. "Look. Uh, my Uncle Wally, told me you called him about finding the truck. Uh, I didn't know if you wanted to talk to me too." It was the only thing he could think of to try to recover.

"Could you hold a second please?" It sounded like she was moving.

"Sure." Dan sat listening and trying to compose himself after the disastrous start.

He heard a door close. "Sorry, Mr. Williams, uh, Dan. Look, I'm at work. I don't want to be rude or mean, but I have to keep this professional."

"Okay."

"I had a nice time when we met, but if I knew who you were, I would not have let it happen. It could screw up my whole career, becoming involved with a witness in an active investigation. I hope you understand."

"Uh, okay. I —"

"When I saw you at the police station, it kinda freaked me out. Look, I'm sorry, but we have to act like it never happened. It's nothing personal."

"Is that kinda like the 'it's not you, it's me' speech." Dan's stomach was churning.

Angie laughed. It wasn't a nervous laugh but a full-fledged laugh from the gut. Dan could feel some of the tension leave her voice. "Yeah. Kinda like that."

"So if I weren't a witness, things would be fine?"

"Look, Dan. We had a good time. I like you, you're funny and kinda cute. But I'm not looking for anything permanent right now."

"Just kinda?" Dan was recovering a bit now.

Angie laughed again. "Well, not as cute as your dog, but you'll do in a pinch."

"Ouch." It was Dan's turn to laugh. "Okay. I think I understand. I don't like it, but I understand."

"Thanks, Dan, uh, I mean Mr. Williams," she said mocking herself, by lowering her voice when she said his name.

"So, do you need any kind of a statement from me?"

"I think I have everything from your uncle." Dan was disappointed. She added, "But I have your number if I need anything."

"Okay, Detective. And thanks for the explanation."

"Sure, sorry about that. I started to leave a note, but it just seemed too impersonal."

"No problem. Oh, Angie. One more thing."

"What's that?" Angie felt a huge relief.

"When you catch this guy, you're fair game."

Another laugh. "Take your best shot, cowboy." They both hung up.

Dan looked at Syd who sat at his feet looking confused. "Angie says hi, Syd." He leaned down and hugged the dog. The jealous kittens suddenly appeared out of the shadows to get in on the affection, one pouncing on Syd, the other wrapping its front paws around Dan's boot.

~~ Blackie realized he needed to find another car quickly because the area would be swarming with cops soon, and on foot, he didn't stand a chance. He walked to the back of the motel and down a side street, trying to stay on the edge of the business district because he knew he would attract attention in a small town residential neighborhood. He wanted to crawl in a hole somewhere and hide but knew he needed to put distance between Barstow and himself quickly. His grief at losing Tammy was quickly replaced by a burning rage to strike back at the system and people who caused his strife.

He was flat broke because his money was still on the counter in the room. His gun was also gone. Not that he would want that one after what happened. He needed to move fast. His whole world was falling apart, and he felt trapped. A police car approached at high speed with its lights and siren on. Blackie put his head down and turned into the parking lot of a convenience store as it passed. Just as he hit the sidewalk in front of the store, a father and his teenaged daughter pulled into a spot in the middle of the store. They were both laughing and singing to an old Neil Diamond song on the radio. How could they be so carefree and happy? He hated them.

The father turned off the engine, and his daughter protested, "Hey. I was listening to that."

"What? You're not coming in with me? We can sing in the store."

"Yeah right. Just get me some of those little chocolate donuts."

"No junk for you, young lady. We're going to your grandmother's for brunch, and tomorrow you have a big track meet." He put the keys back in the ignition, and the radio came back on. He got out of the car and walked toward the door.

"How about a latte, then?" The daughter yelled after him. He gave her a thumbs up and entered the store. The daughter resumed singing, but at a much lower volume.

Blackie wanted to smash her in the face. He walked over to her door and opened it, then grabbed her by the arm and threw her to the blacktop before she realized what happened. "Spoiled little bitch," he spit the words at her.

"Hey, what the hell?" she was so stunned she laid there as he slammed the door and ran to the driver's side. Blackie got in and started the car. He slammed it into reverse and hit the gas. As she scrambled to get up the right front tire ran over her ankle, and she heard the bone snap. She screamed as car horns blared when Blackie shot out onto the street with the tires squalling. Blackie looked around the car trying to determine what he could use. He laughed at his luck, he couldn't have planned it better if he wanted. He was in a late-model, beige, Honda Accord. What a perfect car to blend in. He slowed down to a respectable speed and headed toward the interstate to get some money.

~~ "Hell no!" Kristoff was livid. "You mean to tell me that you got a lead on this case and not only did you not share it with the head agency, but you went on to pursue it without us and without back up?"

"What do you mean back up?" Walker dismissed the agent with a wave of his hand. "You guys come in here and shove us out of the way. How the hell are you gonna back us up, when you're standing on our throats?"

Walker and Kristoff were both over six feet and were toe-to-toe, when the diminutive DeCicco, who only stood five foot, six, pushed in between them. "You two both need to calm down." They both were forced to take a step back, and DeCicco continued, "Look, Chief, Walker got a call about what he thought was a local shooting, and he went to check it out."

"Local, my ass." Kristoff shot back.

"Hey, do you want every local PD to call you about every domestic stabbing, or gang shooting they get? That would tie you up for weeks," DeCicco reasoned.

"If you didn't think it was related, why the hell did you tag along?"

DeCicco figured a bit of truth would calm him down a bit, so answered, "After talking to you, we decided to grab some lunch so we could talk about what a pain in the ass the FBI is at times. Heh, heh."

That seemed to resonate with the SAC, who smirked. "Very funny."

"Yeah, well we were on our way to lunch when he got the call, so I was in the car." He shrugged his shoulders. "No big conspiracy here, bud."

"I'm still not releasing the other tape."

"They call it video now, you meathead." Walker was still hot. "And what the hell good does it do you now. The woman you were trying to put pressure on, is in the hospital in a medically induced coma. Maybe you should go make them wake her up so you can slap her around?"

"She's in custody now, Kristoff. We need to focus on the male." DeCicco tried to bring them back to the main point. "And we need to see if we can get somebody to come forth who knows the girl. It's probably the best shot we've got." He thought he saw a small opening in the agent's resolve. "Look, I can put him at the scene where the body in the suitcase was found, but she appears outta nowhere. We need to establish a timeline of how and where they hooked up. That can help pin down his movements." He hoped he didn't oversell it.

"Alright, alright, just don't pull this shit again." Kristoff pointed at Walker. "If I find out that you held back on me about anything else, I'll have your ass kicked off this case so fast ..." He didn't bother finishing the threat.

"Great! Now, let's get the new information on the board, shall we?" DeCicco let out a sigh and went to stand by the whiteboard they were using to organize the case. No one moved, but just stood looking at each other, so he tried a different tack. "Hey, Kristoff, what do you say you and I go grab a fresh cup of coffee." The agent didn't respond but did follow DeCicco out the open conference room door. Walker followed them out and turned to go talk to the department's communications group about releasing the video.

~~ Bobbie walked into the garage to see Wally rifling through papers in the glove box of his F-100. "Damn it, Stan," he yelled at nobody.

"What are you fussing about now?" Bobbie asked, causing him to bump his head on the doorframe as he extracted himself from the truck.

"Woman, what did I tell you about sneaking up on a man like that?" he said rubbing the back of his head.

"Are you kidding? A herd of elephants could run through here, and you wouldn't know it with your hearing."

"That's just the high frequencies from listening to you screech at me the last thirty years."

"What is it you're looking for?" she gestured toward the truck. "And why are you cussing Stan when he isn't even here."

"I was looking for the registration for the Las Vegas the car show. I always save the window sticker and put it up on the wall there." He pointed at a row of stickers from the previous car shows thumbtacked to the garage wall. "I didn't even get time to stick this one on my windshield, so I know it had to be in the registration packet."

"So why are you cussing Stan?"

"Because it's not here, and he's the only other one that was in my truck. Well, except for Syd. And I know she didn't take it."

"What would he want with it?" Bobbie ducked down and looked under the front seat of the truck.

"I don't know. What the hell are you doing out here in my garage? Shouldn't you be in the house doing something?" Wally knew when he was starting to lose an argument it was time to change tactics.

"Watch it, buddy." Her eyes narrowed indicating he was pushing it. "I came out here to see what you wanted for lunch. So I suggest you improve your attitude if you want to eat."

"Yes, Dear." Wally wasn't stupid. He was literally saved by the bell when his phone rang. He gave it a strange look as he viewed the screen, then pushed the button to answer. "Uncle Wally's bait and brothel, Wally speaking."

"Hello? Mr. Williams?"

Assuming this was some kind of sales call he answered, "I already said this was Wally. Are you so stupid you don't know who you're calling?"

"Mr. Williams this is Detective Walker of the Barstow PD. Is this a bad time?"

"Oh, no sir. I apologize, I saw the number and assumed it was a telemarketer. What can I do you for?"

"I hear ya. Those guys are a pain in the ass." The detective laughed. "Mr. Williams, we were reviewing all the video from the burger place, trying to track the suspect's movements."

"Doing all that fun legwork, huh?" Wally asked. "Are you making any progress?"

"Yes, sir. Anyway, we can see in the video that the suspect walked past your truck while you were talking to the CHP."

"Really? The bastard was that close to us?"

"He's pretty brazen. And it looks like he reached in and removed something from the front seat of your truck." Walker paused to let it sink in. "Are you missing anything? Do you remember what might have been on your seat?"

"Shouldn't have been nothing on the seat." Wally thought for a minute.

"In the video, you just went to the truck and took something out to show the CHP. Did you leave anything on the seat? You didn't have a gun or other weapon, did you?"

"What? Hell no. Closest thing to a weapon I ever have is a flashlight." He didn't need the cops going there. "I did go back for my registration, and I remember a bunch of stuff fell out of the glove box, and I just laid it on the seat." Wally tried to remember what fell out. "Wait, I was just looking for my registration to the car show in Vegas. It's missing. You think he would have taken that?"

"It's hard to see what it was on the video," Walker answered. "But he stuffed it in his jacket pocket as he walked away."

"Why would he want that?" Wally couldn't imagine anyone taking it on purpose.

"Did it have any personal information on it? A credit card number maybe?"

"I don't think so. I sent a check with it. It would have my address, that's about it. Maybe the tag and insurance policy for my truck."

"That's not good." The concern in the detective's voice made Wally realize the creep had his name and address. "He saw you talking to the CHP, and he grabs something with your address on it."

"You think he would come after me?" It felt like it was a bit of a stretch.

"I don't want to scare you, Mr. Williams, but this guy has acted pretty erratic. You might want to take a few precautions. Just to be safe," the detective warned.

"Well, thanks for letting me know." Wally felt a little uneasy about the whole thing. "Do you know who this guy is yet?"

"No name yet. He seems to have popped up out of nowhere." Walker sounded weary. "I don't think you have anything to worry about but keep an eye out for anything unusual."

"Hey, can you keep me updated on where he is? Is that allowed?"

"To the extent that we know, I'll be glad to share it. But we're not sure where the guy is right now. I doubt he has any interest in you. We're just being cautious. Thanks, Mr. Williams."

"Thank you, Detective." Wally stared blankly at his phone. He figured it would be better not to worry Bobbie, but he would definitely stick closer to home until they caught the bastard.

~~ Blackie headed west through a few towns on the interstate before he dared to pull off again. It felt good to put some distance between the image of the blood-splattered window and himself.

His rage would build every time he thought of his beautiful Tammy dying like that. He thought back to just hours before when they were driving along in the old Ford happy to be heading on a road trip. He could still picture her sitting across from him in the burger joint, looking out at all the old cars with fascination. How could everything change so quickly? Blackie thought back to when he noticed the police car and the two men that ratted them out. The bastards. It was all because of them. Losing the truck and the cash. Needing to rob the liquor store. Everything leading to Tammy sitting in the car with the gun was caused by those two calling the CHP. Now instead of taking a fun trip with a beautiful woman, he was on the run and all alone.

A tear rolled down his cheek thinking of all he'd lost. No. He would not sit and feel sorry for himself. He was no longer a sniveling kid. He was Blackie, and if he could not take his road trip, he would make it his mission in life to kill those men who caused him to lose Tammy. It was his new mission. And he knew just where to start because he had the name and address of the old man. He would find him and beat the name of the other man out of the old bastard before he killed him. Then he would take care of the other one. Think. Where did he put the letter he stole from the old man's truck?

He remembered putting it in the pocket of his jacket as he walked away from the old Ford. He glanced at it in the parking lot and stuffed it back in the breast pocket. Frustration boiled when he remembered he had left the jacket on the bed in the motel room when he went out to check on Tammy. He walked away without going back for anything. He tried to recall the name or address on the form. Nothing came to him. Damn it. He could picture the letter with its logo, but the specific details were just out of focus. The more he tried, the fuzzier they got. He needed to relax and not think about it, and it might come to him.

Focusing back on the real world, Blackie saw a gas station with a convenience store ahead, so he pulled in. There was only one car at the pumps, but Blackie pulled up by the building.

He walked inside and went back by the drink coolers near the rear of the store. Grabbing a six pack of beer, he took his time approaching the counter. The man pumping gas came in to settle his bill, so Blackie stood back about ten feet. He occupied himself by looking at all the junk displayed along the counter to trigger impulse buys as customers waited.

One item was a ceramic pocket knife with only a three-inch blade that was supposed to be razor sharp. Blackie picked one up, admiring it.

There was a television in the corner near the register showing a baseball game. The station went to a quick newsbreak during the seventh inning stretch. The lead story was about the shooting at a motel near Victorville earlier that day. Blackie was transfixed by the story. They did not give many details, only that an unidentified young woman was shot in the face. No word was given about her condition. It looked like they were moving on, and Blackie started to turn away until the announcer said, "In a related story, police believe the unidentified woman may be linked to a carjacking an hour before at the same restaurant where a man from Modesto called to alert police about a vehicle believed to be involved in a murder.

Blackie looked back at the screen just as the clerk was ready to wait on him. "I need to see some ID," the woman said. Blackie ignored her as he listened to the story. "Sorry kid, but if you want to buy the beer, I need some ID. We ID everyone," she repeated pointing to the sign about requiring identification.

"Sorry? Oh, sure." Blackie said as he opened the blade of the knife. He looked down at the blade and made a face. "Can you read this? I think it says where it's made." He smiled at the overweight clerk who looked to be in her early twenties. "I just don't want to buy any junk from China." The clerk leaned in closer to look at the knife.

In one efficient movement, Blackie grabbed the back of her head as he raked the blade across her throat, spraying blood everywhere. The clerk's eyes went wide with realization, and her hand went to her throat. She staggered back a few feet and collapsed as her brain starved for oxygen.

Blackie calmly walked around the counter and emptied the register. He tossed the knife in the hot dog roaster and watched it ride toward the heat lamps on top of an all-beef wiener. Laughing at the absurdness of the image, Blackie grabbed the clerk's purse from under the counter, then spun and walked calmly out the door. Driving down the street with one hand, he searched the handbag and found a cell phone, and to his surprise a .22 revolver.

"I'm coming for you, you old bastard," Blackie said, turning the gun over in his hand. "And I'm gonna make you pay." He was not sure where Modesto was, but it was now his mission and his destination. There was no need to rush because Blackie knew his luck was back and his destiny was set. He was going to enjoy the trip, even without his precious companion, but most of all, he was going to enjoy killing the people responsible for her death.

Chapter Ten - Monday, June 20th

Kristoff called the task force to order and reluctantly acknowledged the local police departments present. Besides his crack FBI team, the room included DeCicco from the Henderson PD, Bartlett from Phoenix, Walker from Barstow, and a sergeant from the CHP. "We've had some developments over the last twenty-four hours we'd like to go over with everyone." He smiled at Bartlett which turned into more of a sneer when he looked at DeCicco and Walker. "I'm not sure if you have all met Detective Bartlett yet. She's our distinguished representative from the Phoenix PD." Angie gave him a slight smile and nodded to the rest of the room. "To the best of our knowledge, this unsub started his rampage in her backyard."

Bartlett's face remained impassive, but DeCicco jumped in, "What the hell is that supposed to mean, Kristoff? The FBI has field offices in both Phoenix and Las Vegas so I would say it's your backyard too."

"Just stating the facts, Detective." He spat out the word detective as if a bug was in his mouth. "I wasn't implying anything. We're all professionals here, and if anyone is insecure about their own competency, I suggest they wear a helmet to the next meeting." Before anyone could interrupt him again, he moved on. "Yesterday, after the female shooting victim was found, a car was hijacked from a convenience store approximately a quarter mile away. We are pretty sure it is our unsub based on the description. The cameras at the store only caught a glimpse of him because the one that should have recorded it was damaged."

"Do we have the information on the car?" someone asked from the back of the room.

"Late model Honda Accord. Tan in color and the license plate number is on the information sheet we will pass out, although this guy has been pretty quick to switch plates before," the SAC responded.

"Do you realize how many gold and tan Accords are out there?" the CHP sergeant lamented.

Kristoff continued, "He pulled a young girl out of the car and took off in a westbound direction." He looked around the room. "Shortly after that, there was a robbery and murder at a gas station ten miles west of there. The suspect drove away in a tan Accord." He paused again to let it sink in. "We are going over the video now but have already confirmed it is the same guy. He did switch the plates when he was at the gas station. We think he is still heading west."

"Who was killed?" Walker asked.

"He murdered the clerk in cold blood. Picked up a ceramic knife from a display right at the counter and slit the woman's throat." Kristoff drew his hand across his own throat to demonstrate. "This freak is devolving. He tossed the knife in the hot dog machine. You know, the kind that spins them around like a Ferris wheel, then stood there smiling as he watched the victim's blood begin to dry on the blade."

"Sick bastard." Several people grumbled throughout the room.

"So we put out an APB on the car. We've updated the BOLO for him to include the new vehicle." He held up his hand counting off the measures on his fingers. "Unfortunately, the unsub has resorted to all cash transactions, so we can't track him with a credit card."

"Have you put the plate number in the ALPR system yet?" the CHP sergeant asked. "If he heads to LA, there are automated license plate readers all around the perimeter of the city."

Kristoff looked over at a second agent who nodded. "Yes, my team has taken care of that."

"What about the girl who was shot?" DeCicco jumped in. "Do you think he might come back to either finish her off or take her?"

"According to a couple that was coming out of their room, the unsub bolted as soon as the gun went off. So he probably thinks she's dead." Kristoff pointed at a picture of Tammy on the whiteboard. "We're not exactly sure of their relationship, but I've kept the fact that she is still alive out of the media. I'm trying to protect the girl either way."

"Oh, so now you're trying to protect her after you let her think she shot the liquor store clerk." DeCicco's temper flared. "Have you stopped to consider that you're probably the cause of her shooting herself?"

"Look, DiCicco. You are only here as a courtesy. If you keep trying to disrupt this task force by laying blame, I will have you tossed out on your ear." Kristoff's face was beet red.

"How can I help, sir?" DeCicco's voice was soft and calm.

Kristoff stared at him, apparently unsure if he was asking how he could assist in getting himself thrown out, or help the team. Finally, Bartlett spoke breaking the tension, "Agent Kristoff, has the FBI made any progress on identifying the suspect, or unsub as you call him?"

A smile slowly crossed Kristoff's face. "Not yet. This unsub's photo and prints are not in any of our databases. Given his looks and the proximity, we're leaning toward him possibly being an illegal."

~~ Wally arrived a few minutes late Monday morning and went right to work. Dan was busy milling couplers for a custom steering shaft for a company that supplied aftermarket parts for early model International Scouts, so he didn't question his uncle or give him a hard time. Usually, Wally would come in with some wild story about how he was late because he was saving the world or grumbling about whatever it was that delayed him. Today there was nothing.

Dan also noticed Syd watching Wally a little closer than usual. She didn't go over to him but laid so she could see where he was at all times. Even the kittens seemed to notice the somber tone of the morning and chose to sleep tangled together in the enclosed bottom of a cat tree Dan made for them out of scrap wood from around the shop.

Sitting at the small table in their lunchroom, which was actually just a corner of the shop, Wally quietly ate his sandwich. "What the hell is wrong with you?" Dan decided on a direct attack.

"Can't a man eat his own lunch in peace?"

"A man can but not you. I've never heard you so quiet." Dan paused, but Wally ignored him. "I've sat here many a day wishing I could get you to shut up so I could eat my lunch without your constant yammering."

"Well, enjoy it while you can."

Dan continued eating in silence for a few minutes. "Seriously, are you alright? Did somebody shoot your dog or something?" Syd raised her head at the mention of the term.

"Did Aunt Bobbie find out how much you spent on that transmission in your truck?"

"Screw you, kid." Wally finally cracked a smile. "And she better never find out, neither."

"So what's got your panties all in a twist today?" Dan pressed his uncle.

"Oh, nothin'. Guess I haven't been sleeping good the past few nights. That's all." Wally's forehead creased with annoyance. "Get off my ass, will ya?"

"I know. Aunt Bobbie took up playing the tuba in bed again, huh?" Dan was sure this would get him going.

"It was the accordion, and no that's not it either." Wally didn't take the bait.

"Okay then, be that way. You old grump. See if I care what's keeping you up at night." Dan threw a potato chip at his uncle. "You probably sleep on the toilet anyway, as many times as you go to the bathroom at night." That didn't even get a response, so Dan decided to drop it.

At three o'clock, Dan finished his batch of adapters and added them to his load to go to the powder coater. He walked over to where Wally was working and tapped him on the shoulder.

"What do ya need?" Wally asked.

"Do you mind taking this stuff to be shot?" He handed Wally the large cardboard box with all the items.

"You trying to get rid of me?"

"Hell, yeah." They both grinned. "Oh, and take the trailer with you. That last batch of telescope mounts is supposed to be ready for pickup today."

"Okay." Dan was surprised there was no argument, but he let it slide. Wally walked from the shop and backed his Tacoma up to the trailer they used to haul stuff. He got out and hooked it up, then left without saying another word. Something was definitely going on.

Dan sat at his desk doing his least favorite part of the shop work. He needed to write proposals for new projects people wanted. Dan preferred working for people who knew he was honest so he could just charge time and materials, but some of the local government projects required putting things out to bid. Dan decided to expand into that area because it was more lucrative. He was busy working on a spreadsheet when his phone rang.

"This is Dan," he answered.

"Dan, this is Angel, at the powder coaters."

"Oh, hey Angel, What's up?"

"That's what I was gonna ask you. What's up with your uncle?"

"Nothin' that I know of, why?"

Angel seemed to struggle with how to put it. "Well, we were trying to help him load the trailer with all those frames you sent." He paused.

"Yeah?" Dan prompted.

"Well, we were trying to fit them all on, and he just got mad, dropped the trailer and drove off."

"He disconnected the trailer?"

"Yeah. He mumbled something about 'not having time for this' and just left. Is he okay, man?"

"I don't know, Angel. Something seems to be up with him. He was kinda quiet here today."

"So what do you want me to do with this stuff?"

"I'll come down there now. No worries." Dan saved his spreadsheet and started shutting down the computer while still on the phone.

"Okay, See you in a bit." Angel hung up.

Dan dialed Wally's number. Wally picked up on the third ring.

"Yes, sir," Wally answered sounding completely normal.

"Hey uncle, everything okay?"

"Yeah, good as can be expected. Why? Do you need something?"

"Well, I just got a call from Angel. He said you got mad and dropped the trailer and left."

"Yeah, so?"

Dan wasn't sure what to ask. "Uh, why did you leave?"

"Listen, I ain't got time to stand around while a bunch of paint sniffing idiots tries to figure out how to load a couple of frames on a trailer. I attempted to tell them how we did it, but they wouldn't listen. So, I figured I'd leave the trailer, and they could screw with it all they wanted. When they figure it out, they can call me, and I'll go get it."

"So you just dropped the trailer and left?"

"Damn right I did. And I'd do it again." He could tell his uncle was getting pissed, again.

"Okay. Okay. I just wondered what happened."

"Did they ever figure it out? Do you want me to go back down there and get it?"

"No. No, uncle. I'm on my way down there now. Don't you worry your pretty little head about it. I know you're a busy, busy man."

"Damn right."

~~ Blackie sat in a taqueria on the outskirts of Victorville, trying to decide if he should go back to the interstate, or use backroads. The Mexican restaurant he entered had a TV behind the counter. He saw a news flash come on the TV's Spanish station. Since he spoke very little Spanish, he could not understand the announcer, but it was easy to tell the story was about him because they showed the convenience store and the gas station. Next, a picture of the car flashed on the screen.

"Damn it!" he cursed his luck. But it only made sense. They showed the license plate number several times. Blackie decided he needed to stick to backroads. He figured the police would be watching the interstate closely, so his chances would be better on the smaller roads. Plus, he was in no hurry. Blackie had no idea where Modesto was, but he knew about LA so he figured it must be near it. He didn't know the geography of California and assumed it was a relatively small state since the only cities he'd heard of were Los Angeles and San Francisco. All the lower states were small compared with his home state of Texas.

Blackie headed west on 18 toward Palmdale enjoying the sparse landscape that reminded him somewhat of the area near El Paso. He was not comfortable in Las Vegas, and it was good to get back out into open country. Blackie needed to think of a more permanent plan for a vehicle. While he was sure his fate was of more importance than being arrested by some stupid local cop, there was no need to push his luck. Lady Fate occasionally needed assistance.

In Palmdale, he saw a sign for Los Angeles, so he turned south on Route 14. Near the tiny town of Acton, he saw an older man struggling with a load of junk on the side of the road. The guy looked like a typical desert rat in dingy jeans, faded plaid shirt, and a well used straw cowboy hat. On a whim, Blackie stopped.

"Need some help, mister?"

The old guy must have been hard of hearing because he jolted then acted surprised when he looked over his shoulder and saw someone a few feet away. The beat-up old Chevy pickup had rickety stake sides, and the old man was rearranging a rope to secure the load. "Damned load shifted on me when I hit a crosswind." He didn't turn around but kept arranging the rope. "You scared me. I thought you were the CHP." He shook his head. "Last time the bastards wrote me up, 'cause I didn't have the load tarped."

"Here, let me help." Blackie deftly climbed the side of the truck and secured the section of the load that pushed through the rope.

"Thanks, Sonny. Damned arthritis in my knees, won't let me climb like I used ta." He looked down at his stiff legs. "Can't hardly bend 'em to get in the cab. I end up trying to lasso the load so I can strap her down."

"Think that'll work, now?" Blackie asked as he climbed down.

"I only got a few more miles, anyway. Should be alright." He looked at Blackie, frowned and stuck out his hand. "Nice of ya ta stop. Most people now days don't give a tinker's damn 'bout other people."

"You want me to follow you in case you have any more problems?"

"Nah. You don't need to go to so much trouble."

"No trouble. I'm not in any hurry.

"Well." The old-timer made a show of taking off his hat, pulling a bandana out of his back pocket, wiping the sweatband and his forehead, then replacing it. "Suit yerself." He hobbled back to the cab and slowly climbed in. The old Chevy complained but finally started, and he pulled onto the highway. Blackie followed the heap for a few miles before it turned right onto a dirt road. After a few more miles, it turned right again onto a dirt track, which led through the sagebrush. Blackie watched the load shift a few times but hold as the truck bounced through a few ruts. Finally, they came to an eight-foot-high chain-link fence. The old man stopped and slowly climbed out of the pickup to unlock the gate.

Inside the compound were several small outbuildings, a camper trailer, and two buildings about the size of a one-car garage. Blackie saw a couple of old utility trucks and several cars that looked like they'd cooked in the sun forever. The old cowboy pointed to a place for Blackie to park. He pulled into the spot and climbed out of the Honda. A large dog that looked to be mostly Shepard ran to sniff him. A smaller mixed breed came yapping behind.

"Don't mind them." He said shooing the dogs away. "You like them damned jap cars?"

Blackie laughed. This guy was definitely from a different era. "I don't know. They're pretty good cars."

"Ahh, they just got newer factories than us, after we kicked the shit out of 'em." He eyed the Accord suspiciously. "What's your name, kid?"

"Most folks just call me Blackie. What about you?"

"I guess most folks call me Ace." Blackie noticed an ace of spades logo painted on the mailbox out by the dirt road. "Got it from the war. I was the youngest pilot in my unit to make ace, kicking jap ass."

"You were in World War II?"

"Yes, sir. Flew an F6F Hellcat from a carrier." He stood a little straighter. "I wasn't old enough at the beginning of the war, almost missed all the fun. I'll tell ya, kid. It's not easy to forgive and forget the bastards that blew your best friend's brains all over you. I still don't like seein' so many of their damned cars everywhere."

"Wow."

"Can I get ya something ta drink, Blackie?" Ace unlocked the front door of the camper and gestured him inside. "I got beer and water. Might have some iced tea left."

"What are you drinking, sir?" Blackie found new respect for the old guy.

Ace reached in the refrigerator and pulled out two beers, handing one to the kid. "Grab a seat. Make yourself comfy." Ace plopped down in a well-worn recliner. "'scuse the mess. I don't get much company."

Blackie looked around the cluttered trailer. In the back, he saw a made bed. A few dirty dishes and containers of food sat on the counter. The place looked lived-in, but it was not dirty. Above his head, on a shelf over the couch, protruded the handle of a pistol.

Ace saw him notice the gun. "That's my government-issued .45." He stood, reached up and pulled it down, handing it to the boy. "Never got shot down, so didn't have to use it."

Blackie was surprised by the weight of the gun. He never held an M1911A1 before. He turned it over in his hand, admiring it. "I got me a .22 revolver in my car. This is a cool gun."

"I always got one within reach, living out here. Can't take no chances." He nodded his head to emphasize the point. They sat drinking cold beer as Ace pointed to a half dozen pistols and rifles within the tiny living room and kitchen area of the small camper trailer.

"What do ya say we unload that junk?" Ace said after a while. With Blackie's help, they unloaded it quickly. The load consisted of most of a John Deere lawn tractor, a couple of fenders from a type of car Blackie didn't recognize, an engine they needed a cherry picker to remove, and several older heads from an engine.

"What are these from?" Blackie said setting down one of the heads.

"Boy, you can't tell a genuine Hemi head when you see one?"

"A what?"

Ace pointed at the heads, and at the motor they unloaded. "That there is a 440 wedge motor. I plan to bore it out and put them Stage V Hemi heads on that sum na bitch. Guy didn't know what he had. I should get more than 600 horsepower."

"What are you gonna put it in? Your truck?" Blackie looked around. It seemed to be the only thing running.

"C'mer, Boy. You gonna learn something today." He led Blackie over to a large building and removed a padlock. Shoving the door open revealed a 1965 Plymouth Barracuda.

Blackie looked confused. "You're gonna put a racing engine in this old car?"

"This is a classic. I bought this car right off the showroom floor. The first one sold in this county back in September 1964. Has the original 318 in it, but I'm gonna turn it into a fire-breathing muscle car."

"Isn't it worth more, if you keep it original?"

"Screw original. Oh, I'll keep the original engine, though I don't plan on selling it. But I'm sure gonna have some more fun with it." Ace patted the fender of the car affectionately.

"Aren't you a little old to be —"

"I ain't dead yet, Kid. You don't think I can drive this thing?"

"No, I meant to do all that heavy work?"

"I'm a little slower than I use ta be. But if you wanna stick around, I'll teach you how to build a race engine." He looked at Blackie and winked.

"Seriously?"

"Hell yeah. Gotta pass it down to somebody." They closed the garage and went back to the trailer for a few more beers. Blackie found himself excited about the prospect of learning to build engines.

Since he never had a strong male presence in his life, the idea of being taken under Ace's wing meant a great deal to him. It wasn't until he was falling asleep on Ace's couch that he thought of Tammy and the promise he made to avenge her.

Chapter Eleven - Tuesday, June 21ˢᵗ

Wally sat at the table in the Otters' clubhouse/garage drinking a cup of coffee. He was early, so he picked up one of the old car magazines and thumbed through it, to keep himself busy. Unable to concentrate on anything, Wally tossed it back on the table. Waiting was not his favorite activity, even if he did arrive thirty minutes before the meeting he arranged. Since most of the gang were retired and had been off the clock for quite a few years, they were not known for being prompt anyway. Stan was the first to show. He came in carrying what looked like a starter wrapped in a newspaper.

"What the hell are you doing up so early? You're usually one of the last guys here." Stan laid the starter on the table.

"Well, good morning to you too," Wally grumbled. "What are you doing with that?"

"Oh, Ralph was having intermittent starting problems on his '63. Relay was worn out. Contact ring was so corroded it was a wonder it ever started." Stan grabbed a cup to get some coffee. "So what's this big meeting about?"

"I thought you were working on the brake lines on that '63?"

"I was, but every time I tried to start it to bleed the damned power brakes, I'd have to sit there for fifteen minutes until the starter would finally catch so I pulled the starter out."

"Oh man, he's gonna owe you big now." Wally nodded toward the door as Ralph walked in. He winked at Stan who knew to go along with him.

"Definitely," Stan spoke louder now to make sure Ralph would hear him. "It's probably gonna end up being a thousand-dollar job."

"What is?" Ralph asked, wondering what they were talking about.

"That '63 of yours." Wally set the hook. "Stan had to pull the starter and replace the relay."

"What? Really?" Ralph looked at Stan. "I didn't tell you to do that. I coulda replaced the starter."

"Didn't need replacing. Just a relay." Stan strung him along. "I couldn't get the brake lines done, 'cause the damned thing wouldn't start."

"Yeah, but …" Ralph started to protest but stopped.

"Relax, we're just busting your balls." Stan finally admitted. "You know I don't like to let anything out of here unless it's right. It took me all of fifteen minutes."

"Screw you guys." Ralph relaxed. "What's so important that Wally, of all people, called a meeting?" About that time the rest of the crew, or at least those who didn't work, shuffled in.

"Yeah?" Tommy chimed in. "And why aren't we meeting over breakfast?" He, along with Bob and Bill, jockeyed for access to the coffee then sat around the table.

"I need some help," Wally said as he looked around the table. "Dan and I saw that '68 of Bob's at a burger joint in Barstow and called the cops. The good news is they got the truck back, but the bad news is they think the guy got my name and address."

A chorus of 'hows' and 'what the hells' followed.

"Apparently the kid walked by my truck as we were talking to the CHP and grabbed my registration for the Vegas car show off the front seat," Wally explained.

"You sure?" Teddy asked.

"Well, I can't find it, and they saw him take something that looked like a piece of paper out of the window. Had it on security tape."

"Shit. How can we help?" Stan asked.

"I'll roundhouse kick that bastard in the teeth if he shows up here." Tommy threatened. The others broke into laughter. "What?" he added looking offended.

"At your age," Wally laughed. "You couldn't roundhouse kick his ankle."

"Seriously, what do you need us to do?" asked Bill.

"Well, I have this map of California that I got from triple A. I marked where we last saw him at the diner. I want all you guys to keep an eye on the news, and the papers for anything we can find to track this bastard. We'll keep track of his movements and be ready if he shows."

"How will we know it's him?" Stan asked.

"I got a picture of the kid. It's from the security tapes too," Wally answered. "I'll post it on the bulletin board with the map."

"Let's get some copies made. I can go to one of those mailbox stores or the library." Tommy suggested.

"Hold on, you dinosaur." Wally took out his cell phone and took a picture of the snapshot. "There, not I got it on my phone." Stan and Bob did the same.

"I ain't got no camera-phone," Tommy complained as he pulled his antique flip-phone out of his pocket.

"Aw hell, I'll make you a copy," Wally grumbled. "That phone of yours can take pictures, but by the time you managed to find it, the guy would have bashed your head in."

"Does this guy have a name yet? Like the Desert Strangler or something?" asked Stan so we can know a story is about him.

"Not that I know of," Wally admitted. "Maybe I'll check with Dan's girlfriend."

"Whoa, that sounds like a story." Tommy sat up, hoping to get the lowdown.

"It is, but I'll have to tell you later. Right now, I need to get over to do some work for the lover boy." Wally stood and headed for the door.

Tommy protested, "Wait! It was just getting interesting."

~~ Detective Bartlett sat at the conference table at the task force meeting working on her laptop and listening to Kristoff drone on in the background. On her screen, she was making airline reservations to return to Phoenix. Bartlett had already reached her limit of tolerance for the credit-grabbing showboat who was running things. After she turned down his offer to go to dinner the previous evening, he started making snide remarks again about how Angie let the unsub slip through her fingers. DeCicco, who was sitting beside her, glanced at her screen.

"Are you bailing on me?" DeCicco whispered. "Now he will only have me to flirt with." He smirked and looked straight ahead at his laptop.

"I don't know. Walker looks like he has nice legs." She glanced quickly at DeCicco who brought his hand to his mouth to cover a smile. "Maybe if he wore tighter slacks," she added. DeCicco, coughed into his hand trying to control himself.

An agent stuck his head in the room to tell Kristoff there was a visitor outside with relevant information to the case. Kristoff sent one of his underlings out to talk to the person, who came back a few minutes later with the visitor in tow. "Sir, I thought the whole group might want to hear this?" the underling said.

The SAC scowled at first but became distracted by the attractive woman following the agent. "I'm SAC Kristoff. Ah, what a nice surprise to have two beautiful ladies in the same room. I'm delighted." He looked from the visitor to Angie, sure his charm was melting their hearts.

Ms. Auer, Tammy's lawyer, was as unimpressed as Angie. They glanced at each other, and both rolled their eyes and gave a slight smile of acknowledgment. "I have to say, Mr. Kristoff, that my primary focus in getting dressed this morning was to bring delight to the hearts of men like you." You could see in his face that Kristoff was unsure how to take it.

"And you are ..." Kristoff finally asked raising one eyebrow.

"Erin Auer. I am Tammy Dotson's attorney." The SAC recoiled noticeably at the news. "I have pertinent information relevant to the investigation of this task force. But first I have to ask about your intentions toward my client."

"By intentions you mean will she be charged?" A slight tip of her head was the only response. "We have a video of your client shooting a man."

"My client was under duress and was being controlled by the madman you have let rampage across the country."

"As you can see, we have significant resources dedicated to his capture." He swept his arm around the room, indicating the task force.

"Why do you say she was under duress?" Angie spoke, breaking the tension in the room.

"My client managed to get a letter to my office and to a friend of hers, explaining she was being forced to leave with the suspect. She gives a description of him, and everything she knew about him. She was terrified."

"Why didn't she just leave?" Kristoff tried to take control back.

"You have seen what this man is capable of." Ms. Auer looked around the room at some of the pictures on the whiteboard. "She tried to leave once. But he tracked her down. He even managed to get her fired from her job, so she was financially dependent on him." She knew she was stretching the truth a bit, but she was determined not to be bullied.

Kristoff wasn't buying it. "Is that why she shot herself?"

"The gun went off accidentally. Tammy was in the process of trying to leave again when the killer came charging toward the car. She grabbed a gun to try to make him stop, and it went off."

"May we see the letter she sent to you?" Angie asked, wondering if the SAC ever took a class in de-escalation.

"I would first like assurance that my client will not be charged."

"No way!" Kristoff spat out.

"I'm afraid, Ms. Auer." Angie put both hands out, palms down gesturing for things to calm down, "that we will need to see the letter before we can make any promises. Besides, determination of who gets charged is made by the DA's office, we only make recommendations."

"I understand that. Here is a copy of the letter." She handed it directly to Angie. "As a woman, I'm sure you can understand the terror my client has experienced, not to mention the trauma of the gunshot."

"I assure you, I will make sure the DA reads this," Angie promised.

"I'm the Agent in Charge here! Give me that letter." Kristoff came around the table toward Angie.

DeCicco stood quickly and moved in front of her. "Shut the hell up, Kristoff." Walker, who was at the end of the table, stood too.

"What the hell are you gonna do?" Kristoff said to DeCicco, who was about 4 inches shorter than Angie. He stopped and lowered his arms.

The ridiculousness of the situation stuck DeCicco. "I was gonna grab my phone and video Detective Bartlett kicking your ass. Heh, heh."

Angie turned to the lawyer. "Thank you for coming in Ms. Auer."

Chapter Twelve - Wednesday, June 22nd

Tammy opened her right eye and wasn't sure where she was. She raised her hand to her face and felt a large bandage over her left cheek that also covered her eye. Everything was a bit hazy, and strange faces stared down at her. She was transfixed by one of them because it was a beautiful woman who seemed familiar. "Are you an angel?" she asked, expecting it to disappear instead of answering. Her speech sounded strange. It was difficult for her mouth to form the words, and they came out barely recognizable. It felt to her tongue like some of her teeth were missing. She had IVs in both arms and heard the steady beeping of a monitor near her head.

"Almost." A smile spread over the face. "I'm your lawyer, silly."

Tammy blinked and looked around at the other faces. One was an older, motherly looking woman. Beside her, a young black woman in a white uniform dress and wearing glasses smiled. "Boy, are we glad to see you awake," she said. More of the room came into focus.

"Where am I?" Tammy tried to ask. She winced with pain.

"You're in the hospital, Sweetie," the angel answered. "Barstow Community Hospital. Don't try to talk. You need to rest to heal."

"Why?" Though it came out sounding more like wooie.

"You were shot," the older nurse answered this time. "Your mouth has been injured, so you need to take it easy. We have a small whiteboard for you to use for questions and answers if you hurt too much to talk." She laid a small board in Tammy's lap and handed her a marker.

"Can I see?" she wrote.

The nurse held up a small mirror while saying, "You're all bandaged right now, dear." The image staring back at her in the mirror looked like a mummy. One of the eyes was bloodshot and appeared to be blackened. She let out a cry at the sight of herself.

"Honey. You're lucky to even be here." The nurse gently but firmly took back the mirror.

The lawyer asked "Tammy, do you remember anything? We're not exactly sure what happened. The best we can piece together is that you had a gun in your hand and it went off accidentally." Tammy shook her head slightly, searching the void that was her memory.

"What was the last thing you remember?"

"Not sure. Getting fired?" Tammy wrote in response. Two men appeared from a corner of the room, jockeying to see what she wrote.

"Okay. Well, you rest now," the young black nurse said. She seemed to be in charge. "Everyone, that's enough for now. She needs rest." She shooed the men out of the room but allowed the lawyer to stay. The older woman stepped closer to the bedside. "Tammy, I'm Dr. Carter. I was your trauma surgeon. You've had some significant damage to the jaw and tongue. You lost a few teeth too. But don't worry, it's nothing that we can't fix. I have to tell you, it will be a long road back. You've already proved you're a fighter, so I know you'll do well. Now you rest, and I'll be back to see you soon."

~~ Blackie spent the day working with Ace tearing down the engine the old guy brought home. At first, he was extremely cautious with both the tools and the motor, afraid that he may break something and be humiliated at his ignorance.

"Boy, you ain't gonna break anything we can't fix," Ace chided him. "Besides, we're tearing this one apart, it ain't rocket surgery." The old guy chuckled at his own joke. Blackie never worked with an older man who joked with him to correct him, instead of yelling and telling him he was stupid. He began to relax and go at the task enthusiastically, absorbing everything Ace told him.

They worked until almost six o'clock with his patient mentor slowing down to explain each part and what it did to make the engine run correctly. When they stopped, Blackie was coated in grease from head to toe, glad he was provided with coveralls, since he only brought the one set of clothes.

"Do you know how to cook, kid?"

Blackie shook his head. "Not really. I can make us sandwiches. I worked at a Subway for a week once."

"A man's got to know how to feed hisself. You can't be dependent on a woman to take care of you. Sometimes they just up and run off."

"Yes, sir."

"Now, I'd say the same thing to a young girl. She ought to know a thing or two about cars, and fixin' things. Never get yerself in a position where you can't make it on your own." He looked at Blackie and winked. "That way, if you decide to take up with somebody, you're doin' it 'cause you want to, not 'cause ya need to."

"Makes sense."

"Now grab that skillet over there, and I'll show you how to make corn pone, while I warm the pot of beans left over from yesterday." He opened the refrigerator and took out two bowls. "These beans got ham in 'em, so I know you ain't Muslim, are ya?"

Blackie wondered if the old man thought he was middle-eastern because of his darker complexion compared to Ace. "No." He stopped what he was doing and looked at Ace.

Ace chuckled. "I know ya ain't. Don't be so thin-skinned, Kid. If people think they can get to ya, they'll ride ya into the ground." He elbowed Blackie's arm affectionately. "Besides, I could tell you was Mexican."

"Only part," Blackie responded.

"Yeah, well you don't have to worry about me. I like Mexicans. Had myself a Mexican wife once. The second one." Ace's looked at the ceiling. "That one was too danged religious to be good in bed. Always felt like God was watching her. But she could cook. Oh man, she could cook."

Blackie started thinking about Tammy. He was sure they must have had a good time in bed, but he drank too much to remember exactly. He missed her, and a sad look came over his face.

"Oh, now I done it. Didn't mean to get you thinking about home, kid. Us bachelors do alright. We can spend our days building a Hemi, without some woman a-yapping at us."

Blackie smiled and went back to tending the skillet.

~~ "What do you mean, he's disappeared?" Kristoff screamed at the CHP sergeant. "Are you guys totally incompetent?" The policeman stared straight ahead, stone-faced, trying to contain his temper. "Does the FBI have to come and hold your hands and teach you to chase down a bad guy?" The SAC seemed to enjoy humiliating others. "It's not that hard. Now, there are only about three routes out of that little pissant town where he was seen last. Did you put a roadblock on each of those, so you can catch him? No. Not until hours later. And now it's been two frigging days, and he could be anywhere." He waved his arm at the map of the western United States. "And your job, along with mine, just got a whole lot harder."

"Hey, Kristoff," It was DeCicco.

The SAC viewed him as if he were a lower life-form. "Why are you still here, DeCicco?"

"Mostly for the camaraderie. Heh, heh." There were a few chuckles from the others until Kristoff glared at them all. "Did you federal boys have any luck coming up with an ID on the unsub yet?"

Kristoff glanced over at one of the other agents who shook his head briefly and looked down at the floor. "Uh, no."

"How about the girl, uh Tammy? Any decision on her status been made yet?"

"We're still analyzing the tapes."

DeCicco stood rocking from his heels to onto his toes. It was an unconscious habit he developed when surrounded by superior officers, and tall people. "Well, then why don't you get off his ass, and work on your own issues?" There was a stunned silence, and everyone could see the SAC's face redden. He shot the detective a look of death, spun and walked out of the room.

The CHP Sargent gave DeCicco a quick nod. One of the other agents said in a mock whisper, "Careful detective, your punching above your weight class." DeCicco didn't care, He always hated bullies because he'd endured them a lot as a kid.

~~ Erin Auer anxiously sat in her office waiting for a client meeting to start on the hour. She was reviewing the file in front of her. As a lawyer, Erin used an app on her phone to track her time down to five-minute increments so her time could be correctly billed. When the phone rang, she hit a button on the apps screen that stopped the clock and started another app with an open field for her to either add something new or select from a list of billable clients.

She picked up the phone on the first ring. "Erin Auer."

"Ms. Auer, this is Detective Bartlett from the Phoenix Police. We met at the task force meeting the other day."

"Oh, the one Prince Charming was leading?"

Angie smiled. "That's the one."

"Did he bully you into turning over the letter after I left?" the lawyer asked, referring to the confrontation with Kristoff. "I thought there was going to be a brawl for a few seconds there."

"We ended up playing nice. I think Kristoff realized that he crossed a line. He even volunteered to make a copy for me."

"Really? I hope you didn't fall for false regret."

She heard the detective chuckle. "No, I told him copying was woman's work. I don't think he got that it was a joke until the others laughed."

"Well, what can I do for you, detective?" As much as Ms. Auer was enjoying the conversation, she had a client meeting in a few minutes.

"Actually, I think it's what I can do for you. You should know there was an additional video from the liquor store that exonerates your client. The unsub is shown forcing the gun into her hand. The look on her face as she holds it is pure terror. And it went off when he grabbed to take it back."

She thought of how they used the first tape to paint her client. "That bastard. Can you send me a copy of the second video?"

"I'd lose my job. But if Kristoff tries to use it to bully Ms. Dotson any more, I wanted you to know it exists. They'd have to disclose it if charges were brought."

"Is that likely?"

"I don't think so. Between the letter and the second video, I doubt that any DA would bring charges." Angie sighed heavily. "I don't want him to cause your client any more grief. She's been through enough."

"Thank you, detective. You're certainly more than just a pretty face."

"Shhh. You'll blow my cover." They both chuckled as they ended the call.

~~ Wally looked at the screen of his cellphone as it rang. It was a 916 number he didn't recognize. He started to ignore it or use his standard trick of sending a text message saying 'I'm on my way.' Something made him answer it. "Who the hell is this?"

"Uh, Mr. Williams? Wally Williams?" a voice on the other end stuttered.

"The hell it is. I'm Wally Williams, and I stopped calling myself years ago."

"Huh? This is John Sinclar, a reporter for KCRA in Sacramento. Mr. Williams?"

"What the hell do you want with me? I don't even like your news. That old married couple gives me the willies."

"Mr. Williams, I've been following the string of murders in southern California. I've been working with affiliates in Las Vegas and LA. And your name keeps popping up."

"What do you mean my name? You accusin' me of somethin', you son of a bitch?"

"No. No. Mr. Williams. Please. I understand you've helped the police. You're a witness. I'd like to interview you."

"What for? I didn't witness any of the crimes." Wally started to hang up.

"You could be the key to catching this guy. The police are stuck. They have lost track of him."

"Really? The dumb bastards won't tell me anything. I wondered why I didn't hear anything in the last couple of days." Wally and the Otters were monitoring all the news sources they could find, and nothing hit their radar.

"We would like to do a piece on the story and get it out to the public. Someone has to have seen something? Will you help us?" The reporter was sure he had a nibble now.

"What the heck could I do?"

"We were going to do a recap of what is known and need some background from you on what you saw. I understand you, and your nephew helped recover a stolen truck?"

"Well, yeah. We did do that." Wally admitted. "It was an old '68 F-100. I recognized it from when we briefly met the owner." The hook was set.

They arranged to have the interview later that afternoon. Wally was surprised when the crew actually showed up an hour early. They wanted to get the layout of where they could shoot, and get things set up before 'the Talent' arrived. That was how they referred to the reporter.

By the time they left, Wally was out of patience and sorry he bothered with the whole thing. They were all over his house and shop, taking video of his truck, his car lift, and every angle of the place. Wally was uncomfortable with his privacy being so violated. The reporter assured him they would only use a small subset of things, and the rest was for background. After the 'talent' left, Wally threatened to kick the ass of the whole crew if any of his tools were missing later.

Wally awaited the news anxiously that evening. He didn't even tell his friends about the interview because he was unsure if he came off looking like an idiot by the time they finished. The opening shot was of Wally standing in front of his house with the reporter. He was introduced as anyone's next door neighbor who suddenly got caught up in the world of a serial killer. Wally didn't really think about the fact that the guy was a serial murderer and was a little thrown at first.

The heart of the interview was Wally describing how they casually met Bob at the Eloy truck stop and then learned later he was murdered. Wally explained that he owned a similar truck years ago.

"Is that how you recognized it at the restaurant?" the reporter asked.

"That's part of it, but I recognized a few unique things about that particular truck." Wally was starting to enjoy himself. "The kid tried to disguise it by changing the plate numbers and spray painting the sides of the truck white. The dumbass. Oh sorry, can I say that?"

The reported just smiled, knowing they would beep it out. "Go on Mr. Williams."

"Anybody could tell it was done with a spray can. There were a couple of other things too."

"What sorts of things?"

"I'm not sure I should say." Wally hesitated.

"But they've recovered the truck, haven't they?" He could tell the old guy wanted to brag.

"I guess you're right." Wally looked intently at the reporter. "There was a sticker on the driver's door window, from a club that changed its name a while back. I knew Bob kept it on there. He was a member."

"That would certainly narrow it down." The reported prompted.

"What sealed it for me was that Bob welded a plate on the bottom of the stake pockets. The came from the factory open. I meant to ask Bob why he did that." Wally looked lost in thought, remembering.

The rest of the piece was used to bolster Wally's credibility by showing quick shots of his hot rod '54 pickup and his shop. Wally was also wearing his Otters Hot Rod Club t-shirt which the reporter asked about.

"Yeah, the Otters and I have been tracking this dirtbag. If the creep shows up around here, we'll be on him like a chicken on a Junebug."

"Well, thank you, Mr. Williams." The reporter ended the segment by noting the suspect's trail had gone cold and requested that the audience call authorities if they saw anything that might help.

Wally looked over at his wife. "Well, that didn't come out too bad."

"No, except for you daring a serial killer to come to visit us," Bobbie commented. "That wasn't the brightest move there, ya think?"

"Don't you worry. Tommy Tailpipe said he'd roundhouse kick that guy back to Phoenix."

"Oh, jeez. That'll sure help me sleep tonight."

Michael L. Patton

Chapter Thirteen - Thursday, June 23rd

Blackie and Ace stopped working on the engine to grab a sandwich. Blackie was in the trailer's kitchen throwing potato chips on his plate when he heard Ace turn the TV on. The old guy hadn't watched the thing the entire time Blackie was there, and he doubted it even worked.

"Just want to catch the weather," Ace said, lifting his chin to indicate the set. "Rest of its just drivel. Ain't been any real newsmen since Walter Cronkite retired."

Blackie didn't know who that was, so he sat on the couch and balanced his plate on his legs, He munched a few chips and kept a wary eye on the noisy box, hoping his story died down in the past few days.

A few minutes into the broadcast the female anchor launched into a new story. "And now for an update on the potential serial killer on the loose in California here's a followup from our sister station in Sacramento."

Blackie stared intently at the TV and saw a reporter introduce the story, about a string of murders that started in Phoenix and ended in the small town of Victorville, California.

"That's only twenty miles from here," Ace said as he bit into the second half of his sandwich.

The screen went to the interview of Wally standing in front of his house. Blackie was mesmerized and leaned in to see the number on the frame of the door. It was 1731. Now if they would only say the street name. The news story confirmed it was in Modesto and gave the man's name as Wally Williams. "Gotcha now," Blackie said under his breath.

Blackie listened as the old man gloated about how he found the truck and knew it was Bob's. He would show that old goat who was smarter. When Wally talked about his friends the Otters tracking the killer's movements, Blackie wondered how much information was out there.

It was when Wally called him a dirtbag and practically dared him to come and get him that Blackie knew what he must do. He was enjoying his time with Ace so much he was thinking of settling down here with the old guy. Blackie really liked Ace, and it was the perfect set up. He was out in the middle of nowhere. They would never find him. Ace was the first man in his life who actually took time to teach him and treat him like he had potential. But now, he would have to go to Modesto, to kill this old jerk, and all his friends. Maybe he could just take a break. He would only be gone a few days and then come back. Sure. That way he could do both.

The story on the TV went into details on the murders and carjackings. Before he realized it, Blackie found himself staring at his own picture. His face was less than three feet from the screen. Because he was angry at the guy in Modesto, he wore the same scowl as when he slit the clerk's throat at the gas station. He turned to see Ace looking at him. The old man's eyes went from the screen to his face and back again.

"You?" was all Ace said.

Blackie saw Ace's hand move down to the little pocket on the side of his recliner. He assumed the old man was reaching for the television remote. When the hand came up with a snub-nosed .38 revolver, Blackie froze.

"You killed all those people?"

"Look, Ace, I ain't done nothing but help you with the motor." Blackie pleaded.

"Can't abide your kind." The old man said softly with a look of disappointment in his eyes. The look Blackie saw all his life. As the old man reached for the cordless phone beside him on an end table, he took his eyes off Blackie for just a second to locate it. The young boy's reflexes were too fast for the octogenarian, and he grabbed the gun and twisted it, so it wasn't pointing at him. But by bending the old man's wrist, the gun pointed back at Ace. Ace resisted and tried to pull his hand back; but suddenly the gun went off with a thunderous blast inside the small trailer. The bullet entered below the old man's sternum and traveled up through his heart. A look of surprise registered on his face.

"Shit!" Blackie screamed. Ace slumped in the chair, taking his few last labored breaths as he died. He still faced Blackie. The look of disappointment would be his death mask. It burned itself into the boy's memory. Tears streamed down Blackie's face. Tears of loss. Tear of sadness. Tears changed to anger. It would be the anger he would carry away with him. Anger and determination to kill that meddling old bastard who continued to cost him so much.

~~ Dan was also eating lunch and decided to turn on the news to see if the serial killer was mentioned. He hoped the guy, who looked Hispanic, would head down into Mexico and try to disappear. Maybe they could catch him at the border. Instead, he saw his uncle on the screen acting like Sam Spade, going over how he helped recover the truck.

"Oh man, do you see this, Syd. What the hell is he thinking?" The dog looked up from her food bowl when she heard her name. Dan kept a bowl of dry food for her. She seemed to like to eat lunch with him, so they often ate at the same time. In the evenings Syd would get a small can of the wet food. She self-regulated well and her weight stayed the same.

Dan grabbed his cellphone and dialed his uncle who was taking a box of peaches to the owner of the powder coating business. After Wally's drop the trailer incident, Dan figured it would be a nice gesture, and Wally reluctantly agreed.

"It ain't my fault he's got a bunch of dumbasses working for him," Wally protested.

The phone rang a few times before Wally answered. Syd went back to her lunch. "Don't worry, I played nice," was how Wally answered the phone.

"You better, 'cause you're a much bigger dumbass than anyone he's got working over there, Uncle."

"Well, hello to you too." Wally wondered where this was coming from. "What put a bug up your butt so quick? I just left there forty minutes ago."

"I just saw your big interview. What are you doing, trying to bait the killer?"

"No," Wally said indignantly, "but I ain't scared."

"You should be scared, you old fart. You ought to go to church and pray he doesn't see it."

"Let 'im come," Wally said, but he wondered if that was a bit much.

~~ Kristoff pounded his desk as he watched the TV in the corner of the conference room. "What the hell does that old fool think he's doing? He's gonna get himself killed while making every law enforcement agency on this case look bad." He turned his anger toward Walker. "Couldn't you control your witnesses, Walker?"

Walker jerked to attention in his seat. "What? What the hell do you expect me to do, arrest him?"

"Didn't the local news run that past you before it aired? You need to control the narrative better."

Walker was on his feet now, pointing his finger at Kristoff. "First, I was never designated as the communications officer on this team. Second, that story originated in Sacramento, which you would know if you paid attention instead of jumping to conclusions. And third, maybe we should get that old bastard to run this task force. He seems more competent than who we have now." He stormed out of the room and slammed the door.

DeCicco, who dealt with Wally first hand, just snickered at the thought of anyone controlling what he said. He looked from his laptop at Kristoff and the others, "He's got a point." The detective focused back on his screen. The air dripped with tension.

Michael L. Patton

Chapter Fourteen - Friday, June 24th

Blackie grabbed a blanket off Ace's bed and wrapped the body in it. Because he was so far out in the country, he wasn't worried about anyone seeing him, so he was dragging the body across the yard when a UPS truck pulled up the to the gate. Fortunately, the body was partly behind his car, and Blackie was not sure how much could be seen. When he looked up, the driver waved at him, stepped out of the truck, and opened the gate. He jumped back in and pulled into the yard. Blackie walked around the end of his car and approached the driver with the .38 tucked into the belt of his jeans. Ace's dogs ran to meet the driver like an old friend.

"Hey. How are you? Got a package for Ace." The driver smiled so he must not have seen anything.

"Hi. I'm his nephew, Frankie. He's inside laying down. Said he was tired."

"Oh, darn. I usually sit down and chat with the old guy for a few minutes. Try to time one of my breaks so I can do it. Man, with this new computer system though, they monitor everything." He nodded at the truck.

"That sucks." Blackie took the offered package. "You guys got a key to his gate?"

"Yeah. Ace tried a box outside but lost a package or two, so he gave me a key. I'm not supposed to do things like that, but Ace is one of my favorite customers. Really cool guy, but I'm sure you know." He looked at the trailer as if hoping Ace would come out to talk.

"He's definitely my favorite uncle." Blackie lied.

"Well tell him I was asking about him. Hope he feels better." The driver stuck out his hand to shake, so Blackie reciprocated. As he did, the sleeve of Blackie's shirt revealed a bloodstain. The driver's eyes locked on the blood on Blackie's arm. His face turned white, and he jerked his hand back without completing the handshake. He turned and sprinted toward the truck, but Blackie took out the pistol and fired. The bullet hit him behind the right ear and exited damaging most of his face. The driver fell a few feet from the door of the truck, with Ace's dogs barking and running over to him, thinking it was some kind of a game.

"Stupid dogs." One of them was actually licking the bloody exit wound of the driver. Blackie considered the dogs as poorly trained and annoying, so he shot both of them too.

Now there were four bodies to get rid of, and a UPS truck to hide. Blackie stripped the driver of his uniform. He was only slightly bigger than Blackie so the outfit could be used as a disguise. Blackie found a key fob on the belt as he removed it from the body. He pressed one button, and the door to the cargo area of the big brown truck popped open. Another one unlocked the doors of the cab. It looked like the truck started by pushing a button, as long as the fob was close enough. There was a hand truck in the back also, and Blackie used it to move some empty fifty-five-gallon drums beside the van. He loaded one body and one dog in each drum, installed the locking rings on the lids, then loaded the drums in the back. He would dispose of both the vehicle and its content away from Ace's compound, in case he wanted to use it in the future. Perhaps a nice fire at the bottom of one of the area's canyons. According to the driver, the company monitored the location of the trucks, so he wanted to move it quickly.

Blackie put on the uniform and started the big truck. He drove out of the compound and locked the gate. The big boxy vehicle seemed ungainly at first on the narrow roads, but the boy soon began to get comfortable. Once he got to the main roads, he was surprised how many people waved at him. People always seemed glad to see the UPS guy. That gave Blackie an idea. Instead of sending the truck down into the canyon or torching it, he backed up to a drop off along one of the narrow rural roads and rolled the barrels out and over the edge of the cliff. Blackie watched as they tumbled and bounced down the hillside into a culvert filled with brush. The lids stayed on so it would be a good long while before the bodies were found.

Maybe he could use the truck to throw the cops off his trail. The brown trucks were everywhere, and no one paid much attention to them. Yes, he could use it to hide in plain sight. Remembering what the driver said, he found the driver's handheld computer and ran over it with the truck. He scanned under the dash and in the wheel wells for any kind of GPS device. Nothing. He looked back in the cargo area and found a black box, about the size of a cable box. He smashed it using a brick and a small club the driver probably used to check the tires. When the little red LED on the front of the box went out, he assumed it was disabled. Blackie walked out to the side of the van and was glad to see this particular one was a diesel. He knew some of them were propane and had no idea where to refuel if it was one of those. Diesel was easy. He was all set to execute a misinformation campaign that would keep those trailing him going in circles.

Blackie knew his ultimate target was in Modesto, so he headed north. It was fun sitting up high in the box truck watching the world go by. He planned a routine. He wanted to keep the UPS truck safe so he would drive into the edge of a town. Then he could pull up to a house in the middle of the day when fewer people were home. Next, he'd sit on a street long enough to identify a house where a woman appeared to be at home alone. Walking to the door in the uniform and carrying a package should almost always result in someone coming to meet him. If not, a ring of the doorbell would bring them out. To implement this plan, he first headed up Interstate 5 and stopped in the small town of Buttonwillow.

As he approached the first house after parking a few doors down, a lady who looked to be in her seventies came to the door just as he was started to ring the bell,

"Is it Kenny's day off?"

"Yes, ma'am it is." As she reached for the package, he pulled a custom-made tactical combat knife he found in Ace's trailer and pointed it at her throat. The stunned woman slowly backed into the house stuttering. Out of sight of the street, he slashed her throat and shoved her backward into a chair in the living room. She slumped and gasped while clutching her neck. She was dead within a minute. He moved quickly, to find her keys, and drove her car out of the garage. He didn't really need money, but found a liquor store, and shot the clerk three times as soon as the cash drawer was open. Leaving the car a few blocks from the old lady's house, he was back in the UPS truck and on the road within thirty minutes. Blackie found a truck stop and parked in between two rigs, listening to the radio for any news of his exploits.

After hearing nothing for an hour, he crossed over to Highway 99. This time he struck in the town of Delano. He left the truck on the edge of the parking lot of a garage so it would look like it was there for repair. He took a small package and walked into a nearby neighborhood, disposing quickly of the young Hispanic woman who answered the door. Taking the minivan in the driveway, he crossed back over to Kettleman City, There, he hijacked a car in the parking lot of a gas station. After almost being caught because of the truck, he decided to change cars with every crime to confuse the stupid cops. It would also help to keep changing his appearance, so he was wearing a large sweatshirt over his uniform so as not to give away his disguise. No one was killed, but he did drag a woman several hundred feet down a street during the getaway. Blackie calmly drove back to Delano, parked the car and returned to the safety of his UPS truck. He continued in it until late evening when he entered Modesto.

~~ Wally sat in the Otter's clubhouse watching three television screens set up to monitor the killer's movements. After days of complete silence, it seemed like the suspect was on a sudden tear. The guy suddenly popped up in three small towns in the southern San Joaquin Valley, leaving a trail of crimes. Wally put three red post-it flags on the map, one for each of the people that were killed, and a yellow one for the hijacking.

"He's definitely headed this way," Stan observed.

"Thank you, Captain Obvious," Wally wise-cracked.

"Hey pal, just because he's coming here to kill your ass, don't mean you got to get snippy with me."

"Maybe you should leave town for a bit, Wally," Bill suggested. "No use taking chances."

"Yeah," Tommy joined in. "Nobody would blame you for not wanting to deal with a psycho."

"Screw this guy," Wally answered. "Besides, you guys have seen the Rottweiler I've got at home."

"I thought Daisy was a pit bull?" Stan looked from the map to Wally.

"Daisy is. I'm talking about Bobbie." Wally answered.

Tommy rolled his eyes. "You better not let her hear you say that."

Stan laughed, "That psycho will be the least of your problems."

Bill wasn't falling for the misdirection. "Seriously, Wally, what are you gonna do? This guy seems to be on a rampage."

"Other than keep my eyes open, and my friends close, I don't know what I can do, Bill," Wally admitted. "But I'll tell you what I'm not gonna do. I won't be giving any more interviews. That's for damned sure."

~~ Blackie slept in the back of the UPS van in a sleeping bag he found in Ace's trailer. This time he took a change of clothes with him in a small backpack he got from the last stolen car.

He left the truck parked behind a strip mall containing a UPS Store on McHenry Avenue and walked two blocks to a 7-Eleven for coffee. Blackie felt energized knowing he was close to his target. He didn't realize how big Modesto was, which would make finding the 1731 address more difficult. However, Blackie was enjoying the hunt so much that his enthusiasm was undaunted. As he came out of the convenience store, a harried mother, stopped at the curb and left her car running to just pop in and grab some cigarettes.

Blackie slipped behind the wheel and drove around the corner thinking how fate was on his side. His thoughts were interrupted by the voice of a three-year-old child in the car seat in the back.

"Who are you?" the tiny voice asked.

Blackie squealed to a stop. "Get out." He spun around to face the child.

"My mom says I'm not supposed to go anywhere with strangers." The child seemed unafraid and indignant.

"Get out of the car."

"I'm not allowed to walk to the 7-Eleven alone either."

Blackie watched the mother running around the corner of the building, screaming and pointing at the car. He turned back around and squealed out of the lot, heading down a side street, making several turns.

"You're driving too fast. There might be kids in this neighborhood, you know."

"Shut the hell up, kid." Blackie pulled to the curb and got out of the car.

As he opened the back door, the young boy scowled at him. "You're not a nice man."

Blackie unlatched the child from the seat and lifted him to the sidewalk. "There, now, get lost kid." He slammed the passenger door and jumped back in the car.

"You're gonna be in big trouble, mister," the kid yelled as Blackie drove away.

Racing down the street, he saw the smart-mouthed brat in his rearview mirror standing on the curb with his hands on his hips still yelling at the car. "I should have cut the little bastard's throat," Blackie muttered to himself.

It took Blackie a while to get his head back in the game, as he drove aimlessly around. He pulled onto Highway 99 and headed north blindly following the flow of traffic, soon finding himself in Manteca. He found another liquor store on the east side of Interstate 5 and pulled into the lot. Blackie could remember his mother saying that if she ever owned a business, it would be a liquor store because it was mostly a cash business. That made it easy to cheat the IRS. However, it also made it prone to robberies, which was what he was here to do.

This time he didn't even pretend he was a customer. Blackie just walked in and looked around to ensure the clerk was alone. Once he confirmed no one else was around, he walked to the counter and smiled at the vaguely Asian looking man behind it. The clerk had one hand on the register keys, and the other braced against the desktop. In one swift motion, Blackie grabbed the knife from his belt at his back and thrust it just under the man's ribcage bursting his heart. The clerk took a surprised breath upon the impact and stared at the blood pooling on the surface of the counter as if trying to figure out where it was coming from. Suddenly, his knees collapsed, and he fell to the floor, without uttering a sound.

Blackie started around to the register but stopped in his tracks when he saw a short, older Indian woman in a sari, holding a pistol. "Stop right there!" She thrust the gun forward, but her eyes were on the knife in Blackie's hand covered in her husband's blood.

The adrenaline flowed, and Blackie felt invincible. He let out a breath to calm himself, and asked, "Have you ever killed a man?" Her eyes went from the knife to his eyes, then to her husband lying crumpled on the floor. It was all the hesitation he needed. The combat knife slashed across her wrist, severing the ligaments that controlled the fingers gripping the gun. It clattered to the floor.

She stared at her useless hand and the blood seeping up the silk fabric of the sari. "Please."

Blackie backhanded her, the handle of the knife amplifying the impact of the blow. He stood over her looking at the bloody, broken figure before him, then turned and walked out. He'd made his point.

~~ The FBI was notified as soon as any crime happened remotely matching the M.O. of the unsub. Kristoff was convinced the killer was going after Wally, ordered the task force be moved to Modesto. Since the closest FBI residential facility was in Stockton, they coordinated with Modesto PD and booked a conference room at the Clarion Inn Conference Center. While they were traveling to set up a facility there, Kristoff visited the crime scenes in Delano and Kettleman City.

Angie reluctantly rejoined the team at the insistence of her boss. Just the thought of being in the room with Kristoff was enough to make her skin crawl. She was glad to see DeCicco still tagged along. As quirky as he was, he was harmless and balanced out the stiff suited federal agents well. She debated digging out her old wedding ring but doubted it would act as any kind of a deterrent to Kristoff.

Angie arrived at the hotel midafternoon and dressed to go for a run to help reduce the tension she felt. It was a gorgeous day in the middle eighties outside. The temperature would already be approaching one hundred back in Phoenix, so a midday run would be a nice luxury. She had her smartphone and headed out to wander the maze of streets. She figured when she felt tired she could use her phone to find her way back. Enjoying the day and pushing her body, she soon forgot all about the unpleasantness tomorrow would bring.

~~ Dan stood at the counter of the electrical supply store checking his email.

"Looks like somebody's got a big project." The store owner knew Dan his whole life. Since he was a kid, he came in with his dad or his uncle whenever they worked on a project that required materials.

"It's actually two smaller projects, Dan answered. "Most of it is for a customer, but I'm getting some for Uncle Wally's shop."

"He keeps coming in here, looking at 'em. Each time he shakes his head, and says they're too damned expensive, and leaves." He laughed. "I told him, I'm cheaper than anyone around here."

"Crazy old goat, will give you the last dime he has, but won't spend it on himself." Dan pointed at the pile on the counter. "Since I've got enough to get a little better price, I figured I'd throw some in for him."

"He'll still raise hell with you."

"Yeah, I know. I'll just say I ordered too many and these lights were left over so he might as well take them." Dan often used such ploys to get Wally to accept anything.

"I know he's been eyeing those T-8 LED shop lights for at least a year, so I'm sure he'll jump at the chance."

"At his age, he needs all the light he can get."

"I hear that," the shop owner agreed. He helped Dan carry the boxes out to his truck. "You tell your uncle I said he should hire a real electrician to install these. That ought to get him riled up."

"It doesn't take much to spin him up these days," Dan told him about Wally's drop-the-trailer episode.

"That sounds just like the ornery old fart."

Dan climbed into his truck and headed toward his uncle's house. He was going down the main drag near his place when he saw Angie running on the bike path beside the street. At least it looked like Angie. His attention was brought back to the road when the driver beside him honked because Dan's truck drifted into his lane. He finally found a place to turn around and headed back to catch her, but she was gone. "Damn it." Dan cruised the streets around where he saw the runner, but there was no trace of her. Finally giving up, he drove to Wally's house convincing himself it couldn't be her.

He planned to leave the lights in the shop so Wally would find them. Dan swore his Aunt Bobbie to secrecy regarding their origin.

After dropping the lights off, he went back to the area where he'd seen Angie but still had no luck.

Chapter Fifteen - Saturday, June 25th

"**Damn** it, I am tired of being two steps behind this guy." Kristoff was on another rant. The detectives and agents around the conference tables all rolled their eyes. The task force was trying to gather as much information as they could on the movements of the unsub. The theft of the car with the little boy was dismissed as a local issue at first and didn't make their radar. It wasn't until four hours later that the car identified in the liquor store murders was linked to the carjacking in Modesto. It was Detective Bartlett who put it together.

"Have we located that car yet?" Bartlett asked the liaison for the local Modesto PD.

"Not yet," he answered. "How long does this guy usually hang on to a car?"

"Depends," DeCicco answered. "He seems to ditch them as soon as they are used in a job and are hot. It's likely to turn up soon, but it may be in a town miles from here."

"What time was he at the liquor store?" Kristoff asked. He was standing at a board with their timeline on it.

"Surveillance tape said 11:05," one of the agents chimed in. Kristoff added it to the board.

"The store was in Manteca. It's 3:30 now. He could be in Oakland by now."

DeCicco asked the SAC, "Do you think we should put a team on the old guy in case the suspect goes after him, now that he's in the area?"

"I was just thinking about that." Kristoff pointed at the map. "If it were yesterday, I would have said yes, but now it looks like he went right past Modesto and is continuing to head north. I was wondering if we should try to get ahead of him and move the task force to Sacramento."

Detective Walker jumped in. "My guys down in Barstow found the registration the unsub stole from Williams' truck in the hotel room. Maybe the guy memorized it. I was sure he was going after Williams, but now he seems to have left Modesto, so I don't know."

"Could we at least put some local guys on it?" DeCicco pressed.

"Maybe we could have them cruise by a few times, but I doubt we need to have a protective duty."

"Here's something I found almost as an aside from the car theft this morning," Bartlett said. "Buried in the notes of the interview with the little boy, he made a comment that wasn't followed up. The patrolman asked him why he wasn't scared of the driver, and the kid said that he comes to their house all the time, but that he didn't like the UPS guy anymore." She looked up to blank stares. "Since we know it was our unsub, do you think he looks like their regular UPS guy, or do you think he was dressed like one?"

"Could be either," DeCicco said.

Kristoff wrote 'UPS?' on the board. "Do we know how many Hispanic UPS drivers there are in the Modesto area?

"Approximately forty percent of the drivers in Modesto are Hispanic, sir," one of the agents answered.

"Damn!" DeCicco exclaimed, looking at the agent in surprise. "What are you psychic?"

"No. As soon as Detective Bartlett mentioned it, I ran a sequel query on the department of labor database."

"Impressive."

"Perhaps now you'll learn to appreciate what the Federal government can bring to bear on this investigation, DeCicco, and you'll learn to cooperate." Kristoff couldn't miss a chance to gloat.

"I love the resources of the federal government," DeCicco admitted, smiling at the SAC. "I just have trouble with some of the assholes controlling them."

Kristoff could see it was time to divert attention. "Well, if we haven't detected anything new by tomorrow at this time in this area, I think it's time to move north."

"Wait. I think Bartlett's got something there." It was the CHP sergeant. "Do you think this guy's a UPS employee? It would be a great way to get people to open the door for you."

"Ugh, I'm not feeling it," Kristoff replied. "But if the CHP wants to throw resources at it, go ahead."

"I'll at least check to see if they have reported any missing trucks." The sergeant walked out of the conference room, calling on his cell phone.

~~ Blackie ditched the stolen car on the edge of a place called Robert's Island which was part of the delta area west of Stockton. He hitchhiked back to Manteca east on Highway 4 and south on Highway 99 back to Modesto. His last ride dropped him on McHenry Blvd. a few miles from the UPS truck. From there he walked to the truck. Blackie drove it to a local strip mall and was sitting at an outside table of a burger joint when he saw the pickup of the old bastard he was searching for. There was no mistaking a customized truck like that one. It was definitely the nosy old bastard. He knew fate would lead him to the right place. Blackie quickly jumped into the brown truck and followed down one of the main drags hoping he would not lose him again. Just as he was losing hope, Blackie saw the old Ford make a right onto a side street a quarter mile ahead. He followed it a few blocks over and saw him turn in an alleyway leading to a decent sized garage which seemed to be added beside one of the cookie cutter homes.

Blackie drove past slowly and circled around the block to the front of the house. There it was, 1731, just like in the video. Perfect. He parked the delivery van a few houses down and pretended to be doing paperwork on a clipboard hanging from the dash, while he watched the house. Blackie heard a dog barking in the yard. Probably greeting the old bastard as he arrived home. He would have to deal with it, but now he knew where his target was. Blackie would take his time with this one.

~~ Blackie went to a grocery store a few blocks away and picked up two pounds of freshly ground hamburger. Thirty minutes later, he returned to the old bastard's place after leaving his truck in the parking lot of the store. The backyard was surrounded by a six-foot high redwood fence. Apparently, the residents liked their privacy. When he first walked up to the yard, the dog behind it barked ferociously. It sounded big, and as he glanced through the spaces between panels, it looked like a pit bull. Darn.

The old bastard yelled at the dog. "Daisy shut the hell up. What's all that racket about?" Blackie crouched behind the fence and tossed a palm-sized piece of hamburger through the small gaps between the boards.

"Hey, Daisy. Hi, girl." He whispered as he tossed some more meat. "Is it good? There ya go. Good, girl. Good, Daisy." It didn't take long before she was eating right out of his hand and getting used to his scent. He even gave her a few pets and scratches between the ears. Before half the package of ground beef was gone, the dog was making an entirely different noise. It would talk in a sort of a yowl to try to get Blackie to give her more food if he took too long between handfuls.

"Shut up, ya crazy dog. I just fed you an hour ago." It was a female voice this time. The old bastard's wife?

Blackie hurriedly fed her the rest of the beef. He stayed there and petted her, getting the dog used to him being close. He was just starting to reach through the fence and pet her again when he heard the back door open, and the old guy came out talking on his cell phone.

"I just came home for lunch and to grab my portable band saw, for something we're doing at the shop. I'm leaving in a few minutes."

Great. Blackie figured he could trail him to the shop where the other jerks were who claimed they were tracking him. He would follow each one and deal with them individually when they left their shop or clubhouse. What was it the old man called them, the weasels? Something like that. Stupid name. He left the alley and hurried back to his truck, then pulled down the street. When the old Ford pulled out from the alley, Blackie followed it at a distance. The brown truck wasn't the best vehicle to use for tailing someone, but the old guy seemed to be in his own world. Blackie was surprised as he kept going for more than twenty minutes to the town of Patterson. Finally, he pulled up to what looked like a new metal building with an apartment built into the back of it.

Blackie smiled as he cruised by and saw some kind of shepherd-looking dog come trotting out of the garage to greet the old man. It was followed by the young guy who helped screw up Blackie's life by calling the cops at the diner in Barstow. Blackie continued down the street. Fate was once again on his side leading him right to his destiny. He was going to kill them both.

~~ Wally left early, claiming the Otters had a few new leads on the killer.

"Why don't you guys just leave that to the cops? All you've managed to do so far is probably get yourself targeted," Dan teased.

"You met those cops, we're a hell of a lot smarter than them."

"Angie could run circles around all of you and not be out of breath."

"That's just your Johnson talking, now," Wally said climbing into his truck.

Dan stood and waved as his uncle pulled out of the driveway. He was ready to close the shop and head upstairs to take a shower. His hand moved to hit the button to close the rollup door when a UPS truck pulled in. That was not unusual, but the time was definitely off. The regular guy always came around three o'clock.

Dan waited as the brown suited driver came out of the truck and approached him. He wore the brown UPS hat above wrap-around sunglasses. The driver was surprised by a sudden growling, then a bark as Syd lunged from of the shop to position herself at Dan's side.

"Syd. Knock it off. You know better than that."

The guy stopped in his tracks, his eyes fixed on Syd. "Hi, uh, is he okay?"

"I'm sorry. I don't know what's wrong with her. She won't hurt you." Dan looked down at her, puzzled. The UPS guy took another step, and Syd lunged in front of Dan, teeth bared, growling. Dan grabbed her collar.

"Whoa. Easy there, doggie." Blackie threw his hands up and took two steps back. "Sorry, as I passed, I thought I saw one of our cards in your window indicating you needed a pick-up."

"No. There was a pick-up earlier today." Dan explained, still watching Syd, "But I never use the card. I always schedule my pick-ups online."

"Oh, okay." The driver back peddled away from Dan and Syd, quickly and climbed back in the truck. As he turned slightly, Dan thought he could see something in his belt behind his back. It almost looked like a hunting knife handle, but Dan was sure it was some type of new scanner or something. He watched the driver back out and take off down the street.

"What got into you? That's not like you," he scolded the dog. Syd put her ears back and followed him into the shop.

Chapter Sixteen - Sunday, June 26th

As Blackie drove back toward Modesto, he was livid. That stupid dog. If it wasn't there, he could have taken out the young guy with one strike of the knife. The guy completely bought into Blackie being from UPS and had no guard up whatsoever. With the uniform, and the hat and glasses that he'd found in the truck he looked like every other driver in the state. Blackie was within ten feet of striking distance. The next time he went to Patterson, he would take some special hamburger laced with ground glass. He planned to take out the young guy, then wait for the older one to find out. He wanted the old bastard to squirm. Blackie hadn't decided if he would kill the other members of that stupid car club before the old bastard, or after.

No matter now. Blackie was so frustrated he decided to kill the old man first. Tonight. He took his time because dusk was settling, and he still wasn't sure how he would gain access to the old man. However, he was pretty sure the old man's dog was neutralized. When he got there, Blackie cautiously walked down the alley and passed the house trying to determine the best approach. He decided to climb a telephone pole beside the back corner of the garage. The garage had been extended so it wrapped around the side and part of the back of the house. After feeding the dog more hamburger, Blackie went back to the far side of the garage. He used the pole to gain access to the roof. As he suspected, the roof on the back section was added using corrugated sheet metal. He carefully looked for skylights or other means of access. The dog occasionally cried for more food, but it was a much different sound than the warning bark when she was aggressive.

"Rowl, ow, wowl." He would hear every minute or two from the gluttonous mutt. He finished the roof inspection concluding there was no easy access. Since he was in no hurry, he decided the

233

only way to get in, was to remove a roof panel. He took out the knife and used the back of the blade to remove the sheet metal screws that held on the trim around one panel in the corner of the shop. Once he removed the trim Blackie could see through a separation in the sheets, there was a car lift under the corrugated roof. The old man must have covered the lift area last since it looked like an addition. He worked on the screws holding the section of sheet metal. It was slow going using the knife and trying to keep the noise level down. "Rowl, ow wowl."

Blackie almost dropped the metal knife on the roof panel when the old man suddenly yelled out the back door, "Shut the hell up, Daisy. No more food 'til morning. Now, go to sleep." Blackie waited a few minutes before resuming. After an hour, he raised the edge of the panel some, but not enough to slide through. The pole he climbed had a street light on it allowing the boy to see inside the garage. It took another forty-five minutes before he had access. Blackie slid his feet in and held onto the metal frame on the top of the wall, swinging in mid-air about four feet above the cab of the old man's prized hot rod. He figured if he dropped directly onto the roof, it would cave in the sheet metal and make quite a racket. Blackie moved like a kid on monkey bars until he was over the bed of the truck. He intended to land on the rolled side rails of the bed, which were much more stable and hoped his sneakers would suppress the noise.

Blackie let go and dropped. His feet hit the rails with one on the bed wall on the side of the truck and the other on the rail just behind the cab. What he didn't account for was his butt grazing the roof enough to push him forward. He fell face first into the truck bed with his arms extended and bent at the elbows to cushion his fall. With a whump, his palms landed on the wooden floor of the bed as he stifled a grunt. He couldn't tell how loud his landing sounded to others because it echoed against the metal sides. His hands stung but he wasn't injured.

Blackie lay still a minute to see if anyone heard. The only response came from the dog. One quick bark of surprise, and then another request for more hamburger. "Rowl, ow, wowl."

He stood and climbed over the tailgate, then dropped to the concrete floor. The light coming through the roof opening was dim. Blackie stood for a moment letting his eyes adjust until he could navigate. He could just make out the tops of the four posts of the car lift.

The lift was directly in front of the entrance, with what looked like a shop area perpendicular to it. The only way to pull a second car into the shop area was to raise the lift, but Blackie noticed that the Toyota was parked outside. So it was easier to park on the lift if it happened to be down, and that was where the '54 Ford was now. He used the posts to navigate and felt his way with his hands. He located the closest lift post and saw a wall about three feet to the right of it. Confident that he found a path around the lift, he moved a few steps forward, holding his hands at shoulder height in front of him. As he took the third step, something steel hit him at the solar plexus level, knocking the wind out of him, and causing him to throw his foot sideways to catch his weight. What the hell was that?

Blackie's foot hit a five-gallon bucket on the floor with a bunch of metal scraps extending from it causing it to fall over. Wham! Bang! It sounded like the roof of the garage crashed down.

Blackie's left hand reached out to protect him from whatever hit him. It was hard, metal, and it was immovable. A large bench vise? Who the hell would put a vice there? He was still gaining his balance when the lights came on in the garage, momentarily blinding him.

~~ Wally was stressed when he got home that evening. After talking to the Otters, he was convinced the murderer was in the area. Stan and the others tried to reassure him the guy moved on since the murders in Manteca were north of them, but Wally would have none of that. The killer was close, he was sure of it. Wally came home and tried to relax and watch a baseball game. It was hard to get into it because he was trying to figure out what to do next, and because that silly Daisy kept begging for food even though she was fed. Bobbie yelled at her, and Wally told her to shut up too. Maybe the dog was sick or something.

The dog seemed to settle down a bit other than one sudden bark, and Wally was finally beginning to enjoy the Giants leading the Dodgers when an awful racket erupted from the garage. It sounded like Daisy crashed through the side garage door, or a meteor crashed through the roof. Wally jumped up and headed for the garage door, he started to just charge out there, but at the last minute grabbed a shotgun from the closet. He opened the door and flipped on the switch just inside the door that controlled the garage lights.

Even though Wally thought to grab the gun, he was still not prepared for the sight awaiting him in the garage. Inside the door was a room that was the original garage, but was now used mostly for workbenches, tables, toolboxes and racks for storage. The lift containing his truck was perpendicular to the entry room, with a large roll-up door at one end. Standing by it and the vice was the killer looking completely disoriented.

Wally brought the shotgun up and pointed it at the intruder. "Don't move. Asshole."

Hearing Wally's tone, the dog suddenly began barking ferociously. "Daisy, shut up. Lotta good your barking is doing now."

Blackie looked around the room as if assessing his routes of escape. The only path out was past Wally.

If the intruder tried for the large door behind him, Wally knew he could cut him down with one blast. If he headed toward the exit to the yard, he would have to walk across the room in a clear field of fire of the twelve gauge. Wally expected him to put his hands up, but instead, he watched closely as the boy's face changed from one of surprise to a confident sneer. He took a step forward as his right hand disappeared behind him. It produced a large combat knife that the kid rolled in his hand over and over. Wally almost couldn't believe what he observed. The transformation was unmistakable. With the knife in his hand, it was as if some outside force took over the boy's body. It was frightening to see as if staring into the face of pure evil. The killer took another small step.

"I told you to stop. This is your last warning." Wally was surprised when it came out almost as a question. The killer must have sensed a crack in resolve because he smiled.

"You ever killed a man?" he hissed. Wally felt confused by the evil, confident smile.

Wally couldn't believe the change in the killer's stature. His shoulders went back, and the knife stopped spinning in his hand, ready to strike. It was as if he grew a foot in height. He was within twelve feet and Wally was suddenly surprised at how far he had moved already. "Never killed a man, but then I was never dumb enough to bring a knife to a gunfight either." Wally racked a shell into the chamber of the shotgun. The sound made the killer hesitate. That was enough to break the spell.

"You ever even shot at a man?" The killer practically spit the words out from the sneer. He regarded Wally as something pathetic.

"Shot a man in the leg once," Wally responded. The killer's head tilted a bit as he took in this information just as the gun went off with a thunderous blast! The killer's body spun ninety degrees as the bottom half of his leg exploded in a red mist. He fell hard back against a workbench but caught himself with his arms. He looked more angry than in pain, and he righted himself shifting his weight to the remaining leg and turned toward Wally.

"Now I'll have to kill your whole family."

Rather than subsiding, Wally's anger came to a boil. "That first one was for threatening my family. This one's for Bob." The gun's blast shook the room again! The killer dropped face down on the concrete floor. The knife skittered across the room.

Wally went back to his story. "Yeah, I shot a man in the leg once. Bastard didn't stop coming at me, so I shot his other leg out from under him." He stood over Blackie, then knelt in the middle of his back with one knee. Using two straps he grabbed from the wall, he put a tourniquet around each of the killer's thighs to stop the bleeding.

"No. You're not going to die today. You're gonna spend the rest of your life in prison. And with no legs, you won't be a threat to anyone ever again."

~~ The task force members were crowded in Wally's living room. Police and FBI technicians scurried in and out of every door. Statements were taken from Wally several times. He was patient the first few but was not quite so cooperative toward the end. Aunt Bobbie just wanted the mess in the garage cleaned, and everyone out of her house.

Dan rushed to their home as soon as he heard the news. It was hours before he was able to even speak to Wally. When they discovered the UPS truck down the street, he realized what almost happened to him, and he was shaken.

"Mr. Williams, we're going to need a statement from you, too," Kristoff said when Dan explained about the killer's visit to his place. Kristoff looked around the room. "Detective Bartlett, can you do me a favor and take this man's statement?"

The detective walked over to where they stood. "Sure. I would love to take his statement."

Kristoff looked at her wondering about her sudden enthusiasm. Maybe she had a change of heart. "You know, detective, I was very impressed by your work on the team. If you ever think of joining the Bureau, I'd be glad to put in a good word for you. Maybe you could even join my team."

Bartlett was still looking at Dan. "I don't think so, Kristoff, I'm already tired of carrying your ass." She put her hand on Dan's elbow and led him away.

DeCicco, happened to be walking up at that time and said, "Hey Kristoff, you gonna put in a good word for me too?"

"DeCicco, you've been nothing but a pain in my ass. Why would I do that?"

"Well, sir, rumor is that you walk around with a sharp stick up your ass, so I figured I was a natural fit for the team. Heh, heh."

~~ Tammy lay in the hospital bed sinking into despair. She was homeless, no job, and now there would be enormous medical bills. Even the basic things Tammy relied on were gone. She talked with a bit of an impediment because of the damage to her tongue and jaw. It would take months or years of speech therapy and multiple operations to recover. She had an awful scar just below her left eye that destroyed any prospects of …. Suddenly it hit Tammy that she always relied on a man to make her whole or to subsidize things when she was unable to get what she wanted. Now with the scar and the slight deformity caused by the loss of tissue, she was no longer pretty. She would have to rely on her own brains, skills, and personality to make her way in the world. Tears rolled down her cheeks as she realized how dependent she had been. Rather than feel sad, she was suddenly relieved all of it had ended. She would have to be self-reliant from now on. That independence came with a price but she suddenly felt free, at least for now. She knew she had a long hard road ahead of her while learning to completely redefine herself. Blackie had left more than just physical scars that would have to heal.

Ms. Auer walked into the room and saw her crying. "What's wrong, Tammy?"

"Oh, I was just fretting about hospital bills," she lied.

"They're all taken care of."

"What? How?" Tammy couldn't believe it.

"Your medical insurance."

"But I don't have insurance. I don't even have a job."

"Sure you do." Ms. Auer smiled at her. "When you were admitted, I explained to them that you worked for me."

"But I don't."

"You do now. If you want to. I need a person around the office to do filing, and general office work, as well as an office manager. I'm sure you can handle it. It should help until you get on your feet. It comes with health care and two weeks of vacation."

"Sold!" Tammy said. "Oh my, gosh, I can't thank you enough." She threw her arms around the lawyer's neck. Suddenly she pulled away, looking serious. "What about the charges?"

"That's what I came to tell you. All charges were dropped." Tammy resumed the hug, and the lawyer explained, "Between the letter and the video, it was a slam dunk for proof of duress." Tammy relaxed for the first time in weeks.

~~ Dan and Angie walked outside to the alley to get out of the bustle of the house, so he could give his statement. Angie was visibly shaken by the close call Dan survived. She tried to keep it professional, but he couldn't miss the occasional smile she gave him as he went over the details of the past few weeks. Dan acted casual as he gave the information, trying to remember everything he thought would be needed. Once the statement was complete, she said, "You'll have to stop by the office to sign a copy."

He said, "You know you're fair game now, right."

"What?" Angie feigned innocence.

"After I'm no longer part of an active investigation, you're fair game, young lady."

"Oh, you think so, huh?"

"I know so."

"Well, we do still need to get through the trial, you know."

"Shit. Okay. The trial, then you're fair game."

"And what about the 700 miles between us," Angie asked, raising her primary concern.

"I thought about that." He started counting on his fingers. "I occasionally do work for the Whipple Observatory, so whenever I'm down that way, we can get together."

"Okay."

Dan raised a second finger. "I have cousins and an uncle down in Phoenix, who I visit once in a while."

"Bit of a stretch, but I'll let it slide."

"Then, when you join the FBI, you can transfer to Stockton or San Francisco." He held up a third finger.

"You think so? Why don't you move to Phoenix?"

"Because the only thing hotter than the women in Phoenix, is the weather."

Angie leaned in and gave him a lingering kiss. "Really?"

Dan stepped back, breathless. "I stand corrected."

As Angie walked Dan back to the house, she said. "You hang on to that Syd. She's a special dog. And make sure she keeps up her math skills."

Dan laughed and let go of her hand.

"How do you know his dog?" DeCicco asked coming up behind her.

"I, uh, from the statement," Angie said turning a bit red.

Dan changed the subject. "What's gonna happen to that kid?"

DeCicco shook his head and sighed. "Well, we have him for at least six murders in California, two in Nevada, and one in Arizona. So I don't think he'll be on the street in the next fifty years."

"So he'll be tried as an adult?" Dan asked.

"I know he will be in Nevada, and all three states technically still have the death penalty," DeCicco looked at Bartlett. "But he is most likely to be executed in Arizona."

Angie nodded. "Given the special circumstances of this guy, I'm guessing they will go for it too."

DeCicco held up the several inches thick case file. "His only hope is if California decides not to extradite him so the other states don't kill him, now that this state has gone soft on executions."

"Even though he's likely to lose both legs?" Dan asked.

"Yeah, he is a juvenile, and now a cripple. He may get some judge who goes easy on him but by the time all three states are done with him, he'll be an old man." DeCicco assured him. "He's just lucky your uncle saved his life."

"My uncle didn't do it to be a nice guy. He wanted the kid to have lots of time to think about what he'd done

"I hear the arraignment date will be set as soon as he's out of the hospital. And I'll be working on putting the evidence together for the Arizona case, so you don't need to worry about him coming back here," Angie said.

DeCicco gave Dan a reassuring smile.

They were interrupted by Kristoff waving the detectives back in the house to prepare for a press conference. Angie looked back at Dan and smiled as she entered the door.

Chapter Seventeen - Monday, June 27th

"**What** are you doing here?" Dan asked as Wally walked into the shop the next morning.

"Last I heard, I worked here."

"With everything that happened yesterday, I thought you'd take a few days off." Dan put down the piece of metal he was working on. Syd came over to wag good morning to Wally.

Wally let out a big sigh. "I just want things to get back to normal."

"Did you get everything wrapped up with the police?"

"Pretty much. I'm sure they'll be back with more stupid questions. The bastards took my vice as evidence 'cause there was some blood on it. Had to unbolt it from the stand. The idiot that came for it thought he would take the stand until I told him the foot was buried in a half yard of concrete."

"We all told you that vice was in the way, didn't we? I mean who puts a free-standing vice in the middle of the primary path into their shop?" Dan had been teasing Wally for years on the placement of it.

"Well, that damned vice was the only thing that alerted me the bastard was there. That vice saved my life. The damned dog sold me out for some hamburger. The killer still had a little in his pocket."

"So now you're trying to tell me you planned it as part of a security system?" Dan laughed at the audacity of his uncle's claim.

"Worked didn't it." Wally stood his ground.

"I still can't believe I didn't recognize that asshole when he showed up here," Dan admitted. "But he looked like every other driver jumping out of the truck.

"When you see people out of context, it's easy to do. I saw my doctor at the grocery store once and had no idea who he was until

Bobbie told me when we walked away. And we talked to him for five minutes." Wally shook his head, remembering. "I'm just glad you had the smartest dog in the world here to protect you." He patted Syd on the back. "You're a good dog, Syd." She did her happy walk, tail wiggling so hard her whole back half moved side-to-side.

"Have you heard anything about what's gonna happen to Bob's truck," Dan asked Wally.

"Yesterday, Detective Walker said Bob has a nephew who is interested in it. I'm glad it will stay in the family. The kid used to go fishing with Bob whenever he was in town. Sounds like a good kid."

"I thought his brother's family was in Alaska," Dan said.

"No, He moved up there after the divorce. The wife and nephew still live in Henderson."

"It's just as well. You don't need another damned Ford anyway."

"Screw you kid. That truck was a classic. At least Bob had a nephew who appreciated a fine machine when he saw one."

"Yeah, okay, I left a few things for you over on your bench." Dan nodded in the direction of Wally's work area. "You want me to put on some coffee?"

"See. Now there you go trying to be nice to me," Wally scolded his nephew. "That's definitely not normal."

"Get your own coffee then."

"Now that's more like it." Wally wandered over to his workbench to grab his mug for coffee. "What the hell's this?" he asked looking at something on the bench. Wally picked it up, holding it where he could read it.

"I thought you could use a new coffee mug," Dan said, waiting for a reaction.

The front of the mug contained a badge-like insignia on it with 'Uncle Wally's Detective Agency' written above and below it. "Well, I'll be damned." Wally chuckled.

THE END

Dear Reader,

Thank you for reading this book. If you have borrowed this book through Amazon's Kindle Unlimited e-Book subscription program, I kindly ask that you close the book here or at the end. This will ensure that the author is properly credited for the book borrow. Thank you. If you enjoyed Death by the Devil's Hand, would you please write an honest review? You have no idea how much it means to get a new review. You will also help all the people out there who use reviews to make decisions. Thank you so much.

If you enjoyed Dan, Wally and Syd and their special relationship, sign up for my guaranteed SPAM-free mailing list.

https://mailchi.mp/870edbe6ec1c/michaelpattonwritessignup

You can follow more frequent information and news about the author at his blog here:

https://michaelpatton.blog

Or if you would like to send me a note directly use the following email address.

michael.patton.writes@gmail.com

Let me know what you think, and I'll also let you know when my next book is available.

READ DAN AND SYD'S FIRST ADVENTURE!

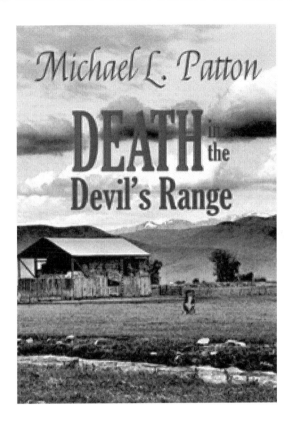

"Michael Patton is a natural storyteller whose characters are realistic and enjoyable. His dialogue flows naturally and with a sprinkle of humor to keep things interesting. DEATH IN THE DEVIL'S RANGE is a crackling good story with plenty of twists and turns – a fun ride!" -Dan Ames, USA Today Bestselling Author of THE JACK REACHER CASES.

BUY IT ON AMAZON

ABOUT THE AUTHOR

Michael has been writing poetry and short stories since he was in the third grade. He has had several articles published about his motorcycle adventures and been included in a regional anthology of poetry and stories. This is his second novel, so please leave a review to let him know what you think. He lives in northern California with his wife and his best friend Cyrus, their cat.

Made in the USA
Middletown, DE
11 March 2020

86214637R00154